WINTER HAVEN

WINTER

Athol Dickson

HAVEN

BETHANYHOUSE
Minneapolis, Minnesota

Published by Bethany House Publishers
11400 Hampshire Avenue South
Bloomington, Minnesota 55438

Bethany House Publishers is a division of
Baker Publishing Group, Grand Rapids, Michigan.

Printed in the United States of America

Library of Congress Cataloging-in-Publication Data

Dickson, Athol, 1955-
    Winter haven / Athol Dickson.
        p. cm.
    ISBN 978-0-7642-0164-6 (alk. paper)
    1. Maine—Fiction I. Title.

PS3554.I3264W56   2008
813'.54—dc22

                                                                            2007036289

For Ann and Beverly and Jim and Preston,
The Vickerys and the Flemings,
Who know the secret to the mystery.
And for Luke Hinrichs,
Who made the story better.

ATLANTIC OCEAN

EVANGELINE'S FOLLY

The Jetty

Evan's Boat

GIN GAP COVE

WEATHERLY

Fallen Giant

BLACK PEBBLE BEACH

The Stones

Blueberries

the forest

N

WINTER HAVEN
i s l a n d

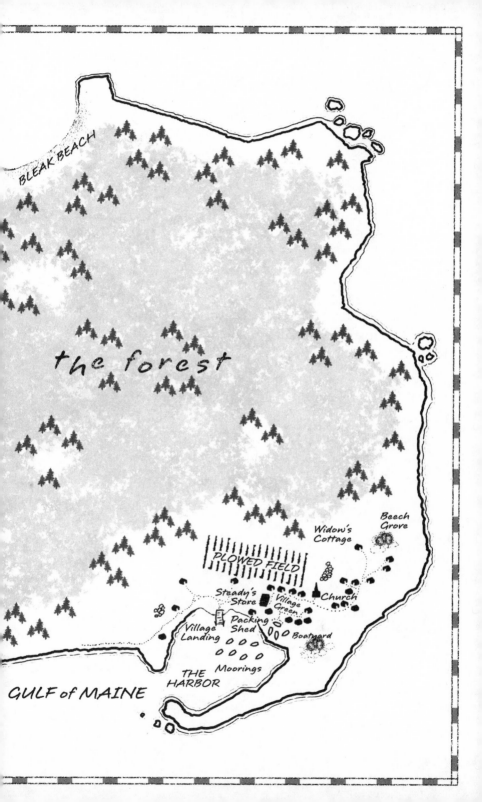

Listen, Stranger! Mist and Snow,
And it grew wond'rous cauld. . . .

—SAMUEL TAYLOR COLERIDGE,
The Rime of the Ancient Mariner

one

THE GULF OF MAINE lay easily beneath the mail boat's keel, passing gentle swells below the vessel like a mother's soothing stroke upon a baby's back. This was misery to me. The slow rise up, the slow sink down, the laborious roll to one side at the crest of every swell, the inevitable correction back the other way as the boat slipped toward the trough beyond—all of it had worked upon my stomach without mercy.

I groaned. "How much longer?"

"Ain't far now, hon," replied the big woman at the wheel.

We had been at this all morning, doing only eight knots because of the impossibly dense fog that contained us—me and the woman and one other passenger, a man in a vaguely martial khaki vest that seemed to contradict his baby face and the look of perpetual astonishment behind his thick eyeglass lenses. The man chattered on and on, a bottomless source of useless knowledge, unaffected by the little vessel's endless rolling. He spoke to the woman about ancient boatbuilding techniques, the rules of cribbage, internal combustion engines, and of course the weather. He said the fog was thicker and more widespread than usual because of a strange temperature pattern in the area, with daily highs a full ten degrees above normal while the seawater remained as cold as ever. He said the damp warm air moving slowly over the frigid sea caused the mist to rise. He said this was called "advection fog," although I considered it affliction fog since he simply would not stop talking.

The woman at the wheel sat on a cushioned swivel seat, swaying easily with the mail boat's ceaseless roll. There must have been some kind of autopilot in operation because the red and callused hands at rest upon her broad lap never moved. A foghorn sounded every minute or two. The lonely moan seemed to emphasize our isolation. Sometimes I looked up to see the woman's eyes flicking between the formless wall of white before us and the black screen of the radar, where a green line slowly made its rounds, picking out a distant blip here and there but mostly undisturbed. I felt the vibration of the engine rising through the soles of my shoes. Slouching helplessly on a hard bench in the deckhouse, back pressed against the wall, I closed my eyes. My head nodded with the awful motion. I breathed through my mouth to avoid the sickening smell of diesel and the faint odor of the contents of my stomach.

I had already thrown up twice. The first time came too suddenly. I made a mess of my wool sweater and blue jeans. Desperately embarrassed in spite of my wretched condition, I did my best to clean my clothing with freshwater in the tiny restroom below deck and then returned above to suffer. The second time had come with enough warning to allow me to stumble to the stern's safety rail, where I clung for fifteen minutes as the Gulf of Maine streamed by. I then reentered the cabin to collapse onto the bench beside the owlish passenger, and suffer.

At least the man and woman had the good sense not to try to draw me into their conversation. Occasionally I focused on a strangely disconnected splash as the bow caught a bit of ocean unawares, but mostly I remained deep inside myself, seeking out a place where nausea did not exist, willing it to grow and push away the queasiness. By way of a distraction, I thought back to how this awful journey started, back in Dallas, with a ringing telephone.

Sitting in my little office cubicle, at first I had been fascinated by the man's strange Yankee accent; then slowly I began to realize what his exotic speech might mean, and I made myself take notes, going through the motions as if it were just another business call, asking about expenses, trying to work out the exact figure it would take to ship the body home.

I remembered offering vague noises in response to his final dreadful words and hanging up the telephone as quickly as I could. I had been in hot pursuit of six dollars and seventy-three cents before it rang. Six dollars and seventy-three cents was a firm number, a known commodity that must be dealt with properly. Desperate to be doing something, I had tapped an arrow on the computer keyboard and watched the cursor slip down the debit column on my screen. I was searching for a missing entry. I needed to get back to that. I forced myself to focus. I would not stop in the middle of a ledger, not when I was close to perfect reconciliation.

Then came Kenneth's voice behind me.

"Knock knock."

In defense against the mail-boat nausea, I forced myself to think of Kenneth's face reflected on the computer screen, his square jaw and straight nose and teeth as white as photocopy paper, his movie-star good looks. I had kept my back to him. If I showed my face, he could read my mind; I was sure of it. He had caught me staring more than once and smiled a knowing smile, and I had been ashamed.

"So, Vera," said Kenneth. "That the Daimler thing?"

"Uh-huh."

"How's it coming?"

"The ledger's balanced. I still have to figure out what they did wrong on the depreciation schedule."

Although it had been a relief to speak of numbers, I wanted to get on with my work. I dared not let my situation show. The handsome man was my employer. Boundaries must be maintained. I kept my back to him and started typing.

He said, "You have plans for this weekend?"

My fingers paused on the keyboard. "I worked last Saturday, and both days the weekend before that."

"I know. And I really appreciate all your hard work lately. Don't know how we'd get by without you. But this thing's come up . . ."

I tapped the arrow key, sending the small white cursor on my screen hopping from entry to entry, under my complete control. My eyes followed the motion, ignoring his ghostly reflection. I said, "It's not right to work on Sundays. I need to go to church." I did not mention my father's vacant stare, although he too was a weekend obligation.

Kenneth said, "If it was anybody else, I'd say they'd have to spend all weekend on this, but hey, nobody's as fast as you, Vera. Put in a little overtime this week, you can get it done by end of day on Saturday. Then you can take Sunday off and be good and rested for the presentation Monday."

"Presentation? But Monday's my birthday. You said I could take it off."

"Wow, that's right. But I mean, it's Pendergrast. What can I do?"

Suddenly I could not see the cursor anymore. I needed a tissue, but the box was behind me and that meant I would have to turn toward Kenneth. I removed my glasses and wiped my eyes with the palm of my right hand, doing it surreptitiously, as if I was only tired of staring at the screen. My palm came away smudged black from eyeliner, something I had just begun to wear after overhearing one of the other women refer to me as "mousy." *"Poor Vera. She might be kind of attractive if she just made an effort."*

"Hey," said Kenneth. "You okay?"

I sniffed. I was a stereotype, a joke, a mousy accountant, and that was just the start. The tears were coming freely now. "I got a call a minute ago. Someone found my brother."

Kenneth's voice turned a little wary. "Found him?"

"They said his body washed up on a beach. In Maine somewhere."

I heard nothing for a moment; then his hand was on my shoulder. I felt the heat of his palm through the artificial fabric of my blouse. "Hey, Vera. I'm sorry."

I nodded, looking down at the keyboard, wiping my eyes and nose more openly.

He lifted his hand. "Here," he said, dangling a tissue over my shoulder. I used it to blow my nose. "I don't remember you talking about a brother."

"I haven't heard from him in a long time."

"How long?"

It was easy to remember because of my birthday. "Thirteen years, next week." I turned toward him at last, but only to reach for another tissue. He had backed away to the opening of my cubicle. I wished he would just leave.

He said, "What are they going to do with the, uh, him?"

He meant the body, of course. "I told them I'd wire some money so they can ship him here."

"So you're not gonna go to wherever he is?"

Sniffling, I shook my head. "Too much work to do."

"You're a real trouper, Vera."

I did not know what to say.

After a moment, Kenneth continued, "Uh . . . you know I feel sorta funny asking this, but since you're not going anywhere this weekend anyway, that thing I was talking about . . . Pendergrast wants it yesterday. I barely talked him into waiting until Monday. Of course I'd do it myself, but I have this party thing Saturday night with about fifty people coming over and I need to get the condo ready. And hey, maybe it'll take your mind off things, you know? I mean, we could put it off if it was any other account, but you know Pendergrast, he—"

I interrupted to stop the unbearable flood of words. "All right."

"Really? You sure you don't mind? 'Cause I could, uh, maybe . . ."

"Just give me your notes before you go."

"Thanks a lot, Vera. And about your brother . . . I'm really, really sorry."

Fifteen minutes later he dropped off his Pendergrast notes, and then I was alone in the office, the last one there as usual, listening to the sound of my own keystrokes amidst the gentle background hum of the building's air-conditioning system, the artificially cooled air necessary although it was only late April.

How I had dreaded the coming summer heat in Dallas, the relentless, suffocating omnipresence of it, ninety percent humidity at dawn, drawing moisture from my body even in the short walk between the parking garage and the office building, forcing me to sit at my computer with sopping underarms all morning. I often brought my own lunch to avoid going outside at noon. But quitting time awaited me, a twilight crossing over searing concrete toward my car, arriving at the apartment soaked with sweat, taking a second shower before yet another solitary dinner on a lap tray in the glow of yet another rented movie.

Alone in the cubicle, I wiped my eyes again. I stared at the entries on the screen and considered that I must write the Pendergrast report, and after that, another, and another, until I reached the end. But would I ever reach an end, or would there always be reports, always errors to identify, transpositions, duplications, outright fabrications? This work had become my life, a treadmill with no stopping point, no prize, no sense of arrival, and no more meaning than the Texas heat, endless and impersonal.

Then I thought, *It must be cool in Maine*, and just like that, I knew I had to go.

Now, rolling with the mail boat, I remembered calling Kenneth to request bereavement leave, his hollow-sounding wishes for a pleasant trip, my shock at the cost of a last-minute flight to Boston, and the acrid scent of long-extinguished cigarettes lingering in my rental car upholstery. I recalled the drive from Boston's Logan Airport to the small town in Maine with the strange name of Pemaquid, and my surprise that you could go halfway across two New England states in the time it took to get from Dallas to my childhood home in Mount Sinai.

Last night in Pemaquid I had treated myself to a lobster (the memory made my stomach roil), and then I slept uneasily on a lumpy mattress in a rustic motor inn—the Mariner's Rest Motel—which was walking distance from the little harbor. Earlier that morning I had found where the mail boat was docked, and the woman at the wheel had warned me the round trip would be a full day's cruise unless the fog lifted, which the owlish know-it-all assured us was unlikely.

Somewhere on the Gulf of Maine, I tried to imagine the return trip in the afternoon, this endless agony of motion rivaled only by my grief at Siggy's sudden reappearance as a corpse. Rocking weakly as the waves passed beneath the keel, I imagined my brother stowed like so much baggage on the stern deck. With that thought I began to wonder if it might be possible to cry and throw up simultaneously, and in the weakness of the moment I made a terrible mistake, a mortal error far more serious than my sorrow or my illness.

I allowed myself to dream of Siggy.

Knowing I was going to collect his body, it seemed safe enough to let my brother in again, or so I told myself. Of course I really knew there was no safety in my memories. I had no excuse, yet against my better judgment I gave him access to my thoughts.

After all those years it was surprising how easily he came: smiling, eyes averted as they always were, seeing something else, Siggy in his private world, head in constant motion, dipping and rolling, with sunlight slanting through the gaps between the shrunken, baking shingles of my parents' attic, and the folding hallway ladder out of reach. I saw the structure of God's dwelling place atremble in the heat up there, as if paradise were far away instead of just above my head. I could never reach that high, and Siggy would not send the ladder down, although I begged.

I remembered Siggy saying, " 'Behold a ladder set up on the earth, and the top of it reached to heaven.' " In spite of the danger, I allowed myself to be a little girl again, looking up beyond my older brother to the rafters and the joists of paradise, papered as it was with glossy covers of *The Mighty Thor*, Siggy's comic-book hero soaring in the wake of his magic hammer. I saw

Siggy's bright Crayola scenes, childish sketches of his precious Vikings, sometimes fighting storms at sea, sometimes warring with each other, but always sailing on in spite of waves taller than their vessels' masts, and oceans of blood, and disembodied limbs. In Siggy's heaven, physical afflictions were nothing.

Siggy in the attic nodded and rolled his head without control, much as mine was rolling now aboard the mail boat. He looked at everything and nothing, saying, " 'Between us and you there is a great gulf fixed, so that they which would pass from hence to you cannot.' " The little girl I used to be had stomped her foot and crossed her arms, demanding to ascend, but Siggy merely laughed his silly donkey-braying laugh as sweat beaded on his forehead, way up in the furnace of his heaven.

The sideways motion of the mail boat finally eased. I lifted my head into the here and now. I opened my eyes, and tried not to think of what I had just done.

Beyond the cabin windows was nothing but white fog. The woman at the helm reduced our speed and placed her hands upon the wheel, somehow cutting off the autopilot. A jagged green mass appeared at the top of the radar screen. We must have reached the island.

The sound of the boat's foghorn changed. There was a slight reverberation to it now, as if the moaning echoed from a nearby solid structure. A bell tolled lethargically in the distance, the sporadic ring of metal on metal growing slowly louder until the mail boat ghosted to within twenty feet of a rusty buoy. Through the drifting mist I saw the bell atop the buoy swing from side to side, clanging two times with the passing of our bow wave. The buoy disappeared into the fog behind us, ringing two times more at the insistence of the mail boat's wake. I felt a strange regret, as if the passing of that lonely sign of man had signified my one last hope of rescue.

"Here we are," said the woman at the helm, turning *r*'s to *h*'s.

Both the man and I sat up straighter. Staring ahead, I saw a dark form looming in the wall of white, and suddenly it was there before me.

According to the guidebook I had purchased at the airport, at nearly fifty miles offshore, it was the most remote of islands in the state of Maine, a granite rock of less than ten square miles adrift at the fringes of the continent, with no roads, no cars, and just one village, population eighty-three in winter and barely double that in summer, a tiny settlement that shared its name with the island itself.

I watched it growing in the mist and thought how different this moment was from what I had expected. In the years since Siggy disappeared I had sometimes failed to keep him from my mind. Sometimes in weak moments I had imagined him a man grown tall and strong without me. Sometimes I had dreamed my brother might be cured, might be living out a life somewhere, sound of spirit, mind, and body. Sometimes in unhealthy moods I had dreamed those dreams in spite of the awful thing such dreams unleashed. But never had it crossed my mind that I might find my brother's body in a place like Winter Haven.

TWO

M Y GRIEF, NAUSEA, and momentary lapse of discipline forgotten, I watched in fascination as the boat approached what seemed to be some kind of dock, although the structure towered a full twenty feet above the tiny harbor's tranquil water. The woman at the wheel lifted a radio microphone to her lips and said, "Winter Haven, Winter Haven, Winter Haven, this is the *Ulysses*. Steady, can ya see me yet?"

A voice crackled on the radio. "Just now got my peepers on ya, Marge. Meet ya at the landin'. Over."

"All righty," said the woman. "Out."

Drawing closer now, I noticed several other boats at rest upon the water round about. They were simple craft with graceful lines much like the mail boat, except a little smaller and with scrapes and rusty places, apparently in poor repair. The woman steered past the spindly dock and turned, and through the fog I saw a man descending along a steeply angled wooden ramp. The incline led down to a floating platform just beside the dock. As the mail boat coasted very slowly forward, the woman put the engine in neutral and left the wheel to throw a line. The man caught it neatly. In less than three seconds he had it wrapped around a cleat upon the platform. The line went tight. The boat was stopped.

A dozen seagulls dipped and wheeled above the man, mocking him with discordant calls. Ignoring them, he reached across the narrow bit of water between the platform and the hull to grab another line off of the boat. "How ya doin', Marge?" he said.

"Not too bad," called the captain and mail carrier from the cabin, where she had returned to kill the engine.

When the man had tied the second line to another cleat with the automatic expertise of long experience, he turned back toward the boat. "Dr. Thorndike?"

My fellow passenger said, "Yes, sir," and I looked at him more closely, surprised that anyone who seemed so young could be a doctor. Of course, I often got the same reaction when people learned I was a CPA. And now that I paid closer attention, I realized he might be ten years older than I had thought at first.

The man on the dock said, "Somebody from the university called a while ago. Wanted ya ta call right back, on account a somethin's gone missin' at the lab or some such thing."

Grabbing two pieces of luggage, the passenger leapt from the boat onto the platform. "My cell's not working out here. Can I use your phone?"

"You betcha. At the store. Up the ramp, third buildin' on the right."

As the doctor rushed away, the man turned his attention to me. "I'm guessin' you're Miss Vera Gamble."

Before I could reply, the woman called, "Help that poor girl off this boat, Steady. She like to chummed all the way across."

"Sorry to hear it. Come on, Miss Gamble. Let's get ya on dry land."

Still uneasy on my feet, I strapped on my small backpack, then took the man's extended hand. I felt the roughness of it like sandpaper against my yielding palm. I stepped up on the vessel's bulwark and then back down to the floating platform beside him. The platform rocked with the addition of my weight. In my lingering weakness I stumbled just a little. The man's grip on my hand tightened and was quickly joined by his other arm around my waist. I felt embarrassed when he touched the wet spots where I had done my best to clean my sweater, but he did not seem to mind and did not release his hold until I had completely regained my footing.

"Thank you," I said.

"Welcome to Winter Haven, miss. Wish ya was visitin' under better circumstances, though I'm glad ya came."

I could see he was a man of fifty or thereabouts, medium height, with well-established creases on his face that spoke of habitual good humor and a life out in the elements. He wore a day's growth of heavy beard, a pair of blue jeans, scuffed brown work boots, and a red and black plaid woolen jacket. I said, "Are you the man who called about my brother?"

"I am. Steady Wallis."

"The police chief, right?"

The man smiled. "'Chief' might be puttin' on airs, seein' as it's just me, but I am the law on Winter Haven, for what it's worth. And the harbormaster. Also own the general store. And I do a little lobsterin' in season."

"Postmasterin', too," said the woman on the boat as she passed a white plastic box across to Steady Wallis.

Taking the mail he said, "Ayuh, that too, though it don't pay worth a hoot."

Laughing, the woman left the man and me standing on the platform and busied herself in the cabin. After a moment she called, "Don't ya wait on me, you two. I'll be along shortly."

Nodding, Steady Wallis indicated the ramp up to the dock. "Shall we?"

I set out up the ramp. "It's so steep."

"Got a wicked big tidal range out here, Miss Gamble. If ya stayed with us a few more hours ya'd see her rise to almost level, what with a full moon tonight and all."

I paused at the top of the ramp. An ethereal mist drifted just above the ground, but it was thinner than it had been on the water. Up here, it floated in discrete layers, putting me in mind of pipe smoke hanging in my father's study. Except for the complaining gulls and the reverberating clatter of the woman doing something back down on the boat, I heard no sound at all. I felt disconnected in the silence and the fog. After crossing a wide gulf that I never saw to reach that shrouded place, I wondered if the island was a dream. But I refused the thought as quickly as it came, having given up on visions long ago. Instead, I focused on the many true things to be sensed from where I stood—worn and blackened dock planks firm beneath my shoes, orange and bright red lichen splashed across a granite boulder standing like a sentry where the dock caressed the island, and the mist itself, cool and moist upon my cheeks. I saw a row of nine or ten buildings following the curving harbor shoreline, with dark geometric hints of other structures farther back inside the fog. White painted siding or weathered shingles sheathed all the structures. None was taller than two stories, and most were only one. Few had any form of porch or shelter at their entrances; most had only a simple set of wooden steps. The windows were small and widely spaced, composed of many tiny panes, like those of houses I had seen in photographs of ancient Europe. Leading from the dock to all these buildings was a trail of crushed seashells. It led to the far edge of a clearing just behind the village, where a monolithic wall of evergreens dwarfed the man-made structures. Much larger than any living creature I had ever seen, they seemed as tall as mountains.

"Look at that!"

"What, miss?" The man stared at me.

"How tall are those trees?"

"Oh, them. Two hundred fifty, maybe three hundred feet, I expect."

Squinting through the fog, I understood the guidebook's phrase "old-growth forest" as I never had before. Back in Texas I had seen an oak tree some people said was standing before Washington was president, but here were things that surely lived upon this island before Columbus sailed, before the crusades, before Charlemagne, perhaps even before the time of Christ.

Steady Wallis cleared his throat. "I don't mean to hurry ya, but Marge will wanna be gettin' back to it pretty quick I expect, what with slow goin' in the fog and all."

"Yes. All right."

"Would ya like a meal before I take ya to the, ah, to your brother?"

Mindful of seasickness I said, "I don't think I'll ever eat again."

He chuckled. "Oh, that'll pass."

We left the shell path and set out across the grass along the harbor side. Dew soon soaked the toes of my sensible shoes, though it was no longer morning. A man and woman appeared in the fog, walking toward us. The darkly bearded man carried an axe. His shoulders were very wide beneath his plaid flannel shirt. He made me think of Paul Bunyan. Beside him, the woman's gray-streaked hair was wild, as if she had just survived a storm.

"Nathaniel. Rebecca," said Steady Wallis as they came close.

"Steady," replied the man.

Steady Wallis said, "Would ya mind settin' this inside the store?"

"All right," the man said, passing the axe to the woman in order to take the white plastic box containing the mail.

"This here's Miss Vera Gamble," said Steady. "Come to take her brother home."

The man said, "Awful sorry 'bout your brother, miss."

"Ayuh," said the woman. "We'll keep ya in our prayers."

I said, "Thank you," and the strong man and windswept woman continued on into the fog.

Steady Wallis and I walked in silence until, a few minutes later, he paused before a little shed. It clung to a level place above a precipitous drop from the grassy field to the harbor, which lay about twenty feet below. The shed looked somehow durable and tenuous at once, with weather-battered siding and a blanket of lush moss thick upon its shingles.

"Here we are," said the man.

"What is this place?"

"Used to be kind of a fish-packin' shed, I guess ya'd call it. Our fishermen kept their catch on ice in there till the buy boat come to pick it up. Lately we ain't caught enough to justify the ice."

"A fish-packing shed?"

He turned and looked me in the eyes. "I'm awful sorry we couldn't do no better for your brother, Miss Gamble."

I shook my head. "No. I understand. Can I see him now?"

"Whenever you're ready."

I hesitated, staring down at the black, motionless harbor. The shed leaned slightly toward the cliff. It seemed dangerously near the edge. I thought of someone pushing the whole thing into the harbor, with me inside. I could not seem to free myself of this odd notion even as Steady Wallis began asking questions. Why was my brother on the island? Was he traveling on a yacht or workboat? Had he been sick lately? Did he know anyone on Winter Haven? Did he have any enemies? Did I know if anyone would profit from his death?

I did not know the answers to his questions. I told him this over and over again. Finally I said, "It sounds like y'all might think somebody killed him."

Steady Wallis looked off into the fog. "Not really. There's no sign of violence. But a body washes up like this, I got to ask these things, ya understand."

"Where did he . . . where was he, exactly, when you found him?"

"Place called Bleak Beach, over on the windward side."

"Bleak Beach? What a strange name."

"Whole thing is awful queer, ya ask me. Young fella like that, he don't just up and die for no reason, but Doc Belamy come from Monhegan to look him over—did an autopsy I guess ya'd say—and he couldn't figure out what killed your brother."

I frowned. "I assumed he drowned."

"Don't appear that way. Doc ain't exactly got the latest equipment here to work with, but he's a pretty smart old cuss, and his best guess is hypothermia. We're thinkin' your brother mighta fallen off somebody's boat pretty near the shore, maybe the others in the boat didn't notice, an' he died of the cold before he went under. Happens that way sometimes."

"Did you check with the police in other places? Has anyone reported him missing?"

"Nobody's filed a missin' persons report on him in New England, New Brunswick, or Nova Scotia. But that don't mean nothin'. Maybe the boat was headin' out across the Atlantic. Maybe they're in the Canaries now, or Europe. Coulda been headin' out to anywheres from here, ya know."

I thought about our search when Siggy first disappeared. At first it had been only my father and me, one old man and one little girl, walking the neighborhood where we lived, calling out his name. I remembered my father's initial anger, before he understood the whole truth. I ached to recall my own naïve assumption that Siggy was only hiding, playing some kind of game. The search had soon broadened to include all of Mount Sinai, Texas—both its people and its territory—and then, growing in proportion to my panic, it spread out to include all of Jackson County, then all of north Texas, Louisiana, Arkansas, and Oklahoma. For three weeks, as the law looked far and wide, my father and I walked the fields and woods around our little town. Beside us walked most of his congregation, and dozens of well-wishing strangers from nearby towns and even distant places like Shreveport and Texarkana. Three weeks of that, every day and long into the night, and then we stopped, certain Siggy must have fallen in with someone who had taken him away. In all that time, never did it cross my mind he might be dead. I would not allow it. I decided that my brother was in the hands of well-intentioned strangers, like a stray puppy picked up by kind passersby. For thirteen years I had clung to that assumption in the rare middle-of-the-night moments when I allowed myself to think of him at all.

I said, "His time in the water, did it . . . is he . . . ?"

Steady Wallis patted my shoulder softly, then removed his roughened hand. "Don't ya worry, Miss Gamble. He don't look healthy of course, but it don't look like he was in the water long. And he ain't no worse for lying in the shed. We got no proper mortuary, but there's an ice machine out back of my store, so I been keepin' him good and cold."

I trembled.

"I'm sorry," the man said. "This ain't gonna be easy. But like I told ya on the telephone, I gotta have a positive identification before I can let him go."

I wasn't sure that I would be much help. Thirteen years would have changed my brother more than his short time in the ocean. He was fifteen when I saw him last. He was twenty-eight now. He would be taller and much heavier, of course. He might have whiskers—Siggy with a beard or mustache was an image I could not imagine—perhaps a new scar or two, broader shoulders, a mature hardness in his features. I might not even recognize the man inside the shack. Once or twice on sleepless nights I had been tortured by the possibility of passing Siggy on the streets of Dallas without knowing. Siggy might not know me either, because I also looked very different. I was living in a woman's body, although I often felt like the little girl my brother used to know. I now wore eyeglasses, and my hair, once as short as his, now fell in a wild and bushy mess down to my shoulders. If it were me inside that shack instead of him, would Siggy see the little sister beneath the woman I had become? Would I see him in the man? It was time to find out.

I took a deep breath. "I'm ready."

Steady Wallis pulled on a short length of knotted rope dangling from the door. I followed him inside. The shed had no electricity, but filtered daylight streamed in through the open door to cast itself upon the reason for my presence there. They had laid the body in a kind of open concrete box, one of several in the shed, and then packed it in with ice. The earthen floor had turned to mud because of runoff from a pipe drain at the bottom of the concrete. I imagined the body lying there almost a week while Steady Wallis worked one of the village's few telephones to track me down, while I took three days coming, the ice melting and being replenished all that time. I stared at the body and felt a strange vacillation between relief and disappointment, knowing Siggy was still probably dead somewhere, but knowing that wherever he had died, it was not in this lonely place.

I sighed.

"That's not my brother."

three

THE MAN BESIDE ME moved his feet a little. "It's a hard thing to accept. . . ."

"No. It's not that. He can't be my brother."

"Ya haven't seen his face good yet, Miss Gamble. Lemme move the ice."

"No. He's much too small. It can't be him."

I turned and left the shed. Steady Wallis followed. Outside in the mist again I closed my eyes, lifted my face toward the sky, and breathed in the moisture-laden air that smelled of salt and giant spruces. To come so far after so many years, to know at last where Siggy had gone, or at least where he had ended, only to find it was another person lying there . . .

I should have been relieved.

And I was. But there was disappointment, too. I had been hoping for some closure. Finally.

"Uh, Miss Gamble? I'm sure you're right and all, but the thing is, we found these on him."

Opening my eyes, I turned to see the man holding two plastic sandwich bags. He passed one to me. Inside it was a hand-printed card with a black ribbon dangling from a hole punched in the top. I removed my eyeglasses, wiped the condensation from the lenses with my thumb, and then replaced them. On the card I read:

My name is Sigmund Gamble.
I am not dangerous.
I am autistic.
I live at 821 Carver Street, Mt. Sinai, Texas.
Please call my parents at (903) 321-5555.

Steady Wallis said, "That's the one I told you 'bout on the telephone."

"When you said you found a card on him, I thought you meant a business card."

He cocked his head. "You seen that thing before?"

"I've seen it."

The card was white, laminated in clear plastic, and looked as fresh as yesterday, although I knew it had been written years ago in my mother's sparing and irregular hand. I remembered the angry words my parents had exchanged about this card, unaware that I was listening in the next room, my father insisting it was a risk they could not afford to take—the congregation must not hear the word *autistic*—and my mother standing up to him for once. I had never seen my mother's stubbornness before that day. She was much younger than my father, young enough to be his daughter, and he had seemed so wise, the very image of a patriarch to be revered. She usually deferred to him in everything. But after that day I never knew my brother to set foot outside our house without this card dangling from his neck, even if it was always hidden underneath his shirt.

Steady Wallis said, "That card. It was your brother's? Sigmund Gamble?"

"Yes."

"That part there, where it says 'I am not dangerous,' why does it say that?"

"Because Siggy was autistic. Sometimes he would kind of panic, scream and fling his arms around. People didn't understand."

"But this fella here, he's not your brother?"

"No."

"Strange, ain't it? This fella havin' that card."

I searched for explanations. "He must have known Siggy."

"Maybe." He took the card away from me and looked at it closely. "'Course this here ain't your family's number anymore, but I guess it must be a real small town 'cause the nice lady who answered, a Mrs. Reed, I think, she remembered ya. Told me where your father moved. I tried callin' him at the rest home and got your number from the folks that run the place."

I thought about this stranger talking about my family's business with someone at my father's long-term care facility. I thought about my father's shame when the Alzheimer's first began to show. " 'Physician, heal thyself,' " he used to say. "What will people think?"

"Yes," I said, "Mount Sinai is a real small town."

Steady Wallis cleared his throat. "Your brother's autism. Was it pretty bad? I'm just wonderin' if he could of gotten here on his own."

"What difference does it make? That's not him."

"Well, we got this here thing with his name on it, don't we? Seems like I oughta at least ask some questions."

I took a deep breath. I let it out. How I hated talking about this. "Every case of autism is a little different. Siggy could dress and feed himself, and read, and lots of other things. And he *did* leave home, so who knows what else he could do."

"You're sayin' maybe he could of come out here?"

I shook my head. "No, not really. I don't see how. Not all the way from Texas. Not alone, anyway. He never even spoke in his own words."

"His own words?"

"He quoted from the Bible whenever he had something to say."

"You mean he couldn't say nothin' on his own?"

"I'm not sure he couldn't. He just wouldn't."

"So he only talked in Bible verses? That musta stifled conversation quite a bit."

"You can find a verse for almost anything."

"Yeah, but who can remember it all?"

"Siggy could. He memorized the whole Bible, every word. I guess I ought to tell you, he wasn't just autistic. He also had savant syndrome."

The man nodded. "I heard of that. Like the fella in the movie, did math like a computer?"

"With some savants it's math. Some can play any music on any instrument after hearing it just once. Some paint things after one glance, just as well as Michelangelo except faster. There's this blind woman, a musical prodigy. She can also walk through strange rooms or crowded forests without bumping into anything. Another man, Kim Peek, he memorized more than seventy-six hundred books."

"Seventy-six *hundred?*"

"I know. It's hard to believe until you see it for yourself."

"No, I believe ya. That movie made me wonder what's inside my own head, if ya know what I mean."

"It's a good question. A lot of people think savant syndrome comes from one side of the brain trying to make up for the weakness of the other. Making up for the autism. All savants have some kind of autism."

"Do they now?" The man stared off into the fog. "And he really had the Bible memorized? The whole thing?"

"Cover to cover."

"Ya think any of this might have somethin' to do with what happened here?"

"I don't see how. That's not my brother in there."

"Sure a that, are ya?"

"Absolutely."

"All righty. But it's awful strange, what with this card around the body's neck."

I could only nod.

"Ya got any idea what this is?" He handed me the other plastic bag. Inside was a small piece of metal, dull olive in color, shaped like a sailboat.

I stared at the object. "It looks like a Viking ship."

"Ayuh. That's what they tell me. I sent a photo to the university. They say it's a piece of jewelry from about a thousand years ago. Say it's worth a lot of money to the right collector. We found it in this same fella's pocket."

Siggy had always loved Vikings. He would play the old movie over and over, Tony Curtis and Kirk Douglas fighting on top of a castle tower, swords and shields and Odin and graceful wooden ships. He was captivated by *The Mighty Thor*, his precious comic books, which he treated like museum pieces. But a real museum piece? Even if that was true, it did not seem like Siggy. The Viking pin was corroded and bent. Siggy would have polished it and kept it safe. I said, "It just can't be my brother. How would he get hold of something like this?"

The man cocked his head again. "Ya haven't heard what's happenin' on Winter Haven?"

"What are you talking about?"

He stared at me silently. I felt it was some kind of test, and resolved to wait him out. He was the first to speak. "Ya know nothin' 'bout the Vikin' thing, but the other thing, this card, it was your little brother's, right?"

"*Little* brother? It's the other way around. I'm his little sister."

Steady Wallis frowned. "Ya sure?"

I laughed. "He's almost four years older than me."

"I'm gettin' foolish in the head. Of course you're sure. But this young fella here . . . If he ain't your brother, who could he be?"

The card was Siggy's, and the tiny pin did look like a Viking ship, so there must be some connection, maybe a clue I could follow to find Siggy, wherever he might be. I said, "Let's go back in and look again."

We reentered the low-lying shed. This time I felt no sense of apprehension, except the dread that anyone would feel on viewing a dead body. Steady Wallis approached the corpse and pulled the ice away so I could see the face more clearly. I stepped closer as if drawn by a magnet. Through the open door a blade of burning sunshine slashed across the corpse's face. The stark heat of it spread before my eyes, spilling to the edges of my vision until all I saw was white, nothing but white—above, below, and all around—as if the fog had somehow flowed in off the ocean to lift my body from the earth and hold me floating in its awful vacancy. Then, within the barren whiteness, I saw one color: Siggy, rosy-cheeked, and smiling, and looking all around, although not at me, never at me. Siggy, drifting the omnipresent nothing, saying, "'Fear not, for I am with thee.'"

"Miss Gamble? Miss Gamble!"

Steady Wallis held me up. Somehow I had moved from just beside the body to a wall across the shed. I stood leaning heavily against it, still on my feet but only barely, only because of a stranger's hands upon my arms.

"I think ya musta fainted, miss. Are ya all right now?"

I nodded, unable to speak, unable to believe the nightmare had resumed, and yet, of course it had. I had opened the door to it myself, back on the mail boat. I had only myself to blame for what would happen next. In spite of thirteen years of rigid discipline since I last allowed the horror in, thirteen years of working to forget a single moment's weakness when I let my brother slip into the empty whiteness all alone, in spite of the bloating and the greenish cast to his complexion now, I knew at once it was indeed my long-lost Siggy in that shed. How could I deny it, when the boy before me had not aged a single day?

four

S TEADY WALLIS WOULD NOT let me take my brother home. He said this was no longer just a simple case of someone falling from a passing boat and dying in the ice-cold waters of the Gulf of Maine. "A body that ain't changed in thirteen years has gotta be explained," he said, "before I can let it go."

I replied, "I don't see why," although of course I did.

"On the phone ya never told me he was lost so long ago. Why is that?"

"It's not the kind of thing you think to tell a person. I mean, I just focused on the fact that you found him. I never thought . . . I didn't think it through."

Something changed behind the man's eyes. In the mist outside the shed where Siggy's body lay, he asked me all the questions he had asked before, and many more besides. I answered everything as best I could. Then I tried to change his mind about releasing Siggy, but Steady Wallis was determined not to move the body.

I knew it would be risky to stay. I should have flown back to Dallas, to immerse myself in routine and hope the forbidden door my feckless memories had opened on the mail boat could be closed again. But having laid eyes on my brother I could not bring myself to leave without him, no matter what the cost. I asked Steady Wallis to help me find a place to spend the night.

He led me through the fog across the village of Winter Haven, passing his own general store, and a meeting hall that doubled as a library, and a boatyard where I saw vague silhouettes of vessels on dry land, unnatural and out of place like floundered whales. The broken shells of countless ocean creatures crunched beneath our shoes as we walked. I heard the clanging sound of someone beating on a piece of metal, then a curse was uttered, and the beating stopped. Perhaps a shipwright had just struck his thumb. As we continued, the boatyard dissolved into the mist, even as a pair of yellow squares appeared ahead—electric lights pleasantly aglow beyond the windows of some kind of building. Drawing closer, I saw it was a church. Two women watched me through the glass. I gave a little wave. The women both waved back. Scattered in the ether with the public buildings were about a dozen houses. Although I could not make out details, I thought I glimpsed more structures standing farther from the road, or the trail, as the pathway winding through the village might be more rightly called.

"Here we are," said Steady Wallis.

We stopped at a small gate hanging on a pair of leather hinges. Beyond a short dilapidated picket fence lay a weed-choked yard showing vague signs of a gardener's touch in ages past, and beyond that, near the edge of vision in the fog, I saw a little cottage. The man pushed at the cockeyed wooden gate and took a step into the yard, while I remained where I was, outside on the path of crumbled shells. Though it made my stomach roil to think of pressing him, I had to try again.

"I really wish you'd let me take my brother home."

"I know it," said Steady Wallis, turning back toward me. "And I wish ya could, Miss Gamble."

"But y'all did an autopsy. What else do you need? What difference does it make if Siggy's here or down in Texas now?"

"Somethin's wrong, Miss Gamble. Until I know what's what, it don't make no sense to let go of the only evidence I got."

"He's my brother, not 'evidence.'"

"'Course he is. I'm sorry."

"Please, Mr. Wallis. I don't want to stay here overnight."

The man just shrugged. "We could see if Marge is still here with the mail boat. Maybe ya could go back with her and wait on the mainland. I can send your brother across when we got a handle on this thing."

It was one last chance to escape, probably an opportunity from God, a way to bear up under the temptation. But I could not stand the thought of Siggy traveling alone. I told myself I would be strong. It would be all right. I would not let the whiteness lure me back again. "No," I said. "I'll stay until he can come home with me."

"Don't blame ya one bit. Let's go on an' see the widow."

I peered beyond the worn and peeling picket gate and the unruly yard, examining the widow's cottage doubtfully. The guidebook promised three bed-and-breakfasts on the island of Winter Haven. According to Steady Wallis, all three had only one spare bedroom each. One was still closed for the season and the owlish man from the mail boat had already spoken for another, which left only the Widow Abernathy's place.

Her house had a steep roof in the Cape Cod style with a rough-cut granite chimney rising from the center of the ridge. Like most other buildings I had seen so far on Winter

Haven, the walls were clad in wooden shingles, looking gray and timeworn like the picket fence. I stared at two small windows, one on each side of the front door. They gazed back with malevolence, as if the house were conscious of my visit and did not wish me well. Dry rot at the mullions made me think of how the cataracts had crawled from out of nowhere to obscure my father's eyes. I did not want to think about him back in the nursing home, unkempt, nearly blind and demented.

I followed Steady Wallis to the door, which he rapped upon quite sharply with a rawboned knuckle. We did not have to wait long before a woman flung the door wide open and stood with both hands on her narrow hips, glaring down at Steady. She was tall and frightfully slender, perhaps seven decades old. A simple jet black dress hung nearly to her ankles, close-cropped hair sprang wildly from her scalp in alternating shades of snow and soot, and drum-tight skin clung tightly to the contours of her bones. A sickly odor emanated faintly from the house. The chemical aroma of Mount Sinai's only funeral home rose unwelcome in my memory. With it came my mother lying in an open casket. I gave a quick, involuntary shake of my head to drive the image back. There was so much I did not want to think about.

"Well there. Ya don't have to beat it down," said the old woman, referring to her door.

"Sorry, Ida," said the man. "Didn't know but what ya might be in the cellar."

"Well, I wasn't. I was right there by the window, watchin' ya loaf around my gate."

The old woman bared yellow teeth in something like a smile, and I remembered the malignant presence I had sensed behind the cottage windows.

Steady Wallis said, "Ida Abernathy, this here's Miss Vera Gamble."

The woman did not even glance at me. "What's *she* here for?"

"We was wonderin' if ya'd like to take her in. She can pay."

"She a painter? Not in oils, I hope. Can't abide the smell of linseed."

"No, she's—"

"Well it's too soon for tourists, Mr. Wallis. Ain't finished with my spring cleanin'. Just get in the way."

"Ain't a tourist, Ida. She's come for her brother. Ya know, that boy the cap'n found at Bleak Beach."

Finally the woman turned to look at me. There was a hint of softness in her eyes. "That a fact?"

"Ayuh," said the man.

The widow returned her attention to Steady Wallis. "Why don't she just take her brother home, then, 'stead of loafing with the likes of you out by my gate?"

"We've still got some questions to be answered. About the boy."

"Thought ya said the boy fell off a *yacht*. Fell off a *yacht* and drowned." She put emphasis on the word as if it were an insult.

"It don't look that way no more," said the man at my side.

The woman set her gaze on me once again. This time I was almost certain I saw sympathy there. Yet still the woman spoke as if I were not present. "How long she gonna be here?"

I finally spoke up. "Just a day or two, ma'am. If I can hire a boat to get me home when Mr. Wallis lets my brother go."

The widow ignored my answer. "What I mean is, Mr. Wallis, how long till ya know the way of things with the boy?"

"Hard tellin', not knowin'," said the man. "Couple of days at least, I imagine. Maybe more."

"All right. Be thirty-five a day, seventy in advance, and more every mornin' if she stays longer than two days. I'm assumin' cash will be agreeable. Don't got no *credit card* machine." She uttered those words with the same disdain earlier assigned to yachts.

Steady Wallis looked at me. I answered meekly, "That's fine, ma'am."

The woman lifted one hand from a hip and made a shooing motion. The sickly chemical odor I had noticed before seemed to waft down the steps, chased along by the widow's gesture. "Ya don't have to call me 'ma'am.' Mrs. Abernathy will do. Bring your bags. I'll show ya to your room."

I slipped my backpack off my shoulder. "This is all I have."

The widow glanced at the small pack, which was meant for day-trips. "Don't imagine ya got a change of clothes in *that*."

"I was planning to go back with the mail boat this afternoon."

The old woman sniffed and let her eyes roam over my sweater and blue jeans, which remained moist and stained. "What ya gonna wear tomorrow and the next day?"

"Same thing as today, I guess."

The old woman sniffed again, but before I could speak, Steady Wallis said, "Ida, seein' as she's stayin' unexpected, don't ya think ya could lend her a change of clothes?"

"Man, are ya blind? She'd have to grow a foot and lose a good twenty pound to fit into anythin' of mine."

"I'll be okay," I said. "But I am kind of tired. Would it be okay if I just went into the room?"

"'Course it is, child," said the widow. "Only reason we're still standin' here is 'cause of Steady's nonsense."

With that, she turned to disappear into the house's dark interior. Standing at the bottom of the steps, Steady Wallis looked at me. "I'm sorry. I'd let ya stay at my place, except my wife's got the flu or somethin', and I'm afraid it's catchin'."

"Thanks, but I'll be okay here."

"Sure ya will. The widow's got a mouth on her, but she don't mean no harm."

I left him there and went inside, where the old woman showed me bruskly to my room. I lay down on the four-poster bed, and slept.

It was dark outside when I awoke. I sat up. I reached over to the nightstand and switched on the light. On the bed beside me lay my backpack. I picked it up and clutched it to my chest. I stared at the opposite wall. It was covered with more than a dozen black-and-white photographs, nature scenes mostly, which were a pleasant surprise. I had entered the old woman's house expecting secondhand furniture and frilly junk. I had been completely wrong. Most of the furniture looked at least two hundred years old. Some pieces were so well made and well preserved I believed they must be priceless. And there were no trifles on display, no nicknacks or dusty remnants of an old woman's lonely life. On almost every inch of every wall hung striking photographs and watercolors.

To my untrained eye, each painting seemed to be a little masterpiece, done by a single, expert hand. Opposite my small four-poster bed hung a haunting watercolor of a man at work in a field of grass with an old house in the background. It made me think of another painting, *Christina's World*, the famous one with a girl flopped right down in a field of grass in spite of her pretty pink dress, alone and leaning toward a house on the horizon, leaning on bony arms with a kind of yearning in her skinny frame. I had always felt I knew that girl completely.

The widow's photographs were as perfect as the watercolors, far better than any other photos I had ever seen, except perhaps those famous ones some man had taken years ago, the black-and-white ones of the Grand Canyon and Yosemite with waterfalls that seemed to stream down from the clouds. The pictures on the Widow Abernathy's walls seemed to portray Winter Haven mostly. They showed it as a fierce and untouched place where corruption could not tread. They made it look like all the other mythic places I had always hoped to visit—not only Yosemite and the Grand Canyon, but Yellowstone, and Alaska, and the Everglades, and so many other landscapes known for lonely grandeur.

Suddenly I realized I had achieved my dream. I had come to this uncommon island, this secluded summit of a granite mountain risen from the ocean floor with giant pines and spruces stretching toward the heavens, and houses built by hands that never knew electric tools or machines fueled by gasoline, and roads of shells, and mighty tides, and the endless North Atlantic hidden just beyond the fog. But having risked the journey to this enchanted place, all I wished for was a rented movie and a frozen pizza and the chance to curl up on my sofa underneath a woolen throw with the dead bolt locked on my apartment door, and my telephone turned off, and no one to stare at me or speak of me as if I were not there, and nothing weighing on my mind but balance sheets and ledgers. I longed to go back to a hiding place where they had proper mortuaries for dead bodies, and boys changed into men when thirteen years went by, and I might never dream the awful dreams I knew I had unleashed.

five

T HE BED FELT WARM and soft and seemed to rise and wrap itself around me in a somnolent embrace. I smelled flowers in the sheets and woodsmoke in the air. I smiled with my eyes closed and wiggled my toes and snuggled in to sleep some more, and would have lain there until noon but for the discordant shout that roused me.

"Scat! Scat on outta here ya mongrels!"

My eyes snapped open. I saw fuzzy shapes in the near distance, knew the bedroom was not mine, and came to consciousness confused about my circumstances. I heard a loud slap and the howling of a dog in pain, and the same voice shouting, "That'll teach ya, I imagine!" Then I remembered everything, and felt the dread return.

Cautiously I touched objects on the nightstand until my fingers found my eyeglasses. I sat up and put them on and looked around, confirming memories of photographs and watercolors and oddly bright and cheerful curtains and the unexpected downy luxury of the bedclothes. On an antique chair across the little room I saw someone else's garments lying in the place of mine. Curious, I set my feet upon the old oak boards.

Fifteen minutes later I found my way into the Widow Abernathy's kitchen. It was a cozy room with a floor of old bricks, walls of knotty pine, dark green painted cabinets and a drop-leaf table with four bow-back Windsor chairs below a wrought-iron pot rack. Beyond the table and chairs, the old woman faced a wood-burning cookstove. Wearing a white cotton apron over what appeared to be the same simple black dress, she used a pair of tongs to turn sizzling bacon in a black iron skillet. The old woman did not seem to hear me enter, or else she did not care enough to let it show.

I said, "Good morning."

"Mornin'," said the woman without turning.

"Thank you for the clothes."

"Ya can thank Mr. Wallis for that. He brung 'em by a few hours ago."

I sensed a reproof in the last few words, as if the old woman felt no decent person slept this late. I looked down at the stranger's clothing that I wore—faded jeans and a maroon sweatshirt with the words TEXAS AGGIES in large white letters across the front. "I guess his wife must've gone to school in Texas, huh? Good thing she's about my size."

The widow remained focused on the bacon. "She's considerable taller. Them was Isaac's clothes before he passed."

"Isaac?"

"Steady and Abigail's boy. I suppose you'll be wantin' breakfast. Or lunch."

Before he passed. Did that mean he was dead? Was I wearing a dead person's clothes? Or did "passed" mean something different here in Maine? I wished to ask these simple questions, but something in the way the widow had abruptly changed the subject told me it was best to let the matter go. I said, "Breakfast would be great. Thank you."

"Just so's ya know, it'll be five dollars added to your bill. Cash."

The old woman set a massive meal upon the table—half a pound of bacon, three eggs, boiled potatoes, and four blueberry pancakes, which she called "flapjacks." Then she left the room. I did my best to eat everything, afraid it might be taken as an insult to leave some on my plate, but I was used to only a piece of toast and black coffee for my morning meal, and could not manage even half of what now lay before me. The food I did consume sat uneasily in my belly at the thought of facing the old woman with half the meal uneaten.

Remembering the sounds that had awakened me, the widow chasing off a dog, I rose with my plate and approached the back door. Sure enough, through the little panes of glass in the top half of the door I saw a pair of golden Labrador retrievers lounging in the ragged yard behind the cottage. I paused, listening for the widow's footsteps. Hearing none, I pressed down on the door handle, pushed it open, and stepped outside. Overnight the weather had cleared. There was no hint of fog. On the contrary, it was a bright and sunny morning, and just as warm outdoors as in the kitchen. The air felt fresh on my face, moist and clean and healthy. Mindful of the widow, I whistled softly for the dogs. Both of them perked their ears and rose, tails wagging tentatively, kind brown eyes completely fixed upon the food.

"Come on y'all," I whispered. "Come and get it."

The dogs approached me warily, pausing about halfway to the cottage. I descended to the bottom step and knelt to tip the eggs and bacon onto the soil. Just as the food left my plate, the widow's voice came sharply from behind. "What in the world are ya doin'?"

I stood quickly and turned, hiding the empty plate behind my back. "You have some good-looking dogs," I said.

Although I had heard nothing, somehow the woman stood right there at the top step. She thrust her hand toward me. "Gimme the plate."

Sheepishly, I passed it to her.

The widow glared. "If ya don't care for my cookin', ya only have to say so!"

"Oh, no. It's not that!"

"Mr. Abernathy would have a thing or two to say about this! Givin' perfectly good food to dogs!"

The old woman turned abruptly and disappeared into her kitchen. I followed to find her standing at a deep porcelain sink, running water over the plate. "I'm sorry, ma'am. I love your cooking. It was just too much for me to eat."

The woman scrubbed the plate. "So ya threw it in my yard?"

"I didn't throw it. I mean, I didn't mean to . . . I just thought the dogs would like it."

"Ya thought the *dogs* would like it," repeated the old woman as she rinsed the plate.

I made a final try. "I'm so sorry, ma'am. I really am."

The old woman put the plate into a cupboard by the sink. "Guess there's no accountin' for the way some folks is raised. But I'll not have such ingratitude in my home. You'll have to go."

"Go? Where? Mr. Wallis said there's no place else."

"That's none of my concern." She removed her apron and strode out the hallway door.

I called after her. "Can you at least tell me how to get to Bleak Beach?"

There was no reply.

I crossed the little kitchen, entered the dark hallway to my room, and nearly walked straight into the widow. She stood stock-still in the shadows. Framed by the high collar of her black dress, the old woman's face seemed to float disembodied in the darkness. She said, "What ya want with Bleak Beach?"

"Mr. Wallis said it's where they found my brother."

"Ya got no business goin' there."

"Why? Is it private property or something?"

"Everyplace is private on this island, girl."

"Who's the owner, then? Maybe I can get permission."

"I'm tellin' ya not to go."

"Why not?"

The widow moved a step closer. A frown drew flesh tightly across the bones beneath her face as it hovered above me. "Bleak Beach is right near Gin Gap Cove," she said, as if that was explanation enough.

"So?"

"It's on the windward side, where the wrecks wash in. It's an evil place. Folks has died there, folks besides your brother. Folks has died there since the olden days. Died and disappeared into the soil."

Something from the guidebook I had purchased at the airport came to mind, a sidebar underneath a drawing of a group of men in tall black hats and shoes with thick buckles. "I know about the missing Pilgrims, if that's what you mean."

"It don't start nor end with them. Goes further back and forward. It's come to my generation. And to yours."

The old woman began to tell a story, which in most respects matched the one I had read on the flight to Boston. It was the Winter Haven legend about a colony of Pilgrims shipwrecked on the rocks offshore of the mouth of Gin Gap Cove in the early sixteen hundreds, stranded there through a merciless Maine winter. In the widow's version, it was a woman's charms that caused the lookout to ignore his duty and thus allow the ship to sail into the rocks. To this day those offshore rocks were known by Winter Haven people as Evangeline's Folly, named for the hussy who caused the disaster.

The surviving Pilgrims camped among the great evergreens around the cove. More than half perished that winter from the cold and lack of food. Then had come the spring, when five men set out on a raft crudely fashioned out of giant branches, each limb easily as large as any normal tree. They hoped to reach the mainland and the new settlement at Plymouth, hoped to bring back help. The guidebook's story of the suffering those men endured seemed more lurid with the widow's telling, but her story and the guidebook both agreed that just one man survived the crossing to the mainland and the long walk south through vast forests filled with hostile Indians. When that one man got to Plymouth, a boat was sent to Winter Haven, where a thorough search was made. No sign of the colonists was ever found—no blackened wood from campfires, no broken twig, no remnant of a shelter, no solitary boot print—absolutely nothing.

According to the legend, the rescue party suggested they had landed on the wrong island. The lone survivor was insistent. Had he not endured the deadly winter by hunting game on every hill and dale across that evil place? He knew the island like he knew his own home back in England. This was where he had left his friends and family—he was certain of it, and besides, hadn't they noticed? It was not only his fellow colonists gone missing.

The rescue party realized it was true. There were no chirping birds, no rustling rodents down among the fallen leaves, no sign of deer or squirrels or possum. Except for the silent forest giants, there was no hint of anything alive upon the island of Winter Haven.

It was said the forest had consumed the colony for the crime of taking trees to build the raft, and the animals had fled for fear of what they'd seen. It was said that hikers in the forest on the windward side of Winter Haven still sometimes heard the chopping sound of axes. It was said this was the desperate spirits of the colonists fashioning another raft to send their strongest men for help, doomed to try and try again for all eternity, doomed to linger on amongst the trees they had so foolishly attacked to save their lives.

Reading about the legend at thirty thousand feet above the earth, surrounded by the sleekly modern interior of the jet to Boston, I had smiled at the melodrama of it all, enjoying the distraction from my fear of flying. But hearing these things from a skeletal woman in black mourning, with the chemical scent of death adrift inside a two-hundred-year-old house . . . this was less amusing. I backed a step away from the Widow Abernathy. The old woman smiled, her lips drawn back from yellow teeth. I sensed a light of triumph in her eyes. I stopped and faced her squarely. "You don't really believe that story."

"Why not? You do."

"No, I don't. That's ridiculous. I'm not a superstitious person."

She cocked her head, examining me as if I were a worm, and she a crow. " 'The lady doth protest too much, methinks.' "

"What? What are you talking about?"

"Don't they teach ya *Hamlet* on the mainland? It ain't the *story* I believe. It's what I *know.* Ya simply must not go."

In the face of such a solid prohibition, I felt surrender creeping in. Speaking softly, I said, "I just want to see the place where they found my brother."

"Are ya a complete fool? I lost my husband there! Steady Wallis lost his son there! Ya lost your own kin there for pity's sake! *Ya must not go!*"

The intensity of the woman's words pressed down against me. I felt confined by the narrow hallway's paneled walls and the widow's immovable presence. My only choices were to turn back or to stand my ground. I longed to resist this woman, but it was not in me. Against my will, I nodded. "All right."

"Do ya mean you'll stay away?"

I nodded again. "Yes."

"It's for your own good, ya understand. Only that."

"I know."

"Well then." The widow drew in a sharp breath through her nose. "Perhaps I've been a little hasty, tellin' ya to leave. I suppose ya can stay another day or two, long as ya mind your behavior."

Hating myself for doing it, I said, "Thank you."

She stepped aside, allowing me to pass on down the short hall to my room. Once there, I made up the four-poster bed to save the widow the trouble. Then I sat on the mattress edge, my feet dangling above the floor, hands clasped together in my lap, back straight, eyes on the black-and-white photographs. I sat this way for half an hour, without moving. I tried to pray. It would have been good to ask for help, and maybe for an explanation, but I did not want to complain to the Almighty, not when so many of the words inside my mind could be misconstrued as anger. I dared not take the risk. I had made that mistake once, a long time ago, and look at what it brought: a dead mother, a dead brother, a father who had lost his senses, and me myself, alone for all these years.

I must deny the past. Now, this moment, was the thing I could control, the thing to focus on. But I had broken faith on the mail boat and at Siggy's side in the packing shed. I had failed to shun the first hints of temptation, and now my will was weak. The widow's personality bore too strong a likeness to my father's heavy-handed ways. In spite of years of habit to the contrary, I felt my thoughts drawn back to the first day my mother stayed in bed, my father fixing breakfast, the sour scent of pipe tobacco in his undershirt, the eggs done wrong, the bacon black. In spite of the danger, I indulged my old addiction to the memories of doing laundry, doing dishes, doing my own hair, warnings to be quiet, and a few short minutes with my mother in the dreary darkened room before going off to school each morning, a few more minutes before bedtime every night, my mother's eyes so far away, my mother's fingernails so dirty, and the moment when the truth broke through my childish inexperience, the horrible truth that she would shortly go.

In my mind I knelt beside my mother's bed, laying hands upon her, certain I could draw the illness out. Of course my mother never noticed. She remained unmoving, pale and damp with sweat as ever, leaving me with nothing. I remembered saying prayers without regard for Siggy, or my father, or the poor starving children of Africa. My only plea was for my mother. I had not yet learned to fear God's wrath. I did not staunch my words of anger. Foolishly, I spoke my mind.

"Why are you doing this? What have I done wrong? Why don't you stop it? Stop it! Stop it! Stop it!"

I remembered rising to my feet and throwing things, making firm demands.

"You have no right to do this! I've been good! I've been *good*!"

I remembered my father's face as he burst into my room, the horrified expression just before he gripped my arms and shook me to my senses, yelling, "Never speak to God that way! He doesn't owe you anything. You must accept his will. Accept it!"

Outside in the hall, the widow's heavy footsteps fell as loud as hammers. Startled back into the present I realized where I was, and what I had allowed myself to do again. I slapped a palm against my forehead as if to beat my history into its darkened corner. I focused on the widow's watercolors until the weakness of the moment fully passed, clinging to the colors in my fear of empty white. Finally, grateful that my errant memory had not led to something worse, I practiced what my father once had preached. I closed my eyes and bowed my head. I whispered, "Please forgive me for those things I was just thinking."

With the awful void thus narrowly avoided, I gathered up my jacket and my backpack and set out for Bleak Beach. I dared not say another word to God for fear of retribution, but at least I had enough courage to brave the Winter Haven curse. What were Pilgrim ghosts to me, when I had survived the much more dreadful haunting of the Holy Ghost himself?

SIX

A SHORT MAN WALKED AWAY from me across the village green, moving as if the world might roll beneath him at any moment. Legs spread wide, he charged quickly through the air from step to step, with an instant's pause each time his soles set down upon the soil. It was as if he wished to maximize the time he spent with both feet on the ground. I supposed it was a sailor's wish.

The man had just allowed his name was Zeke, but only after I had asked directly. He was the fifth person I had asked about the way to Bleak Beach, and the fifth one to claim ignorance. I saw the short man reach a woman on the far side of the clearing. The woman's hands busily tied her hair up in a scarlet-colored scarf. She listened to him for a moment, then shifted her eyes toward me. Although the man named Zeke stood facing away, I knew what they were doing, talking about the stranger in town, speculating, assuming the worst about the sister of the dead boy in the packing shed. I had grown up in a little place like this. I knew how these people were.

Everyone was lying, of course. You could not live year round on ten square miles of rock without knowing every nook and cranny. But on the seashell path through the village, in the boatyard, and in front of the old church, everyone's response had been the same. One young woman had not even bothered to reply to me, walking away as if I had not greeted her or asked a question, as if I were not even there. I followed behind the young woman for about a hundred feet, asking questions to her back, until at last I said, "Are you deaf, or just bad-mannered?"

Now, sitting on the front steps of the church, I put my chin down on my fists. Why was this so hard? Was it just the standoffishness of isolated people, or was there something special about me, or my brother, or the place I wished to go? The few Winter Haven people I had met and seen yesterday had been friendly enough, the wild-haired woman who had promised prayer, the wide-shouldered man with the heavy beard and axe, and the two women who had waved as I passed by the church window. What had changed to make them so unfriendly now?

Considering the Widow Abernathy's warning, I wondered if the entire population of this village shared that woman's superstition. Surely not. Surely these were modern people in spite of fifty miles of ocean between them and the mainland. I had seen fairly recent styles of clothing on the women. The U.S. Postal Service came each week on Monday. These people voted in elections. Surely they did not believe the Winter Haven legend, or put stock in a curse upon the island's windward side.

An idea came. Digging through my backpack, I found the guidebook. I flipped to the dog-eared page on Winter Haven and, yes, there was a map at the bottom showing the island. The village and the kidney-bean-shaped harbor were prominent on the southeast end, and I saw a deep gash on the northwest corner labeled *Gin Gap Cove*. I applied mathematics to the problem. The island appeared to be about three units wide from east to west, and two units tall in the north-south direction. If the island was ten square miles, that meant the distance from the village to the cove would be . . . I shut my eyes, visualizing basic algebraic ratios, the hypotenuse of a triangle, feeling calmer, with a task before me I could master. Soon the answer came. About six miles. Maybe a little less. One could only be as accurate as the data available, but say five and one half miles; an easy walk.

I slipped the guidebook back inside my backpack and rose to pass around the corner of the white clapboard church. Stepping through the knee-high grass between this structure and an adjacent house, I reached an open field, bounded to my left and right by a string of village buildings. On the far side loomed the ancient forest. Straight rows of freshly plowed soil stretched between the village and the forest, perhaps two acres of spring planting. Careful to step only between the raised rows, a lesson learned as a child in rural east Texas, I set out toward the giant trees. The fecund scent of fresh-turned earth engaged my nostrils. An image leapt to mind—of a hot spring day, a sorghum field, Siggy and me, just the two of us. . . .

In the middle of the Winter Haven field, I stopped. I knew where such memories would lead: the confusion, guilt and fear. I must not let them enter in. I *would* not let them enter in.

Resolutely focused on the here and now, I continued walking.

At the forest edge I paused and looked back. A figure clothed in black stood at the far side of the field. My eyes were too weak to make out her features. She raised something to her face. A camera? I turned away. Although it was two hours before noon, shadows lay like twilight underneath the towering canopy ahead. I slipped into the darkness.

The ground beneath the lofty evergreens yielded as if my footsteps pressed into the planet's living flesh. Rotten and infested with fungus, a billion fallen needles and the decomposing wood and bark of centuries moldered in my path. Strangely, there was little underbrush. Enormous tree trunks stood like columns built for potent gods, the gnarled bark deeply crenulated with swirls and grooves as if those gods had poured the pines and spruces down from heaven. From these frozen waterfalls of wood sprang limbs the size of normal trees. High above my head the lowest of the interwoven branches clutched at precious sunlight, misers demanding nearly all of it, withholding the currency of life from lesser earthbound beggars on the forest floor. Possibly this eternal darkness explained the lack of undergrowth. It certainly meant easy walking. But if weaving my way between the massive trunks was easy, maintaining a northwesterly direction in the diffuse green glow was not. With only rare breaks in the canopy, I had to zigzag through the forest to get my bearings from fleeting sunbeams.

After walking a long time I paused, suddenly convinced I heard no other living creatures. No birds, no insects, no rodents fleeing from my footsteps. I stood stock-still to listen. Remembering the widow's story of lost Pilgrims, I felt my heartbeat race. Then I heard a clicking sound, probably the fussy chatter of a distant squirrel, and smiled at my own foolishness. Had I learned nothing from my superstitious past? I checked my wristwatch. It was half past noon and I was surely lost. I should have reached the far side of the island by this time. The three hundred and sixty degrees in a compass came to mind, and the twelve stations on my wristwatch. I took comfort in the numbers, comparing them, making allowances. I set out again.

At two in the afternoon I sat on a rock outcropping, bathing in a rare puddle of sunshine where the granite underneath the island thrust up through the thickly matted forest floor to impose a hardness yielding to no seed or root. Surrounded by the timber's brooding wall of darkness, I listened to the wind high in the branches, a lonesome, ghostly sound. I heard nothing else. Nothing. I told myself to remember the clicking squirrel. I must not let an old woman's foolish story beguile my imagination. But it did make sense to think of turning back. I had taken four hours to reach this place. I would need four hours to return, which meant I could reach the village before sunset if I hurried. I had a sudden mental picture of myself in the forest after dark. I shuddered.

Remembering the oppressive heat in Dallas, I whispered, "Think positive. At least it's cooler here."

Rising, I set out again, heading back the way I came. At least I hoped that was my direction. Looking up I saw glimmers of sunshine sparkling beyond the soaring canopy, but these points of light offered no clue of the sun's location. I put one foot before the other, wishing I had not ignored the Widow Abernathy's warning. I would be trapped out in this maze all night. I had not even brought a bottle of water. I would have no dinner. I thought about the Labradors, wolfing down my eggs and bacon in seconds flat. I thought about the card sealed inside plastic, my dead mother's handwriting.

I am not dangerous.

Oh, Siggy.

In the silence I stopped to lean against the lichen-covered form of something that had lived a thousand years exactly in that spot. I sensed the great tree's permanence and changelessness and drew a little comfort from the idea of a living thing that lasted. I saw the grooved and swirling bark as if it were a wooden waterfall again, and realized I was wrong. These giants were not permanent, not unchanging, not poured down frozen from the heavens to remain just as they were. They were geysers flying from the soil in ceaseless motion, flying up right then and there, always moving higher. It was how they reached such startling altitudes, even if the rising was too subtle for a fleeting creature such as me to notice. These pines and spruces had an eternity to change, while I existed in a rigid instant, doomed to live one moment by comparison with them, and then pass on unchanged forever.

But what of Siggy? How could he remain unchanged for thirteen years? And having changed as little as these trees in all that time, had my brother's life slowed down enough to let him wander that dark forest, seeing mighty columns move?

No. Even thirteen years inside an instant was too short a time for that.

I saw Siggy's face framed in ice again, the strange smile on his lips, such peacefulness in his expression. Whatever caused his unchanged condition, it seemed he had found some reason for joy in the midst of so much immobile time. Obviously it was something I had missed.

Imagine if I never found my way back to the village. If I disappeared like Siggy, Kenneth would replace me. The Widow Abernathy would wash the sheets where I had slept and rent the room again. Steady Wallis would do something with my brother's body. My mother's grave would slowly settle into the

earth, untended. My father, who no longer recognized my presence, would not recognize my absence. I would be forgotten
by the world, just as Siggy had been lost to everyone but me.
Imagine if they found my body here. What would my expression
be, the thing upon my face? Would it too be a smile?

As if in answer I felt a sudden warmth caress my forehead. I
raised my eyes into an errant ray of sunshine. In the unexpected
blinding light I saw Siggy racing through a colorless void, stumbling, falling to his knees and elbows, and then rising to look
back. Yet he did not look at me, and I saw no peace on Siggy's
face, no smile. There was only terror as he stumbled off into
the white.

Underneath the giants, I tried to stand against this memory,
this hallucination. But the warmth upon my forehead grew,
I felt my mind begin to burn, and the delusion overwhelmed
me as it had so long ago. I told myself this time it was just a
nightmare, a memory of fearsome dreams. But it felt like here
and now, and memory or not it was beyond my control, an
assault, a violent imposition of a phantom I had seen before,
a seizure that constricted everything, blocking every other
thought until there was only Siggy in the whiteness, just as
he had come that first time on the front row of my father's
church in those innocent days when a wooden pew lay hard
beneath my bottom and I still believed Almighty God trod
softly in my heart.

Now, as then, I could no more stop the scene inside my
mind than I could stop the spinning of the earth. Now, as then,
Siggy was the only color in a universe of nothing. All was white,
white, white as fog out on the ocean except for Siggy's colors,
his cheeks a rosy red and his wispy yellow hair. Against my
will, hating it, I remembered Siggy in the whiteness exactly as

he had appeared when I was a child: floating red-cheeked and encompassed by the golden halo of his hair, looking round at everything but me.

"Siggy!" I called thirteen years ago. Or was I calling now? "Siggy! Where have you been?"

And my brother answered with a shout, " 'The mighty are afraid! The arrow cannot make him flee! He laugheth at the shaking of a spear!' "

Then I heard a terrible sound, a monster's howl of rage, and I sensed the presence of an awful thing, but the horror was pure white in a world of only white and so could not be seen. I could only watch my brother flee, within my memories perhaps, his slender form becoming smaller, ever smaller, until he was a dot of solitary color in a colorless void, Siggy shrinking down into a dreadful moment when he simply vanished.

I was somehow on the forest floor, curled in on myself, moaning. I rolled onto my back and stared up into the sparkling canopy. How could this be happening again? It had been so long. What had I done to deserve this relapse?

I remembered now.

I had thought of Siggy on the boat and in the packing shed. That was my mistake: indulging memories again after all the years of abstinence, asking that morbid question, imagining the worst. What if they found my body here? What would my expression be, the thing upon my face?

I told myself this had not been a seizure like the others. It had only been a foolish indulgence, a daydream I could not afford. It had *not* been a hallucination. I told myself those days were over years ago.

I rose and set out through the gloom. I no longer tried to calculate my position from the slant of sunbeams through the canopy. Although I heard the clicking sound again, I took no comfort from the presence of squirrels, or any other sign of life. I walked below the trees, trusting only in my moving feet, searching ahead for the straightest route to someplace else, anyplace else, so long as I was seen and therefore known to exist.

On and on I walked. I began to check my watch more frequently. The more I checked, the slower time passed by. This was good, because the flight of time was now the enemy. Soon the sun would set. Already it was darker than before. How was it possible to walk all day within only ten square miles, yet never reach the forest's edge, never find the ocean, never see anything at all but tree after tree after impossibly enormous, silent, hulking tree? Was this what had happened to my brother? Had he been lost for thirteen years in this Neverland where there was time enough for trees to grow into giants and the space of only ten miles could be stretched into infinity? It would explain Siggy's unchanged condition. It would make sense of a lot of things. . . .

I stopped.

It made no sense at all.

I had to get control, think logically. I was simply walking in circles without a compass or any way to sight the sun. There was no enchantment here, no frozen time, no expanding space—just a hysterical woman from the city who had gotten lost without her streets and signposts. Obviously, I would spend the night out in this forest, so the best thing was to make some plans. I held my wristwatch close to my eyeglasses, staring hard to see the numbers. It was nearly five o'clock. Sunrise would come at, what, maybe six in the morning? Yes, say six. Keep things in perspective. Think about the numbers. I would walk another hour or so, and when it was too dark to go on safely, I would lie down to sleep. Twelve hours would pass by—only twelve—and then I would have the light again, and another twelve hours to find the village. Twelve hours was seven hundred twenty minutes. Or think of it another way: forty-three thousand two hundred seconds. The numbers were in my favor. Just twelve more hours here, then another twelve to find the village. Yes. It all made perfect sense.

Calmed by precious mathematics, I set out walking again. I kept my eyes up, watching the canopy of needles, searching for a slight break where I might see the setting sun. If I could see it set, I would know which way was west. Then I could lay a branch or something on the ground to point toward the village. I glanced down very rarely, confident from the day's experience that the forest floor was largely clear. Because of this, I almost missed the trail.

Fortunately a small noise caught my attention, the clicking I had heard before, a squirrel, or some other tiny creature rummaging through the composting needles for its dinner. I looked for it and saw a depression in the ground, just the barest hint of a line curving gently off into the shadows. Instantly I knew it was a path. I started running. When my wind gave out, I walked as quickly as I could until I caught my breath. Then I ran again. I began to sweat. My eyeglasses slipped down the dampness on my nose. I paused to remove my jacket, which I stuffed into my backpack. Feeling cooler in only the maroon sweatshirt lent to me by Steady Wallis, I kept moving. I did not want to sleep in this forest. I wanted company, a bed, a roof above my head, and water—glasses and glasses full of water. And although it made no sense, I wanted someone, anyone, to know I was alive and well.

seven

A HEAD I SAW what looked like a clearing. The edge of this vast wood at last? It must be! The path went straight toward it. I walked faster toward the pastel gloaming, striding on the yielding earth, backpack heavy on my spine, my ordeal ended finally. I drew nearer, nearer, until at last I stepped out from the tree line and saw nothing but a pile of rocks.

Disappointed, I moved closer. There was a sense of order to the stones. In the center, overgrown with vines, lay a low, circular boulder at least ten feet in diameter with an almost perfectly level top. A ring of smaller rocky cylinders surrounded it. All of them were nearly identical, as big around as a car tire and about two feet tall. Even through the brush and fallen branches I could tell their flat tops were unnatural. On the far side of the central stone with its ring of smaller satellites, two other boulders stood like a crude pair of columns, perhaps three times taller than I was.

The whole arrangement made me think of photos I had seen of the ancient structure in England called Stonehenge, except this strange grouping was overgrown and untended, and much smaller. I saw a depression in the middle of the large central rock, a place where the surface had been charred black, as if by many fires. Stepping closer, I saw a border etched around the perimeter of the flattened top, where the hand of man had carved planets, moons, and stars into the surface. The workmanship was beautiful. Nothing similar adorned the smaller stones around the outside, but in front of one of them, directly across from the two tall boulders, I saw a break in the decoration. Looking closely I saw words carved into the central stone:

> O thou perfect goddess,
> Receive mine heart,
> An eternal offering to thee.

What I had read of Stonehenge came to mind again, how the druids built it in homage to celestial gods, how they worshiped sun and moon and stars with slashed and burning human sacrifices. Staring at the inscription on the level rock before me, I thought of beating hearts ripped from open chests and cast into the fire. Trembling, I understood the purpose of this forgotten place, the central altar, the sentinels all around it, and the twin pillars brooding godlike over everything. But who had carved these stones to curry favor with the Celtic gods?

Afraid to move my eyes from the sacrificial altar, I backed into the forest until I could no longer see the unholy place. I found the path again and ran as quickly as I could, putting distance between myself and the horrible clearing, casting backward glances, more afraid than ever of the falling darkness. Desperate to find safety, I ran, and suddenly the ground ahead of me was gone—it simply disappeared—and I willed my legs to stop their reckless flight and whipped my arms like cartwheels, stretching for some kind of purchase on a limb, a branch, anything to halt my headlong rush into the open sky.

Somehow I stopped short of running off the cliff.

Rocking on my toes with arms cast back for balance, I teetered at the very brink of a precipice at least fifty feet high, just an inch away from certain death. I willed myself to take a backward step. I then collapsed to my knees, blood roaring in my ears. Breath came in ragged gasps. I clasped my arms across my chest, clutching my elbows. Five minutes passed, maybe more, as my panicked blood and breathing both subsided.

Somewhere in the forest back behind me another squirrel was chattering, its clicking sounding strangely mechanical. I stared at the bizarre place where I had nearly fallen to my death. Ahead of me and far below was a large empty space, almost certainly a cove, perhaps the length of four football fields. Across one hundred yards of open air I saw another granite cliff, almost vertical, which seemed to be a mirror image of the one that fell away immediately below me. These two cliffs ran ever closer to each other toward a point far to my right, where at last they came together to form an intersection that probably looked like a massive V from high above—a pie-shaped slice into the island's granite shoreline, pointing like an arrowhead straight at Winter Haven's heart. In my calmer, nearly motionless condition, I heard the distant roar of surf. I turned left, and there at the head of the cove, between the sheer cliff beneath me and the one across from me, I saw the lavender sunset meet the sea, the gap between the black cliffs framing a glorious view of distant waves and glowing clouds beyond the island's outer edge.

I recalled the guidebook map, the deep gash in the northwest shore, and knew this must be Gin Gap Cove, famous center of the Winter Haven legend.

How strange, to have turned back toward the village hours ago, only to find myself here on the far side of the island anyway.

I remembered the Widow Abernathy's warning. If I had taken one more step, running headlong off the cliff, I would have perished near the spot where they found Siggy, and Steady's son, and the widow's husband, where the storied colony of Pilgrims had disappeared four centuries ago.

I felt a fatalistic sense of destiny. This was indeed a place where time stood still. At least it had for Siggy. I leaned forward to gaze down again, trying to see where I had almost ceased to be. But across the hundred yards or so of empty cove between me and the face of the cliff opposite, I saw nothing below but a dense and strangely settled fog. Like an expansive topping of meringue upon the pie-shaped wedge of Gin Gap Cove, it filled every inch of space, spreading inland to the right, all the way to the sharp notch of the V. It spilled onto the ocean to my left. From high up where I was, the fog reminded me of clouds below my window on the flight north to Boston. The mist appeared flat and solid. Just for an instant it seemed possible to leap and be received with gentle buoyancy by the vapor.

I pulled back from the precipice.

A new sound joined the chattering squirrel, the distant roaring surf, and the moaning wind in the treetops. It was something rhythmic, dull, and closer. I held my breath and listened. *Chop. Chop. Chop.* Perhaps it came from within the fog below. I told myself it was only an axe applied to wood, an autumn sound, straight from the woods of my childhood in Mount Sinai. Yet it was not that exactly. It was something similar, but not that.

The chopping seemed to weave a spell within me, drawing my rebellious thoughts into the Winter Haven legend, into ghosts and eerie disappearances.

"It was said this was the desperate spirits of the colonists fashioning another raft to send their strongest men for help, doomed to

*try and try again for all eternity, doomed to linger on amongst the
trees they had so foolishly attacked to save their lives."*

Shaking my head, I forced the guidebook legend from my
mind. There was a natural explanation for this sound. Of course
there was. But even as I searched for logic, another noise came—a
hiss, or a prolonged whisper, formed of something throbbing
like the energy of ocean waves or the flowing of one-thousand-
year-old bark. I heard it growing louder and almost thought the
sound had formed a word.

Issssss.

With the chop, chop, chopping all around me, I turned toward
the hissing. I stared deep into olive shadows under the colossal
trees, seeing nothing. The fearsome blackened altar in the clearing rushed back to my mind, so like Stonehenge. I thought of
druids and their human sacrifices in the British Isles. Pilgrims
came from England, too. I tried to impose reason, to analyze the
sound. Might it be a snake? I envisioned a black tongue, shiny
and flicking in and out, hissing reptilian warnings. But it was not
that. It seemed too big somehow, and too intelligent.

I hardly dared to speak the word, "Hello?"

I waited, hearing nothing until, perhaps a full minute later, the
hissing rose again, competing with the chopping from below, filling the air with a sense of agony, or anger. As before, I was almost
sure it formed a word. Listening, I thought I understood.

"Where are you?" I said, just a little louder. I waited, hearing
nothing in reply this time but the pounding surf and the ongoing
chop, chop, chop. I began to think the hissing had been a trick of
my imagination, an idle fantasy, but dangerous, like the fleeting
urge to jump one sometimes felt when standing at high places.
I listened until the light was nearly gone, until the lavender

Atlantic sky had turned to violet and black. Then I heard the hissing sound again, except this time it sounded like a sob.

I fled along the cliff top, following a narrow band of soil between the ageless trees and the open bit of sky beyond the edge. Eternal darkness beckoned from my right. On my left and far below lay certain death. Behind was something I could not imagine, and ahead . . . ahead in the waning light I saw a massive tree trunk sprawled across my path, fallen from the forest to hang cantilevered out into midair above the cove, a barrier almost twice my height in repose, which I could only get around by entering the forbidding blackness underneath the trees, where the hissing thing awaited.

I looked wildly for another way. I knelt on all fours at the edge of the cliff and peered down. I saw what seemed to be a ramp, or ledge carved in the stone, spanning from the cliff top close beside me to the translucent haze below. I did not want to descend into the fog, but then, above the sound of distant surf and rhythmic chopping, I heard the hissing, sobbing thing again.

Startled at how close it was, I screamed. My cry echoed from the cliff across the cove and disappeared into the treetops. The sound of chopping stopped. Without another thought, I scrambled down the narrow ledge.

The fog below lay strangely effervescent in the first beams from a rising moon. The rocky path was thin and delicate, a mere ribbon tightly stretched along the sheer drop of the precipice. Winter Haven gave me nothing for a handhold, no bush or crack within the granite. I put my back against the flawlessly smooth stone and edged sideways, moving downward, afraid to stop, afraid to turn back, afraid to move so slowly and yet afraid to hurry. Inch by inch I went, glancing back sometimes to see what might be following. Above, I saw the awful crooked blackness of the forest's trunks and limbs, which gestured toward me in mockery. I grew strangely colder with each downward sideways step. At first I thought the chill must come from so much naked stone sucking heat out of the atmosphere. But while that might account for a few degrees of difference, the temperature dipped lower than the presence of mere granite could explain. I tried to fight my fear with numbers. Was it forty degrees Fahrenheit? Thirty-five? How could it be so cold when the temperature among the trees above the cove was nearly seventy? And the fog . . . How was this fog even possible when I had seen it nowhere else that day? How could it lie only there, only in Gin Gap Cove?

No answers came. Unable to apply logic, my mind concocted images of Pilgrims, of puny axes turned against the very trees looming above me, the ancient sentinels who stood guard in this place a thousand years before the colony's disappearance and would be watching for a thousand more. I remembered poltergeists, the sudden chills they were said to bring, along with the eerie mist of ectoplasm. I began to shake. I did not know if I trembled from fear or the cold or from the strain of holding my position on the narrow ledge. This was folly! I must get myself to level ground again, find a place to sleep beneath the trees, wake up in the morning and follow the path through the forest, where it would surely lead me back to the village.

Determined to ascend, I faced up the trail. And there I saw a pestilent shadow, black and indistinct and streaming toward me like a flock of crows.

With a moan, with no care for the deadly consequence of one wrong step, I stumbled on along the narrow ledge, descending, descending, until I reached the level of the fog. Without a backwards glance I went into the mist. Soon the beaded moisture on my glasses and the fog aglow with moonlight made it impossible to see even the rocky trail beneath my feet. I went on blindly, feeling forward with my toes, clutching uselessly at frigid slabs of stone behind my back, trusting there would be something solid beneath my next step and my next. I tried to hold my eyelids open wider, stretching them to capture every possibility of light, staring downward, whimpering, because of course the floating shape above me would not slow for fog.

I heard something scraping, very close, as if trailing claws along the unforgiving stone. Did this sound come from up above or down below? Was this really happening, or was I drifting in the nothingness of white again, my mind a misplaced thing? Uncertain, I pressed harder back against the cliff face. My effort was futile. I could no more disappear into the rock than I could fly. The sound grew louder, closer. I stared into the whiteness, swinging my head wildly left and right, desperate to see the creature before it saw me. I heard it coming from behind, higher up. No. It was down below and rising. I looked up, and down, and up again, and then I turned and it was there, close enough to touch, black and featureless except for the silhouette of head and shoulders and an upraised axe.

I screamed and leapt into the empty air.

eight

I FELL THROUGH the impossibly dense fog for less than half a second and easily landed. Unprepared for such a short descent, I staggered and then toppled over, finding myself facedown on a bed of gravel, smooth and black and polished by the sea.

"Are you okay?" came a voice from just above me.

I rolled over. A silhouetted form bent down, illuminated from behind by moonlight filtered through the mist. Through the condensation on my glasses, I saw it was a man, just a man. He put the blade of his axe upon the gravel beside me. Leaning on the handle, he knelt and said, "Are you hurt?"

I could not speak.

"Miss, I need you to tell me if you're hurt."

I swallowed. "I'm okay."

"Good. But you're on private property," said the man. "And you nearly scared me to death."

I giggled. The giggle grew and turned into manic laughter. When I paused to take a breath, the man said, "Guess maybe I scared you a little, too."

That set me to laughing again. I had to work to master my hilarity. The man beside me remained silent. Eventually I spoke. "I'm so glad you're not a ghost."

"Ah. You're afraid of haunted forests and dead Pilgrims."

To hear him speak of it aloud, even in the eerie mist and chilling cold, made me feel a fool. This was not funny anymore. I stood and brushed at my knees and adjusted my backpack. "Well, it *is* a scary story."

"I guess so." The man's vague form rose as well. "Keeps the kids home after dark, so that's a plus. Usually keeps you tourist types off my land, too."

"I'm not a tourist."

"What are you, then?"

"I'm . . ." I found I did not know the answer. I said, "I have to go," and set off into the fog, gravel clattering beneath my shoes.

"Miss?"

I kept walking.

"Miss? You might want to turn around."

Just then I stepped ankle-deep into water so cold it seemed to burn my feet. I leapt back onto the gravel bed, which was apparently a kind of beach at the edge of Gin Gap Cove. Stomping on the gravel to get warmth back into my toes, I peered through the moonlit fog. He was hidden somewhere within it. I said, "You could have warned me."

"I did" came his disembodied voice.

"Well, you . . . you . . . Can you at least show me how to get back up to the village path?"

"You have a flashlight?"

"No."

"You're gonna need one."

"I don't see you using a flashlight."

"I don't need one. You do."

"What makes you so special?"

"I know the lay of my own land."

Again I had no reply.

After a short silence he said, "Bring any water?"

I stood silently in the solid fog.

"Miss?"

"I'm here."

"How 'bout a map? Compass? GPS? Anything along those lines?"

I stomped my soaking feet on the gravel again, setting off a loud clattering of pebbles that echoed from the unseen cliffs. I said, "Look, if you won't help me find the path, just say so."

"All right. I won't help you find the path."

I stomped my feet a little harder and blew into my exposed hands to fight the growing chill. "Why is everyone so rude on this island?"

"You think so?"

"Just *mean* is what you are."

"Be a lot meaner if I was to help you go off into the woods alone this time of night."

"Why? What's in the woods?"

He laughed. "Nothing a silver bullet couldn't handle, but I'm fresh out of 'em."

"Stop making fun of me!"

"I'm sorry. But look, you really need to calm down here and face facts. You can't go back to the village tonight. You'll just get lost and end up wandering in the woods all night when you could be lying safe and sound in bed."

"What bed?"

"Well, mine of course."

Something new arose within me then, a familiar fear I sometimes felt when leaving the office alone after dark, walking to my car, past shadows in the empty downtown parking garage. I backed away from the man's voice, trying not to disturb the gravel or step into the water again, trying to gain some distance before he knew what I was doing. I had added only ten more feet between us when he said, "That might have come out wrong. What I meant was, I've got a guest room, which has a bed."

I remained silent, taking one careful step after another through the fog.

From somewhere out of sight, he continued speaking. "We could boil some lobsters. I've got a pretty good chowder left over in the refrigerator and half a blueberry pie. There's beer and wine, apple juice, grape juice, bottled water. Even got a little vanilla ice cream, I think."

I paused, conscious of my empty stomach and my parched throat.

"Come on," he said. "Seriously. You don't want to spend the night out here."

I swallowed. Between chattering teeth I said, "Does your guest room have a lock on the door?"

"Yeah, but I—"

"Do you live with someone? A wife or someone?"

He did not answer at first. When he did, his voice was harder. "I can tell from the way you talk you're not from around here. Maybe people have to ask those kinds of questions down in Atlanta or Nashville or wherever you're from, but we don't treat people that way on Winter Haven. I'm just doing the right thing, offering a good night's sleep and a meal to a lost stranger. A trespasser, actually. In the morning I'll be glad to show you how to get back to the village, but not till then. Take it or leave it. Stay out here all night if you want to. It's all the same to me."

Over the sound of my own chattering teeth I heard the rattle of his footsteps on the beach. Was he leaving? Shivering, I recalled the woods, the silent giants waiting up above, and the hissing and the sobs.

"Dallas!" I called.

The rattle of his footsteps stopped. "What?"

"I'm not from Atlanta or Nashville. I'm from Dallas."

"Whatever."

"Do you think you could keep talking so I can find my way over there?"

He stood and spoke to me until I reached him by the sound of his voice, and then he led me in the other direction, along the black gravel beach. I stayed very close so I would not lose his dark form in the fog. After we had gone a distance that I could not gauge, I noticed the ground beneath my feet was soft again, much as it had been up in the woods. Then we were climbing. After a few more minutes the mist began to clear. Still shaking from the cold, I paused and looked back over the top of the strangely flat and motionless fog.

We had ascended on a path into the notch of the deep V of Gin Gap Cove, heading inland and upward at a rate much gentler than my perilous descent along the granite ledge. I saw the tall black cliffs spreading to the left and right from my central position, angling farther and farther out from each other as they ran away, widening the gap until the cove opened onto the Atlantic with the pair of vertical stone walls framing each side of the distant ocean view. In the center of that view I saw a string of three low rocks about a quarter mile offshore, pure black forms upon a silver ocean. They had to be Evangeline's Folly, the very rocks that wrecked the Pilgrims' ship four hundred years ago according to the widow's tale. In spite of that melancholy notion

I felt a tugging at my heart to see such beauty in the moonlight, the solid slab of fog below, the starry sky above, the cliffs, the towering forest, the ceaseless waves from Africa or Europe, the constellations and the planets, and everything, all of it, rendered in a million shades of gray.

While I stood motionless to take this in, the man continued walking. I turned and hurried to catch up.

As we rose, the air around us warmed until my shivering and my chattering teeth were stilled. Although my feet were still freezing in wet socks, the sudden increase in the air's temperature was remarkable. On the right a tiny stream of water appeared from underneath a sheet of stubborn ice, trickling down the way we had come, gurgling merrily as it flowed back toward the cove and the Atlantic. I saw the full moon shimmer in a little rippled pool, then a few more steps and I was up at the same level as the forest, with Gin Gap Cove behind me and a solid wall of trees ahead.

"Do we have to go in there?" I asked, looking at the forest.

The man paused, turning toward me with the axe over his shoulder. It was my first glimpse at more than his silhouette. His perfection in the moonlight made the breath catch in my throat. I had always considered my boss, Kenneth, to be good-looking, but here was a man who deserved to have his image carved in marble for all time.

"Don't worry," he said. "I grew up in these woods."

He smiled at me then, his straight teeth flashing white in the darkness, the moon dancing in his eyes. I had to look away, lest I betray my awe.

"I'm Vera, by the way," I said, staring down at the little stream beside us. "Vera Gamble."

"Evan Frost."

He stuck out his hand. I took it. I thought how nice it would be to have a hand like it to hold whenever I wished. Suddenly aware I had clung to him too long, I let go with a little flinging motion, as if by tossing away his hand I could make up for showing too much interest. He did not seem to notice. Turning his back to me again, he said, "It's not far now." I followed him into the forest, watching the movement of his khaki trousers and plaid flannel shirt and wishing he would stop to turn his face toward me again.

nine

E VAN FROST WAS AS GOOD as his word. We soon passed
through the oppressive darkness underneath the evergreens; then we reemerged into the open. The distant sound
of surf, never completely gone since I had reached the cove,
was much louder now.

As we stepped out of the forest I saw a structure standing in
the silvern moonlight at the edge of a very long clearing. Beyond
it I saw nothing but ocean. If this was the man's house, then
house was far too small a word. The building we approached rose
from the land as if it had been planted there and grown—low
and rambling on the left and right, climbing gradually to three
stories in the center with a series of steeply pitched roofs that
pointed toward the stars at a dozen different angles. It resembled
the profile of a mountain range and was easily the largest house
I had ever seen, filling the far end of a clearing that required
ten minutes to cross on foot.

Drawing near, I saw more details. Seven chimneys of brick
and stone, perhaps a hundred windows on the one side I could
see, two separate porticoes sheltering eight entry steps each, the
steps rising toward pairs of French doors that were probably
fifteen feet tall. Reaching a black gravel court in front of one

portico, the man led me past a fountain with six tiers standing at the center of an empty pool at least fifty feet in diameter. The huge fountain was not flowing, but if it had been, I believed the sound would have masked even the nearby pounding of the surf.

"Are you serious?" I asked. "You live here?"

"About half the time."

"But this is . . . this is . . ."

"Don't be so impressed. Not until you see it in the daylight, anyway. The old place is a wreck."

Moments later I stood beside him in an entry hall the size of the entire suite of offices where I worked. The ceiling was too high to make out in the darkness.

"Hang on a second," said Evan Frost. "I'll go get the lights."

He left me there, and I was more than willing to wait, looking around at what little I could see of the ornate room. The floor was obviously made of marble or some other kind of polished stone, and I was almost certain I could see raised wood paneling on all the walls. A sweeping staircase rose from opposite the entry doors to arrive at a landing where it split and rose again in separate sections to the left and right. Above the lower landing stood a wall niche large enough to hold a life-size statue of a man on horseback. Yet the niche was empty.

A distant engine rumbled to life, and a palatial crystal chandelier above my head flickered twice. Looking up, I saw only three bulbs glowing in the fixture, with another hundred bulbs or so obviously burnt out. I also saw a filmy network of cobwebs woven through the giant chandelier's arms and made out still more cobwebs higher in the shadowed corners of the lofty space. Beyond them, painted on the ceiling in full color, stretched a glorious mural that consisted of clouds and chariots and cherubs. Strangely, the colors only spread partway across the room. Figures lightly sketched in black and white covered the rest of the ceiling, as if the artist had been interrupted in the middle of the masterpiece.

I heard a sound and lowered my gaze. No longer carrying the axe, Evan Frost reentered the hall. I got my second clear look at the man in the chandelier's soft glow. To my surprise, the light revealed a hint of wrinkles beside his eyes. He was easily a decade older than I—maybe more. Nevertheless, the laugh lines only made him more attractive. Indeed, from the endearing way his sandy brown hair lay across his forehead, to the athletic way he moved, I could not see a single flaw. Just as I had when we shook hands earlier, I forgot myself for a moment, letting my eyes dwell on him, taking in his flat stomach and broad shoulders, the tiny indentation in his chin, the firmness of his jaw, the straight and well-defined nose, and the eyes. . . . When I dared to meet his eyes, I found him looking straight at me with one, while the other wandered off toward something on the right.

In the next instant he looked away, but I had seen what I had seen, a pair of gorgeous eyes, large and brown and clear, and absolutely perfect except for the fact that they did not operate in tandem. Upon discovering this flaw I felt strangely hopeful, as if his random eye might give a woman like me some slight advantage, some right of access.

He said, "You want to help me with the dinner?"

Thinking of my solitary meals of frozen pizza, I said, "I'm not much of a cook."

"Well then, we'll just have to do our best."

He led me through an opening cased in darkly fluted wood, then down a wide, dimly lit gallery. Our footsteps echoed from the marble. At first as I followed, I could only admire the fluid way he moved. Then embarrassment set in. To be so easily infatuated, already thinking in terms of access into his life and unable to remove my eyes from him whenever he was not looking, as it was with Kenneth back in Dallas…. I told myself to turn away from this handsome stranger, to turn toward anything but him for pity's sake, to maintain a little dignity.

In self-defense I forced my attention back upon the house. I looked left and right as we walked down the hall, passing many darkened rooms. Even with most of the lights still off I could tell the spaces were unusually tall, classically symmetrical, and finished in the finest of materials. But the wallpaper was fly-specked and out-of-date, and in the dim glow of one solitary sconce I saw faded, timeworn drapery. Overwhelmed by the building's size and richness, not to mention my intense attraction to the man, I had passed several rooms before I realized none of them were furnished. In spite of all this grandeur, there were no decorations on the walls, paintings or photographs, no plants, tables, chairs, or sofas—nothing to indicate that anybody actually used the house.

A bright light spilled through a cased opening onto the gallery floor ahead. Evan reached the opening first and turned into it, out of sight. Three steps later I also turned, following him into a kitchen.

Like all the other spaces in the house, the kitchen was the largest of its kind that I had ever seen. The walls were clad in a regular grid of plain white tiles that ran up to a smooth plaster ceiling. The floor was also finished with tile, except it was earth-toned in a basket-weave pattern. In the center stood a pine table long enough to seat twenty, but beside it were only two chairs, which did not match. Along the walls I saw all sorts of equipment—stoves and ovens and built-in kettles and exhaust hoods of the type I assumed one would find in a restaurant. Most of these had an old-fashioned appearance, with porcelain finishes and dials and gauges reminding me of Zeppelins and steam locomotives and other machines of a bygone era. Here and there were gaps between pieces of equipment with haphazard bits of pipe and wiring poking through the wall, evidence of antique appliances that once occupied those empty spaces.

"Hey," I said. "What is this place?"

He paused on the far side of a stainless-steel worktable to look my way, one eye drifting to the side. "I like to call it the kitchen."

"Come on, seriously. This . . . this house or whatever it is. This whole big empty place. What are you doing here?"

"Cooking dinner."

"This is really your house?"

"Really." Reaching beneath the worktable, he found a large pot, which he put in a three-compartment sink and began to fill with water.

"All of it is yours?"

"Bet you don't boil too many lobsters down in Atlanta."

"Dallas. I'm from Dallas."

"Oh, yeah." He smiled.

Again I had to look away from the brilliance of it. "Uh, you don't sound like a—what do they call them?—a Mainer?"

"I get that a lot. Guess it's 'cause my folks weren't from here."

"But you said you grew up here."

"Well, here and there. Listen, I'm gonna run out back for a couple of bugs. Come over here and watch this pot boil, will you?"

Giving up on a straight answer, I did as he asked, although I did not like the sound of "bugs." The pot had barely begun to bubble when he returned. It turned out that bugs meant lobsters, which he brought in from someplace outdoors, one in each hand, both of the creatures curling their tails inward like chastened dogs and snapping their claws in furious slow motion. Much to Evan's amusement I declined to take the lobsters from him, or to have anything to do with their demise in the boiling water. I did manage to heat up a hearty chowder after he showed me where it was, already prepared in one of the refrigerators, and then I set a pair of places on the long table with heavy ceramic plates and stainless flatware I found at his direction in an antique white-enamel cabinet. Meanwhile, Evan sacrificed the lobsters and prepared a garden salad. When all was ready, he placed a pair of candlesticks on the table and said, "If you don't mind I'm gonna turn off the generator. Try to save a little fuel."

"That's what the engine noise was when you turned on the lights? A generator?"

He nodded, lighting a candle with a wooden kitchen match. "There's no other power on this side of the island. But it goes through a lot of gas."

"I heard something else out there, you know."

He shifted the match to the other candle. "Yeah?"

"Uh-huh. Back where we were. Was that Gin Gap Cove? I heard something strange in the forest."

"Maybe it was killer frogs or crickets." He shook the match to extinguish the flame.

"Look, I know it sounds silly, but I really do think I heard something."

"Sure you did."

"A voice."

"Dead Pilgrims."

"I'm serious."

"I see that."

"You didn't hear anything out there?"

"I heard you screaming up on the cliff. Gave me the willies."

"That's all?"

Smiling, he looked at me. To my surprise, both of his eyes seemed normal now. He said, "You gonna be okay in here all by yourself while I go kill the power?"

I nodded. He left. I sat alone at the long pine table with the feast before me. The distant rumble of the generator died and the electricity went out, leaving me in an island of candlelight. Evan Frost returned to take his place across the table.

"You didn't have to wait on me," he said. "Dig in."

I looked at the spindly red creature on my plate. "How do I . . . ?"

He smiled his perfect smile. "It's easy. Just do what I do."

Tucking the end of a paper towel over the neck of his flannel shirt, he began to break the lobster apart, gripping it forcefully and twisting it this way and that. After some initial squeamishness, I did my best to match his motions. Although my results were nowhere near as productive as his, soon I found myself with a mouthful of the tender meat. It tasted heavenly.

"Good?" he asked.

"Oh, yes!" I heard myself gushing and immediately felt embarrassed, having again shown unseemly interest. We ate without talking for several minutes, the kitchen silent except for the clinking of forks on plates.

Evan Frost spoke first. "Mind if I ask where you got that sweatshirt?"

I glanced down at the Texas Aggies name across my chest. "A guy in the village loaned it to me."

"Steady Wallis?"

"How'd you know that?"

"Did Steady know you were coming over to this side of the island when he loaned it to you?"

"I don't . . . no, he didn't. Why do you ask?"

Evan lifted a spoonful of chowder to his lips. He swallowed, then took a second spoonful.

"Look," I said, "if you're gonna ask me all these questions, you should at least answer mine."

"I thought I did."

"No, you didn't."

"Sorry. Sometimes I confuse what I think with what I say out loud. Maybe I'm alone too much."

I considered what it might be like—living five or six miles from the only village on an island fifty miles from the mainland, wandering through this gigantic house all alone. I felt a sudden rush of sympathy for the man. "No," I said. "I'm the one who ought to be sorry. I'm way too touchy."

Obvious amusement played at the corners of his lips.

I said, "I'm not usually like this. It's just, I was kind of freaked out before. I mean before we met at the cove. That *is* Gin Gap Cove, isn't it?"

"That's it all right."

"See, I asked for directions there, but everyone back at the village was so rude, and I guess I kind of got to where I expected it from people here."

"Rude? Wonder why. They're usually okay."

"Not to me." I took a large bite of lobster.

"Can I ask what you're doing here on Winter Haven?"

I chewed a moment, then, "I came to get my brother's body."

He stared at me. "A teenaged boy? Washed up on the beach?"

I saw no need to tell the man that my brother was born twenty-eight years ago. "How do you know that?"

"I'm the one who found him."

ten

L OATH TO WAKE THE HORROR in my mind with questions, still I had to know. I said, "Tell me how it happened."

Evan Frost searched my face. "Sure you want to talk about that?"

"Yes. Please."

"Okay, then. I was walking on the beach and I saw him a long way off. I thought he might be alive at first, just lying there like people do on beaches, you know? But when I got closer it was . . . uh, obvious. I mean, you can tell. So I pulled him up out of the water and—"

"He was still in the water?"

"Halfway. Just his legs."

"Why did you pull him up?"

"The tide was coming in. I didn't want him to wash back out to sea."

I covered my eyes with my right hand.

The man said, "I'm sorry."

"It's . . ." I was about to say "It's okay," an automatic response, a way of moving past an awkward moment. But it was *not* okay, and I surprised myself with a more honest reply. "It's been very hard," I said.

I removed my hand and met his eyes, and again I saw they were perfectly normal, both of them focused directly upon me. Had I imagined the randomness before? Was I imagining the sympathy I saw in Evan Frost's eyes now? I looked down at my plate. "Go on, will you? I'd like to hear everything."

"There's not much more to tell. I left him there and went to the village to find Steady. He and I came back around and picked up the . . . picked up your brother in my boat. I guess you know the rest."

"I'm surprised Mr. Wallis didn't tell me about you."

"Steady's a year-round Winter Haven man. They don't usually say more than they have to."

"But it feels like there's some kind of secret, like nobody wanted me to come out here."

"People from away usually get lost walking over to this side of the island. Then they have to be found. It's a lot of trouble. Probably they just wanted to avoid all that."

"I don't know . . . Mrs. Abernathy seemed afraid of Gin Gap Cove."

"Her? Afraid of the cove?" He sounded skeptical.

"Well, not exactly, but she talked about the lost Pilgrims and all. Said she didn't want me coming here."

When he did not reply, I looked up. He was staring at me again. He said, "What was your brother doing on Winter Haven?"

"I have no idea. Steady Wallis seems to think he fell from a passing boat." I put down my fork. "Why?"

Evan shrugged. "Just trying to explain things." He set to work on his dinner. Watching him eat, I wondered if he too was hiding something. But then he looked up to catch my eye on him, and grinned, his laugh lines crinkling wonderfully. In the radiance of his smile I told myself I was being overly sensitive. I should relax and try to enjoy the moment in spite of Siggy. After all, it was a remarkably delicious meal, it had been a long time since I had eaten dinner alone with a man, and never, ever, had I dined with such a good-looking man as this.

The candles burned down slowly as we feasted, until even the blueberry pie and vanilla ice cream were behind us and the dishes had been washed and rinsed and put away. Through it all there was hardly any talk. For some reason I felt no need to fill the time with idle chatter, and neither, apparently, did he. When we carried the candles out into the gallery, I knew little more about Evan Frost than when we had first entered the impossibly huge house, yet I had become nearly comfortable in his company. I had almost forgotten to be nervous in the face of his phenomenal good looks, almost settled into the kind of easy silence I had once enjoyed with Siggy. When Evan spoke to me of bedrooms, sheets and pillows, I had no suspicions of ulterior motives. As he led me back along the gallery, across the entry hall and up the grand stairway to my room, and as we parted at the door, I allowed myself to think he might truly be pleased to have me there.

Alone, I removed the maroon sweatshirt and washed up in the ornate bathroom in my suite. Apparently my host avoided spending money on heating a boiler just as he economized on electric lights, since only cold tap water flowed from the lavatory faucet. Still, it felt good to rinse my face and neck and underarms before carrying the candlestick to the bedside table. In its light I saw the bedroom was much like all the other spaces in the house, far larger than I thought necessary, with rich, outdated finishes on the walls. But this room was furnished, the mattress looked comfortable, the sheets were clean, and I felt at ease enough to slip out of my blue jeans and slide between the covers.

Although the day's events had left me weary, I lay awake in the candlelight a little longer, staring up at the deeply coffered ceiling, which seemed to dance with flickering shadows. Tomorrow I would ask Evan to take me to the place where Siggy's body washed ashore.

Bleak Beach.

What a name. What would such a place look like? Would I sense my brother's presence there, or would the place be unaffected by his passing? Would I find a clue to his strange, unchanged condition, or was that just another question best unasked?

As I entered the indistinct place between consciousness and sleep, where thoughts take on their own momentum and waking discipline is lost, the dreadful foe seized my imagination. This time I did not even think to fight. It thrust me back in time to sit beside my Siggy on the floor of a darkened hallway, me in my pajamas and Siggy, pale and skittish with his bony knees pulled up to his chin. For several days he had been rocking to and fro outside our mother's bedroom, quoting the King James as if his ceaseless recitation might somehow wrestle mercy from the heavens. In my youth I had believed my brother was a holy boy, as my father was a holy man. I asked Siggy for a prophecy.

"Will Momma get better?"

He broke off his endless litany somewhere in Hosea. Rocking like a rabbi at the Wailing Wall, he replied, "'They that be whole need not a physician, but they that are sick.'"

As was so often true, I was not certain what he meant, or even if his words had any relevance to our conversation. Sometimes his quotations seemed unconnected to my world. Sometimes they seemed perfectly apt. I thought a moment; then I asked, "Are you saying Momma needs a doctor?"

"'Thou hast well said.'"

"But Father will make her better. Won't he?"

"'Why then is not the health of the daughter of my people recovered?'"

"Maybe God doesn't want her to get better yet. But Father's gonna do it, right?"

Siggy rolled his eyes up toward the ceiling. His head shook, although I could not tell if the motion had a meaning, since his head was almost always moving. "'In that day shall he swear, saying, I will not be a healer.'"

"He is too a healer!"

My brother's head kept shaking. "'Ye will surely say unto me this proverb, Physician, heal thyself.'"

I saw sorrow in my brother. In my own longing for some kind of security I almost reached out to embrace him, forgetting Siggy would explode at the slightest human touch. I leaned closer, but he scooted away across the floor to keep his usual distance.

"Let's just pray, okay?" I said. "Let's just ask the Lord to heal her."

"'Is there no balm in Gilead; is there no physician there?'"

Fearful of the answer, I asked, "Don't you trust Father's gift?"

"'Faith, if it hath not works, is dead, being alone.'"

"But . . . but . . . 'You can have a miracle today!'" I was quoting, too—the catch phrase of our father's ministry.

Siggy shook his head again. "'I will pray with the spirit, and I will pray with the understanding also.'"

In dreamy memory I left him on the hallway floor outside our mother's sickroom door. I left him with Hosea, reciting every word, picking up again exactly where he had stopped. Siggy's doubt frightened me. I believed my brother had the holy gift of prophecy, but I had also seen people coming by the hundreds to be healed by my father's gift, crowding into the high school gymnasium, and a big tent behind our father's church, and in the VFW hall. I had seen them come on crutches and in wheelchairs, the blind and deaf, the palsied and asthmatic, only to leap for joy and run back home, praising Jesus and my father. Like Siggy, my father had been blessed by God. He would surely raise our mother from her bed when the time was right.

And yet she died.

Grief hit me with the freshness of a new wound. My eyes snapped open. Gradually, full consciousness returned and I remembered where I was, alone in an antique bed, in a stranger's empty mansion on Winter Haven island. At first I was relieved, because it meant my mother had not just now passed away. She had been gone for years, and sorrow was behind me. Then, as I became more alert, I began to clinch my fists and set my jaw. I had lived for years without these dreams and memories. I had made but one mistake, indulging thoughts of Siggy on the mail boat. One mistake should not be enough to cause my ruin, yet it seemed I was careening backward toward the awful thing, the terror at the end of all these memories. Desperate to halt my own decline, I closed my eyes and said, "Please forgive me. Please. It was wrong to think about it in the first place. I know that. And I promise you I'll stop if you'll just let me. Please, just let me stop before it goes too far."

My confession and repentance finished, I stared at the dancing shadows on the ceiling, solving arbitrary mathematical problems to keep my mind where it belonged until my eyelids got heavy. Then, just as I reached over to snuff out the candle, I heard a sound that sent a thrill of fear throughout my body. I had heard the sound before: the terrifying hiss above the cliff at Gin Gap Cove. There, it could have been a trick of my imagination, the treetops whispering in the wind or the distant crashing of the surf, a natural phenomenon morphed by my imagination into something sinister. But within that empty mansion were no trees or surf to form the dreadful noise I heard. Inside that strangely empty place, the thing I heard was real.

I rose to lift the candlestick, tiptoed to the hallway door, and pressed my ear against the wood. In addition to the hiss outside, I heard another sound, maybe a man's voice, maybe Evan Frost's, although I could not be sure. I listened for a long time as the muted noises rose and fell, some human, some otherworldly. I made out something almost like words, perhaps a conversation, but the tone was very strange. I was almost certain part of it was human. The rest had no humanity. It was something more mechanical, a steady drone, like a thousand insects, a plague of them outside the door.

Of course that was ridiculous. It was a trick of acoustics, the way a distant conversation bounced from wood and marble as it traveled down the corridor, the way it filtered through the door. I must be logical. I closed my eyes to better concentrate on what I heard. But I could not stop myself from wondering, if acoustics caused one voice to sound like droning locusts' wings, why did it not have the same effect upon the other? And if it was just two people talking, if there was someone else inside the house, why had Evan failed to mention it? Had that other person just arrived? It was a strange time to be traveling. I wondered what might make a person cross the island through the forest in the night.

Suddenly I heard the ugly sibilation growing louder, and then, as if to overcome that brutish noise, the more human voice rose too, and many incoherent words and noises crashed against the door.

I jerked my ear away.

What could cause such rage?

Might the cause be me?

Slowly, I turned the latch to lock myself in. Then, just as the bolt slid home, there was a sudden puff, a draft from out of nowhere, and the candle's flame blew out.

I was in total darkness.

eleven

I STOOD UPON A GRASSY POINT behind the mansion, high above the island's weather coast. A harsh wind rushed across my ears. Huge breakers crashed with wild abandon against a granite jetty far below. On the slightly calmer water inshore of the jetty, a motorboat bucked at its mooring. Winter Haven seemed to shake beneath my feet with each fresh assault by the Atlantic, yet I barely felt it through the insulation of my worries.

Siggy had begun to come unbidden now, washing over me when least expected, the undercurrent of him carving deep into the soft bottom of my mind like waves across the ocean floor. I had to find a way to stop him. I dared not descend into that emptiness again. I might not be as lucky as before. I might not return this time.

With my feet apart, leaning just a bit into the constant wind, I hugged myself, ignoring the loose strands of hair that whipped around my face. Gulls screeched and dipped and soared above. The sun had risen boldly just a little while before, only to take cover behind an approaching wall of golden clouds. In the morning glow I had already seen the mansion where I had spent the night, the rotten wood, the missing shingles, fallen shutters and peeling paint, an American palace from the Gilded Age in the final stages of decline. But why was such a palace dying?

Like everything on Winter Haven, it made no sense to me.

I wondered if I ought to follow the pathway back to the village, hire a boat, and leave. I had not enjoyed a restful night. I had lain in bed with eyes wide open in the darkness, dreading a relapse into hallucinations, trying to understand what kind of person or thing might make the eerie sounds I heard through the door, hoping what I heard was real. I had gotten it into my head to listen for the click and rattle of someone trying the doorknob. Eventually, against my will, I slept.

Then, from outside the bedroom's ten-foot windows, a mockingbird's endless imitations had awakened me. My prayer the night before had done no good. Through the glass a slice of sunshine had streamed across my face, the glare transporting me to memories of old delusions before my mind was self-aware enough to give resistance. As always, Siggy had come in total whiteness, drawing me in deeper, further from myself. A dream it was, a memory of childhood fantasy, a sweet reunion with him. But even as I longed for Siggy, I fought against him, and escaped, and arose to throw cold water on my face, to dress in another person's clothes, to find my way outside and stand high on that craggy point and watch the waves roll in, and think of things that I had struggled half my lifetime to forget.

"Good morning" came an unexpected voice.

I turned. As it had the night before, my breath caught at the sight of Evan Frost. He seemed perfectly attuned to this remarkable place, as enigmatic as the forest giants, as impregnable as the granite coast, as irresistible as the breakers. Yet I could not help but wonder if he might also be decayed and rotting somehow, like the mansion he called home.

"You just going to stare?" he asked with a smile.

Embarrassed, I turned back toward the ocean. "Who were you arguing with last night?"

"Oh no." He stepped up beside me and, like me, stared out at the Atlantic. "Did you hear more dead Pilgrims?"

"If you don't want to talk about it, just say so."

He stood silently at my side. A rogue wave crashed against the boulders. Much bigger than the others, it flung a salty mist high enough to reach my face. I licked my lips, tasting the Atlantic. I had not meant to snap at him. Along with memories of Siggy, this anger seemed to flow in crushing waves, sometimes falling back, sometimes overflowing me. I had only meant to speak more loudly than usual, to be heard above the wind, the waves, the gulls, the beating of my heart. Crazy thoughts assailed me. With one shove I could send the man beside me tumbling down into the greedy ocean. With one step I could leap down there myself. This rage might be worse than my forbidden memories. But why was I so angry? After all, if Evan did not wish to speak about his argument last night, or the voice that sounded like a thousand locusts' wings, it was none of my affair. And if no such voice existed, that was not his fault. I could have repaid his kindness with kindness, but there I was instead, snapping at him like a shrew. If I did not have the courage to pursue the truth I feared, I should simply ask him other questions—about his amazing house, perhaps, and how he came to own it, or why it was in such poor repair. I should at least make an effort to hide this angry shame.

I set out walking down the coast.

"Where are you going?" he called from behind me.

"Bleak Beach," I replied, my decision made sometime in the instant between his question and my answer.

"It's the other way."

I stopped and pushed my windblown hair out of my eyes. Of course it was the other way. What an idiot I was.

A new wave shook the earth. In its momentary thunder I turned and walked back toward him. Reaching his position, I passed him without a look, heading now in the direction he had indicated.

He called to me again. I could not understand his words over the wind and waves that roared together in my ears. I kept walking. He called again, more loudly. "How will you know when you get there?"

"I'll know."

He ran to catch up and gave my arm a pat. "No you won't."

And so I followed him, much as I had the night before, but this time as we walked he taught me the difference between the teal and the black ducks loafing among the swells offshore. He mentioned the countless generations it had taken for the cormorants to stain a giant boulder white. A snowshoe hare bounded across the path, amazing me with its speed, and he commented on its changing pelt. We scared up woodcocks and ruffed grouse, which he identified for me. As the giant pines and spruces loitered along one side of the trail and the ocean undulated to the far horizon on the other, I began to forget my suspicions about Evan Frost, who from the start had met my rudeness with such kind hospitality.

At a wide spot in the path I moved up beside him. "You're quite the woodsman."

He smiled, deepening the wrinkles by his eyes. "Not really. I like it more at sea."

"Oh? So you're a sailor?"

"A mariner, yeah. I used to sail a lot with my parents, but now I'm the captain of an oceangoing towboat."

"Really? I didn't see a towboat behind your house. Just that little motorboat."

"Be kind of hard to get the towboat in there, big as it is and seeing as how it's not mine. Besides, right now they're fixing its running gear in a dry dock over in Portland."

"What does a captain of an oceangoing towboat do, exactly?"

"I work for FHL. You heard of them?"

I searched my memory and realized I had. One of Kenneth's clients owned stock in the company. "They're in shipping—oil and gas?"

"Yeah."

"But towboats aren't for shipping, are they?"

"We do anchor handling and ice management for oil rigs in the North Atlantic."

"Ice management?"

Evan plucked a tall stalk of grass as we passed and put it in his mouth. "Fancy name for moving icebergs around. They break off of glaciers and drift down with the current toward the oil platforms up there."

"They could do some damage?"

"Sure, if we let them. So we tow them off course or use prop wash or water cannons to change the way they're drifting."

"What was that other thing you mentioned? Anchor handling?"

He paused. "This is the way down to Bleak Beach. Better let me go first." He turned off the path between a pair of boulders the size of refrigerators, then stepped down onto the top of another, and down again onto another, then paused to look back up at me. "Can you make it?"

I had already followed and stood atop the big rock directly above him. "Lead on," I said.

Over the next few minutes we picked our way across the pile of boulders, descending about forty feet. At one point he reached up to offer me a hand as I hopped from one rock to another. When we were almost down to the beach, he leapt over a slightly larger gap and turned back toward me, saying, "I'll catch you." Before I could talk myself out of taking the chance, I jumped.

He caught me on the other side, wrapping both his arms around me. We stood that way a moment, our faces very close. I had the feeling that he liked to stand that close. I stared into his eyes and saw both tenderness and strength there, and understood why men would follow him to sea. Then his right eye wandered just a little. He let me go and looked away.

I wanted to tell him not to be self-conscious about his eye. I wanted to say how glad I was that he was finally answering my questions, telling me about himself. I wanted him to know I thought him beautiful. I felt drawn to something in him, as if to warmth on a cold day. But I told myself this was foolishness, an emotional reaction to the majestic and unfamiliar surroundings, which were such a sweet relief from the strange resurgence of my childhood's waking nightmares, and from the shock of finding Siggy lying in a packing shed, totally unchanged at twenty-eight years of age.

I turned to the familiar territory of business. "You were telling me about anchor handling."

"Oh, yeah." He hopped onto a lower boulder. "Oil platforms are kept in place by these big anchors, which are connected to the platforms by big cables, big around as your leg, some of them. Me and the guys, we set the anchors and lay the cables. Sometimes we do it when the platforms are new, and sometimes after the anchors shift."

"The anchors shift?"

"Pretty often, actually. They get powerful storms up north of Newfoundland, you know. Fifty, seventy-five-foot waves. Puts a lot of strain on the anchors. Sometimes it works them right out of the bottom."

He led me down the last few rocks until we were standing on Bleak Beach.

The shoreline sloped up gently from the ocean and ran in a concave arc for about half a mile, but it was not what I would have called a beach. There was no sand. Instead, it was composed of smooth pebbles, mostly polished black like the ones I had seen the night before in Gin Gap Cove. I said, "I can't even imagine seventy-five-foot waves. It sounds very dangerous."

"Well, yeah, I guess. But the *Albert Murray*—that's my ship—she's real sea-kindly, and my guys are wicked good. Most of 'em grew up right here on Winter Haven, so they know the ocean. There's been a couple of us get hurt, but nobody's died so far."

"Nobody's *died* so far? How in the world does a person get started in that kind of work?"

"Like I said, most of my guys grew up here, lobstering with their fathers and whatnot, so it's kind of normal for them. I grew up on the water, too. Summers here every year, crewing on yachts, that kind of thing. It gets in your blood. So about twelve years ago I started working for the FHL fleet, and last year I made captain."

Together we set out walking along the beach. On the left, the waves rolled to a gentle stop, then retreated out to sea across the pebbles. I heard a muted rattle as the water sifted through the stones, like the clatter of a herd of horses cantering across a distant pavement. Compared to the violence of the breakers behind Evan's house, this might have been a different ocean. Compared to Evan's reticence the night before, he might have been a different man. But something still felt wrong, disconnected, about a towboat captain living in a mansion. Trying to be tactful for a change, I said, "It seems like a long way from sailing around in yachts to being captain of a towboat."

"You sound like one of my guys. He calls me Topsider. "

"Topsider?"

"It's a kind of shoe some people wear on yachts, like a moccasin with a rubber sole. Back when I was just starting out as a deckhand, I showed up for work with a pair of them on. Once you do a dumb thing like that, they won't ever let you forget it. It's the best shoe you can wear on a yacht but not so great when you're handling five-inch cable. Kind of like showing up at a ranch to work cattle in a pair of sandals."

I laughed.

He said, "I like your laugh."

Covering my mouth, I looked away.

"You know," he said, "it took a lot for you to come all the way out here alone."

I shook my head. "I had to do it."

"But to come clear to my place from Nashville, all alone. To cross the island like you did . . . I really admire that."

"I'm from Dallas."

"No foolin'?"

Glancing his way again, I found him smiling, because of course he knew where I was from. I took solace in his teasing. It meant he liked me; I was almost certain of it.

We walked in silence for a while. I heard only the clattering of pebbles winnowed by the waves. I began to think of what had drawn me to this place. Siggy, lying on the beach, was such a lonesome image. I was amazed my brother had been found before the animals and elements destroyed him. I imagined Siggy all alone, lying in that wild, forbidding place, waiting for discovery. I could not bear to look ahead as Evan and I walked. I watched my feet instead. To look ahead was to see my Siggy on that beach, which felt so foreign, with our mother's laminated card still around his neck after all the years, drifting in and out beside him upon every tender wave.

I am not dangerous.

Evan spoke. "Mind if I ask you something?"

I glanced at him. "Okay . . ."

"I was just wondering about your brother, why a boy his age wasn't at home."

The question made me shudder. The temptation to revisit forbidden memories was already bad enough; must I face it from this man as well? I said, "It's complicated."

"Right. None of my business. Sorry."

His words brought me back from the brink. They made me realize how badly I wanted to speak of my sins. Maybe if I spoke of them aloud I could pass through untouched. I said,

"I'm sorry. It's just that it really is complicated. But if you want to know . . ."

I began to tell him things I had not shared with anybody. I started after my mother's death, with my father in the living room looking as old as his years, talking tragedy with stern men in suits while Siggy and I listened from around the corner in the hall. The men had asked my father many questions. Their voices had been harsh. As I described the scene aloud to Evan Frost, I almost heard my whispered question to Siggy, "Are they policemen?" And Siggy, with his head in constant motion, his eyes on everything but me, saying nothing. But my brother seemed to understand the accusation in the visitors' dark-suited posture, the danger in their words.

I spoke to Evan of wanting to defend my father, of believing God must have taken my mother that way for a reason. All we had to do was pray and ask God to explain himself. I said, "Siggy blamed my father for what happened. My parents believed God would heal my mother. They never called a doctor."

Evan nodded. "I see."

"You think that's awful."

"No."

"Oh, of course you do. It *is* awful, letting somebody die without calling in a doctor."

Evan Frost did not reply, but I had to keep on speaking of my memories, moving them outside my head, where they could not tempt me quite as strongly to remember something worse. "He ran away from home," I said. "That's why he was here alone."

"Thought it might be that."

"My father was too hard on him."

"After your mother died?"

"He was way too hard on him."

The handsome man stared out at the sea. "Grief can turn you into someone you don't recognize."

Surprised, I glanced at him again. It was as if he somehow understood, and his understanding drew me irresistibly. I found myself talking about the time I heard Siggy screaming, about running to the kitchen to find my father in the middle of the room and my brother standing by the sink, shouting, " 'Every good tree bringeth forth good fruit; but a corrupt tree bringeth forth evil fruit!' " I described my father's wrinkled cheeks, glistening with tears—that had been the most shocking thing—and Siggy's anger set loose in his body, his head wobbling like a top as it spun down, saliva dripping from his mouth.

I told the story for the first time in my life, and many little things came unbidden to my mind, strange things I had no reason to remember. I told Evan how I had focused on a simple wooden plaque above the sink where Siggy stood, how those daring words painted by my missing mother on a calico background had offered comfort in that dreadful moment: *As for me and my house, we will serve the Lord.* I told him how I saw a drop of spittle hit the plaque when my brother slapped the countertop in time with his words. " 'Whoso killeth any person, the murderer shall be put to death by the mouth of witnesses!' "

And our father shouted, "Are you talking about me? *Me?* I didn't kill your mother!"

But Siggy would not let it go. Siggy looked at everything but my father and me, chanting in his singsong voice. " 'Whoso killeth! Whoso killeth! Whoso killeth!' "

I told the handsome man beside me how my father crossed the kitchen in two steps, how he raised his hand to Siggy, how my brother's head had spun and dipped beneath our father's upraised fist, but he never flinched. I relived my own explosion then, my screaming, "Don't hurt him! He doesn't know what he's doing!" and my father, shocked by my outburst, looking from Siggy to me, confusion in his flowing eyes, how tired and old he had seemed as his fist came slowly down. I spoke to Evan of my hope that the worst was over. On Bleak Beach, I drew a shuddering breath and let it out as a sigh. I said, "But then he put his hand on Siggy's arm."

Evan Frost said, "So? If I back-talked my dad that way, he would've beat the stuffing out of me."

"You saw that card around Siggy's neck, right? When you found him here?"

"Well, yeah . . . Oh. It said he was autistic."

"For some reason it terrified him to be touched."

"Poor guy. Was that also why he quoted the Bible that way? Was that the autism, too?"

It comforted me that Evan knew the source of Siggy's words, even if the words themselves had never been a comfort. I explained about my brother. The savant syndrome. Speaking only in quotations.

Evan said, "So he was some kind of genius, even though he had autism? Is that how he got all the way out here from Texas?"

"He wasn't smart like you mean. Not in common sense, or knowing about people. He couldn't tell if someone was happy or angry. He couldn't understand money. I don't think there's any way he could have come here on his own."

We walked on in silence. I had been a fool to think it possible to speak with Evan of these things in safety. I felt the horror rising within. I tried to resist with numbers, counting pebbles as I passed, but my memories had been set in motion and would not be denied. Beneath the gulls and waves I heard Siggy erupt with a piercing cry, high-pitched and continuous, as if our father's touch had burned his skin, and just like that, I lost myself again.

I saw our father set out for the hall. He would not release poor Siggy. Keening with a terror only Siggy understood, my brother meekly followed in his grip. Halfway down the hall, our father reached up and the ladder descended with a groaning of the springs. He shoved Siggy toward the attic. Eager to escape the frightening hand upon his arm, my brother climbed into his favorite place, his strange idea of heaven. As I raised my face to look into the attic, I felt a searing tongue uncoil to lick my cheeks. The asphalt roads were already soft that year, and my mother's candles, forgotten on the patio, had melted into useless pools of wax. Beyond my brother I saw the rafters flicker in the molten air. I begged my father not to send him up.

"He brought this on himself," said my father. "You saw that. He needs time to learn to honor his parents." My father's voice dropped almost to a whisper. "I mean, to honor me."

Above us I saw Siggy smiling, his eyes lifted away, his head a metronome. He said, " 'And they ascended up to heaven in a cloud; and their enemies beheld them. Their enemies beheld them. Their enemies beheld them.' "

"Siggy!" I cried. "Stop it! Father's not your enemy!"

"Be quiet now," said my father. "He'll be fine. He just needs a while to think."

But I knew the bonds between the three of us were tearing. I knew everything would be different after that, even though my Siggy tried to offer comfort, saying, " 'See that ye be not troubled: for all these things must come to pass, but the end is not yet. Our God whom we serve is able to deliver us from the burning fiery furnace, and he will deliver us out of thine hand.' "

As Father closed the attic stairs, the voice of Evan Frost called to me from where I really was, walking on Bleak Beach.

"Are you okay?"

I tried to come back, but the terror had drawn very near this time. I could only nod.

"You seem a little distant all of a sudden."

I said nothing. I should not have dared to speak of the past.

"What's wrong?" he asked.

"I was thinking about Siggy." Even I could hear the dullness in my voice.

"I'm sorry I brought him up."

"No. I need to work some things through, is all."

The man stayed silent. But he had drawn a little closer as we walked.

I vowed not to cry. I had come so far to be in this place. After all the years I finally had a chance to understand why Siggy left, where he went, what he wanted. Winter Haven was the end of him. I should be searching for some hint of what had happened on that beach, not fading into the past. Still, I felt my lower lip begin to tremble. I took it between my teeth and bit down. The pain was welcome. I did not want to play the role of a helpless female. Was I really so weak-minded? Would I really let this man's respect slip away like water through these pebbles just because of grief I should have passed through long ago? I stopped walking and stared down at the beach beside my feet, counting rocks again. I should get a figure for the number of rocks between each step, then calculate the number of steps from the waterline to the edge of the cliffs, then count my steps along the beach and thus arrive at a reasonably accurate estimate of the number of pebbles on the surface of this beach. I should think in terms of math and not in terms of Siggy. I should . . . I would try to . . . to . . .

Evan put his arm around my shoulder. He was hesitant about it, his motions awkward. I could tell this kind of thing did not come naturally, but he did it, and with the unexpected gesture I lost myself to tears. He stood beside me stiffly, his arm across my back, the fingers of his hand spread wide on my far shoulder. Every now and then he gave me a little pat. Perhaps it was a sign of wisdom that he spoke no words as my body convulsed in wave after wave of racking sobs.

Through the long overdue flood I saw Siggy walking off into the afternoon beyond our front porch, my final glimpse of him, too fleeting as he passed beneath the trees on the distant corner, Siggy leaving on my birthday, with nothing but a backpack laden down with candy and his precious Viking things, a dozen editions of *The Mighty Thor*, his favorite comic book, and that *National Geographic* issue with the article about Leif Erickson in Greenland. I saw myself standing on the porch as the bell of Father's church tolled the time.

At exactly four-fifteen in the afternoon I let Siggy go, four-fifteen on my first birthday without a cake, or candles, or presents, or any of the other things our mother used to do. I would not let him make me beg. I would not plead with him to stay. Let him go and let it be good riddance; let him leave me there with nothing but a broken father and a stubborn demand that God must make some sense of this. In my angry silence I almost missed my Siggy's parting words. " 'I go to prepare a place for you. And if I go and prepare a place for you, I will come again, and receive you unto myself; that where I am, there ye may be also.' " I almost missed those words, thinking only of myself, my birthday, my pain, my loss. I let my brother go that day, and for that I would hate myself forever.

When the worst was over and Evan had removed his arm from my shoulders, I felt a different kind of loss. There had been no hint of anything beyond comfort in the gesture, but it had been so very long since anyone had offered even that to me.

He said, "You loved him a lot."

I wiped my eyes and looked out toward the ocean. "He needed me, or at least back then I thought he did."

"I understand."

I heard a hint of sorrow in his words and suddenly I knew why he was good at giving comfort. I wanted to return the favor, but it seemed presumptuous to ask what made him sad.

"Evan," I said, using his name for the first time. "You made me feel better."

He turned to face me. Both his eyes were melancholy, but true. "I'm glad," he said.

"Do you think we could walk a little further? Maybe you could show me where you found him?"

We set out down the beach. In spite of the risk, I was still thinking about the day Siggy left, almost exactly thirteen years ago. I said, "You think there's any cake on this island?"

"Cake?" He smiled. "You're thinking about cake now?"

"Uh-huh."

"You must be feeling better."

"It's my birthday Monday. I was thinking maybe cake would cheer me up."

"No kidding? That was my grandmother's birthday, too."

"Was? She's gone?"

"Yeah. Almost everybody in my family is."

"You must've cared a lot about her," I said, "to remember her birthday."

"Oh, I have help remembering."

"How's that?"

"It's a family secret."

"Okay . . ."

He seemed to sense my disappointment. "I'd like to share it with you one of these days."

Brightening, I watched as a nearby pair of sandpipers chased one retreating wave in triumph, then turned to flee before the onslaught of the next. I had barely noticed the little birds before, but now their antics made me smile. In the aftermath of my tears the air smelled fresher somehow; the ocean seemed less lonely. Until that moment, Winter Haven had imposed a sense of gloom to match my grief, but as I walked Bleak Beach with Evan Frost, I could look into the distance without seeing Siggy washed up in the surf, and I began to wonder if it might be possible to find a kind of peace upon the island.

About a hundred yards farther up the beach a cloud of gulls wheeled madly in a tightly spinning column, flying impossibly close to each other and screeching with more urgency than usual. I thought nothing of it until the wind brought something putrid to my nose.

"Yuk," I said. "I wonder what that is?"

Evan shielded his eyes from the sun with his free hand, staring ahead. "Dead seal probably. Something's always washing up on this beach."

I stopped in my tracks.

"Oh, Vera," he said. "I wasn't thinking."

"It's okay." I went from a flash of grief to another of pure joy at the sound of my own name upon his lips. How strange that I could feel such different emotions in the time it took to take a breath. How strange that I could feel this way about a man who had only spoken my name once.

Evan Frost nodded toward the source of the foul aroma. "I found your brother further up, past that thing, whatever it is. You sure you wanna keep on going?"

The end of Bleak Beach lay about three hundred yards past the dead seal. I knew I would regret it if I turned back. I needed to be in the exact place where Siggy had lain. I needed to stand there in that very place, to somehow put his ghost to rest. I set out again, saying, "It's not that bad."

As Evan walked beside me, his eyes never seemed to leave the dark form on the beach beneath the gulls. I shielded my own eyes as he had done, and saw the way the gulls fought over the unlucky seal's remains. Swallowing, I raised the sweatshirt's collar to cover my nose against the rancid smell. "It's awful!"

Evan slowed our pace. When we were about a hundred feet away, he gripped my arm. "Let's turn around."

"No, it's okay."

He stopped. He would not move. He would not let me go. "Just walk back with me, okay?"

"But why?"

Placing himself between me and the thing on the beach, blocking my view of it, Evan Frost said, "I don't think that's a seal."

twelve

WE RETURNED ALONG THE coastal path in much less time than it had taken to walk out to Bleak Beach that morning. Behind his immense home, Evan led me down a long set of steps carved into the granite cliff. At the bottom he left me standing alone on a floating dock. It projected into a small man-made harbor created by the granite jetty I had seen at sunrise. I watched him row out to his motorboat in a small dinghy. Several waves broke on the far side of the jetty, spraying me with a fine mist. Even though the swells on the jetty's leeward side were much lower than those out on the ocean side, when Evan returned to pick me up, the water surged too violently to let him maneuver his boat against the dock. He shouted instructions over the hammering of the nearby breakers, and at his carefully timed, "Now!" I leapt across two feet of water into the motorboat's pitching cockpit. The instant I fell into my seat, Evan reversed the powerful engines away from the dock. He then threw the throttles forward, and we roared past the end of the jetty into the open ocean.

In spite of the bow's vicious pounding, I felt no seasickness as we flew around the island, the motorboat leaping from wave to wave. This was probably because of the trip's brevity and the shock of discovering the corpse on Bleak Beach. We soon entered the calm waters of Winter Haven harbor. We coasted to the dock, where I stepped from the boat with a line in my hand and tied it to a cleat as if I had been doing it for years. Five minutes later, Evan and I were in Steady Wallis's store.

After hearing our news, Winter Haven's constable went straight down to his lobster boat in the harbor, intent upon recovering the body. I remained on the dock while Evan in his motorboat followed Steady out of sight around the point. Almost two hours passed. In that time, the news of another body washing ashore somehow spread across the village. About two dozen people gathered to wait at the landing. One of the last to show was the owlish man who had traveled over with me from the mainland. Looking out of place with his camera and his L.L.Bean outfit, he strolled onto the dock's far side just as the lobster boat idled into the harbor.

Steady Wallis returned alone. I found myself gazing toward the slice of open ocean visible between the black rocks at the harbor entrance. I hoped to see Evan's smaller motorboat rounding the same point. Surely he was coming back. Surely he was not going to leave me there without even a good-bye. But Steady Wallis docked, and he and another man removed the body from his boat, and still there was no sign of Evan.

They had wrapped the corpse in a bright blue tarp. With my arms crossed, clutching myself, I watched the two men lower their burden into a wooden handcart. They wheeled it up the ramp and off along the shore. Unlike most of the villagers, I kept my distance from the cart. I did not want that smell inside my nostrils again. Soon the men reached the packing shed where Siggy lay. From behind the little gathering of people, I called to them. "Please don't put it there."

Steady turned his eyes toward me. "There's no place else, Miss Gamble."

I tried to think of something logical to say, some rationale for why the dead man ought not to be allowed in Siggy's resting place. Nothing came to mind except the certainty that it was wrong. "Please," I said again.

"I'm sorry. Maybe ya should wait back at my store."

Steady Wallis grasped the knotted rope that served as a door handle. He pulled, exposing the packing shed's interior. Through the open door beyond him, I saw the low concrete box containing my brother's body. I raised one of my arms to lay a palm across my eyes. I left my other arm where it was, across my lower chest in a self-embrace. I stood that way a moment. Then I dropped my hand to look around. The handcart was now empty over by the packing shed, with Steady Wallis and the other man inside. The owlish man had already moved on. Two village women held a whispered conversation while casting fleeting glances back and forth between the shed and me. A nearby man turned away and shook his head. No one offered a smile, or a concerned look, or any other sign of sympathy.

I set out walking.

I crossed the lush field of uncut grass and reached the wide trail of broken pink and white shells that wound through the village. As I passed among the weathered homes, again I wondered why Evan had not returned. He had not even offered me a wave in parting. Disappointment caught me by surprise. I thought we had made a connection on the beach. I had let myself believe . . .

No.

I had no claim on Evan Frost, no reason to expect he would be back. Only a naïve fool would put so much importance on one sympathetic arm around a shoulder and a few minutes of commiseration. It would be pathetic to turn that simple act of kindness into something more. In this, as in the memories of my childhood hallucinations, I must exercise control. I must choose which paths my mind would follow, just as surely as I had chosen the path now before my feet. I must choose to think of nothing but the present. No fantasies of romantic futures, and no blasphemous pasts must cross the threshold of my thoughts.

A trickle of people went by, walking back the other way, toward the harbor. I supposed they had only just now heard about the body. I wondered if they had recently shown this same morbid interest in my brother. Had Steady Wallis laid my Siggy out for all to see? Had these people gathered round to comment on the fairness of his skin, his silky yellow hair, his strange frozen smile? I began to glare at every passing villager. Most did not look my way, but one man smiled and nodded. I did not see his good intentions soon enough to wipe the anger from my face. Startled, he looked away.

Soon the villagers were all behind me. I walked alone along the trail again. I passed the church and several houses. I heard a swishing sound and saw the tall grass near the trail ripple as if a small animal had dashed into it. I felt a tap upon my backpack. I stopped and turned and saw no one.

I searched for the Widow Abernathy's cottage. When Steady Wallis had led me there through fog two days before, I had been in shock. Now I could not retrace our steps. Did the widow live along this narrow trail between the little bungalows on my left, or should I go a little farther down the main trail before turning? One old shingled cottage leaned slightly toward the narrower trail. As with the fish-packing shed, the inclined building frightened me. I reminded myself the cottage before me had been standing there for two centuries or more. It would not tumble in the instant I passed by. Yet I still avoided the narrow trail in favor of the broader path ahead.

I thought I heard the sound of footsteps. I glanced back over my shoulder. Again I saw no one.

I felt another tap upon my backpack. I spun, and received an impression of a willowy figure robed in black. Instantly it disappeared beyond the corner of a house, but not before I glimpsed long black hair, a face as pale as moonlight and diaphanous apparel that seemed to float and flow as if adrift in underwater currents.

Half convinced the vision was a trick of light and shadow, I called, "Hello?"

Hearing only the distant surf, I backed away, glancing left and right, afraid to shift my attention from the spot where the man, or woman, or thing, had disappeared.

"Hello?" I called again.

Again, nothing replied.

Had it been some kind of hallucination? After thirteen years of peace, could I be having new delusions? Not memories of a childhood malady, but renewed attacks, right here and now?

Refusing to admit it, I turned and hurried on along the path. I would think of proper things, healthy things, things that did not lead to wicked doubts and questions.

Something fell to the earth ahead of me. It lay black and shiny on the bleached-white shells. I knew it instantly as the very kind of pebble I had seen at Gin Gap Cove and Bleak Beach. I continued walking, staring down at the glistening surface of the stone. Then, recognizing the danger, I looked away. I would ignore it altogether. I would think of proper things.

A familiar hissing came. As before, it had the quality of wind caressing treetops. It curled and flowed and formed itself into lanky, stringy sounds that might have been a long-dead heathen language. This too must be ignored. Just as my childhood fantasies had never lent themselves to logic, this hissing had no place in rationality, or in faith.

But another pebble fell. Then another, and another, until the little rocks were pouring down all around me—striking the shells, the grass, my head, my shoulders, my legs. It was raining pebbles from a cloudless sky, and this . . . this could not be ignored.

I ran.

I saw a smaller path off to the left. I took the turn and ducked between two houses. Up on a little rise ahead I saw the widow's cottage. I closed the distance quickly. Dashing through the gate and yard, I reached the door and beat upon it frantically. When the widow did not answer right away, I turned the knob. Of course it was not locked. I entered. I quickly shut the door and locked it. Stepping up to a window, I peered out.

Before me lay the cottage's unkempt yard within the low picket fence, and beyond the fence the trail went on to cross a small field, winding away toward other houses in the distance. Off to the left I saw a small beech grove, only partially in leaf. Other than the beeches, path, field, and houses, I saw nothing. Yet something lingered out there, watching. I was certain of it. The only alternative was the far more terrifying prospect that it crouched inside of me.

"What are ya doin', girl?"

Turning, I found the widow standing in the hallway opening. With her had come the sickly odor suggestive of embalming fluid. And like a coroner interrupted in the midst of grisly work, the old woman wore a stained white apron over her black dress.

She removed a pair of flesh-colored rubber gloves from her bony hands. I returned my attention to the scene outside.

"I asked ya a question," said the widow from behind me.

"Something chased me here."

"Did it now? And what was that?"

"I don't know."

I heard the widow cross the room. Reaching my side, she gazed out through the window. "Don't see nothin'."

"It's there. It's hiding."

The old woman's eyes remained on the view outside. "Are we talkin' 'bout a dog?"

"No! It was a . . . like a woman. Or a man. I'm not sure."

"But ya called it a 'thing.' "

"The way it moved and looked, the sounds it made . . . I'm not sure what it was."

Something hit the door. Flinching, I gave a startled cry. The old woman hurried across the room. Flinging open the door, she stood squarely in the opening, staring out with heavy shoes spaced wide apart and fists on slender hips. I peeked past her shoulder. I saw no one.

After a few seconds, the widow lowered her gaze to the ground. She descended to the path in her yard and bent at the waist to pick up a polished black stone. I watched as the old woman rubbed the stone between her thumb and fingers, then raised her eyes to the stand of beeches, and scanned the nearby field. Slowly, the awful hiss rose up to fill the air.

"Evangeline!" shouted the old woman. "Do not test my patience! Get back where ya belong!"

The hissing stopped instantly. Only the distant rumble of the surf remained. The old woman waited, still rubbing the smooth black stone as if it were a talisman. Finally, she turned and climbed the steps again, entering the cottage and closing the front door.

"Evangeline?" I asked.

The widow ran her eyes along my form, from top to bottom. "Ya went across the island. Ya went across while ya was dressed like *that*!"

I looked down at myself, at the maroon Texas Aggies sweatshirt and the blue jeans Steady Wallis had loaned me. "What's wrong with how I'm dressed?"

"Oh, child. Long as you're on Winter Haven, ya better learn to listen."

Shaking her head, the widow walked into the hallway, leaving me alone in the front room. I did not want to admit I had broken my promise not to visit Bleak Beach. I did not want to admit the old woman had been right to warn me to avoid it. I did not want to admit there was something strange about Gin Gap Cove, or that I got lost and nearly spent the night out in the forest. I tried to think of another story I could tell, but nothing else seemed plausible. On such a small island everyone would soon know the truth anyway. Swallowing my pride, I followed the old woman down the hall.

In the kitchen, the widow turned.

I said, "I'm sorry."

"Sorry are ya? Why's that?"

"I should have listened. I shouldn't have gone over there."

The old woman fixed her opaque eyes on me. "Ya should not have come to Winter Haven at all."

"Look. I apologized. What else do you want?"

"I don't want your apology, girl. I'm sayin' this for your own good. I only want ya to understand there's an evil here in Winter Haven. Things at work ya cannot understand."

"I don't believe in ghosts, Mrs. Abernathy."

"Indeed? Why then did ya run so hard along the path?"

I stumbled on my words. "There was something . . . someone . . . outside. I thought I saw . . ." I fell silent.

"Child," she said, "let me find ya a ride home. One of the boys will take ya right across if I go do the askin'."

"I can't leave yet. Not without my brother. Not until I understand what happened."

"Your brother died. There's nothin' ya can learn 'bout that by stayin' here."

"I saw where they found him."

"And did that help ya somehow?"

I looked away. "No."

"'Course not. And now we got another one, dead beside him."

"That's got nothing to do with me."

"Ya know nothin' 'bout what does or does not have to do with ya on Winter Haven."

"Explain it to me, then."

"I've said everythin' ya need to know, child. We all of us made peace with Winter Haven long ago, but ya got no way of understandin' what we have to bear. Ya can only bring more grief."

"I'm staying, Mrs. Abernathy."

The old woman sniffed. "You're filthy."

Again, I looked down at the clothes on loan from Steady Wallis. "I know."

"I cleaned your own things. They're in your room."

"Thank you, ma'am."

"Ya don't have to call me 'ma'am.' I already told ya that."

"I'm sorry."

"Stop apologizin', girl. Makes ya sound so weak."

I swallowed. "Can I still sleep here tonight?"

She stared hard at me, and I thought she would refuse. Then, "Ya know what I charge. Now go clean yourself. I got to get down to the cellar and finish my day's work."

"Can I help?"

The old woman laughed. I did not find it pleasant. Opening the cellar door she said, "Ya know how to dodge and burn a print?"

"Do what?"

"Can ya develop film, girl?"

Suddenly I understood the stained apron, the rubber gloves, the odd chemical odor in the house, and the wonderful collection of black-and-white photographs hanging on the widow's walls. I said, "You took all these pictures?"

"Ya seem surprised."

"No, I just . . . I didn't realize . . ."

"I learned to take 'em from a woman stayed here many years ago. She was a friend of Mr. Abernathy's, but I'm the one he chose."

"They're beautiful."

"Bah! That witch has killed the beauty. I don't waste my time with it no more."

Having no idea how to respond, I remained silent.

The widow continued. "My Mr. Abernathy was an artist, ya know. A great artist. He taught me how to see the world."

"Did he do all your watercolors?"

She stared at me. "Ya never told me where ya spent last night."

The sudden change of subject caught me unprepared. I answered frankly. "I slept at Evan Frost's place."

The woman's eyes turned knowing. "Did ya now?"

"Don't say it like that. It's not like I slept *with* him."

"So ya say."

I felt the blood rise to my cheeks. "Are you calling me a liar?"

"No need for that. Sleeping under his roof is bad enough. Go get yourself clean and change into your own clothes, and then occupy yourself somehow without causin' further trouble. I been at my work below for hours already, and I cannot leave things as they are, but I'll be up and cookin' dinner soon enough." She stepped down onto the narrow cellar stairs, then paused to look back. "Do not open this door, ever, or you'll ruin my prints." With that warning, she shut the cellar door a bit more forcefully than necessary.

I wondered how the widow knew I had run from the thing out on the trail if she had been at work on her photographs as she claimed. She must have been watching. She must have lied to me. I wanted to know why. I wanted all my questions about Winter Haven answered. I crossed the kitchen. I laid my hand upon the cellar doorknob. I willed myself to turn the knob, to descend the steps into the island's rocky bowels and confront the widow there, but the old woman's parting admonition echoed in my mind. I stood with my hand upon the doorknob, motionless. Then I released it, turned, and walked away.

thirteen

THE FOLLOWING MORNING I awoke to the sound of pealing church bells. My first thoughts were of Evan Frost. I had gone to sleep remembering his handsome profile on the beach, his kindness to me there, the strength in his arm around my shoulder as I wept, the comfort of his patient silence as I recalled the things that caused me pain. Why had he not returned with Steady Wallis? Was that too much to expect? Had it all been simple charity? Was I the only one who sensed the possibility of something more?

I rose from the refuge of the four-poster bed and dressed in my own woolen sweater and blue jeans, which had been washed and folded by the widow. In the bathroom across the hall I threw water on my face and looked into the mirror. The young woman I saw in the glass seemed very plain to me, very unremarkable. I envisioned Evan Frost—the man's physical perfection—and realized what a stretch it was to think he might be interested in me.

In the kitchen I found the widow seated at the table, reading a Bible. Without looking up, the old woman said, "Coffee's in the pot. I left some eggs and bacon for ya in the skillet on the stove. No need to take more than ya can eat. The dogs been fed already."

Sheepishly I stepped over to the stove, served myself, and sat down opposite the widow.

The old woman said, "Don't suppose someone like you goes to church."

"Someone like me? What's that supposed to mean?"

"Don't go gettin' your back up first thing on a Sabbath mornin', girl. I only meant most people from away, especially from a big city somewheres, they don't seem to keep the Lord's day holy."

"I go to church."

The widow lifted her eyes from the Bible. "Didn't mean just Easter."

It was as if she somehow knew about all my recent Sundays and working at the downtown office. I said, "I go when I can."

"Well then. Can ya go this mornin'?"

Considering the standoffish ways of Winter Haven's villagers, I had no desire to spend time watching them pretend a piety they clearly did not possess. "I have other plans."

"'Course ya do."

As the widow returned her attention to the Bible, I ate my breakfast with a frustrating sense of guilt. It was true I had not been to church in seven weeks, not since the last time I made the drive to Mount Sinai to see my father. Church for me had always been his church, the one he had led for almost four decades. When I drove out to see him at the nursing home on Saturdays, I often stayed the night and then went alone to his church. I was not certain why. Maybe I just wanted to show his congregation there was a Gamble in the world the Lord had left uncursed.

But lately it had been too hard to bear the vacancy behind my father's eyes, and the disapproval in his congregation's stares. Lately, even when I did not have to go in to the office, I found other reasons to remain at home on Sundays.

I put a forkful of eggs into my mouth and chewed, watching the old woman. I could not forget her knowing look the night before when she learned I had spent the night at Evan's house. Now came this morning's assumption that "someone like you" would not go to church. The widow believed she knew what kind of person I was. I had been judged and found unworthy. Swallowing my eggs, I said, "When do you leave for church?"

"Five minutes," said the widow without looking up.

"I'll be ready."

It actually took nearly fifteen minutes to finish my breakfast, wash my face more properly, make some sense of my hair, and attend to my teeth with a new toothbrush the widow had left for me in the bathroom. The old woman showed no sign of impatience. We set out together from the cottage's front door—I in my thick woolen sweater and blue jeans, and the old woman in a black sunbonnet and a different dress, also black, adorned with two rows of golden buttons at the breast and a gleaming satin collar.

It was another unseasonably warm day. The sky ranged from a pastel shade of blue along the far horizon to something deeper, nearly ultramarine, directly above. I saw a pair of birds far overhead, gliding effortlessly upon the rising thermal caused by so much granite soaking up the sun. I heard the omnipresent growl of distant surf. The widow clutched her leather-covered Bible in both hands and stood aside while I opened the decrepit picket gate at the edge of her yard. I saw a shiny black stone lying on the path of shells. I cast an anxious glance toward the nearby stand of beeches.

"There'll be none of that while you're with me," said the old woman.

I wondered if the widow was a mind reader. I recalled the hail of polished stones that had chased me to her house and the old woman shouting from her open door. I thought about the same black pebbles on the gentle slope of Bleak Beach. I thought about those other rocks, Evangeline's Folly, the menace lying black and low a quarter mile offshore of Gin Gap Cove.

I said, "You never did tell me who Evangeline is."

"Ain't wise to speak of her," said the old woman.

So strange was her reply, I almost let the matter drop. But I was sick of elusion and half answers. "That thing yesterday, the sounds I heard, and the rocks, did it have something to do with Evangeline's Folly?"

The widow stopped dead in her tracks and turned to stare at me. Perhaps there was a glint of madness in her eyes, or maybe it was just a form of suffering. "She's evil, girl. She kills and kills and comes again to kill. I did my best to keep ya from her. I warned ya not to go. Now look at what you've done."

"I haven't done anything wrong."

With a derisive snort, the widow set out at a faster pace. "Come on. We got to do some proper prayin'."

I walked a half step behind the skeletal woman as we made our way along the narrow trail and turned right on the wider path that meandered through the village. Winter Haven people strolled ahead of us and back behind. All the others wore far nicer clothing than I had seen on anyone during the week. I felt self-conscious in my jeans and sweater.

"You'll be fine," said the widow, somehow reading my thoughts again. "Everybody knows ya came without a proper bag."

I felt relieved by this at first, but then I thought about the fact that everyone on Winter Haven knew the details of my traveling possessions. My relief turned to frustration. The self-righteous old woman clearly found no shame in gossip. Still, I kept quiet. With so many of the widow's neighbors walking within earshot, any protest would be fuel for more idle talk.

We drew near to the church. With its thick shakes sprouting moss, and corroded copper cross atop a spire of plain geometry, it had seemed forlorn and unused two days earlier when I sat upon its front steps planning my hike across the island. Now the church had a festive air, its tall front doors thrown open to a little crowd of villagers milling round the lawn, with five or six small children chasing each other through the forest of adult legs until a man dressed in a coat and tie called them inside. Soon the bell high in the steeple started ringing heartily, as the man let the children have a go at the bell's rope. I made a conscious effort not to let the ringing tempt my thoughts toward my parents' front porch and those other church bells, which had marked my final glimpse of Siggy alive in the world.

The widow acknowledged greetings on the left and right as we arrived. Apparently she was an honored member of the community. This surprised me, given her vinegary disposition. She led me straight through the small crowd by the door, up the steps and into the church vestibule. The man in the coat and tie who had let the children ring the bell turned to greet us. His eyes passed over me without pausing and focused on the widow. He seemed uncomfortable in his Sunday best, his deep tan a poor match for the pale blue of his shirt, his jacket verging on explosion due to the pressure of his broad back and thick arms.

The old woman said, "I see from your apparel you'll be doin' the talkin' today, Mr. Honeycutt."

"Ayuh, it's my turn, Mrs. Abernathy."

The widow turned to me. "We don't have a proper minister, ya see, so the men take turns in the pulpit." Then she directed her attention back to Mr. Honeycutt. "I trust you'll give predestination a wide berth."

"Thought I'd speak to miracles today, Mrs. Abernathy."

"Ancient, or the current day?"

"A bit of both, starting in Exodus."

The old woman pursed her lips. "Winter Haven is not Egypt."

"Ayuh, but that's a poor reason not to put no stock in miracles."

The widow tilted back her head and stared at him along her nose. "Just support yourself with Scripture, Mr. Honeycutt, and you'll get no guff from me."

I followed her through a second pair of doors into the sanctuary. It was a simple room, with open trusses above and wide wooden planks on the walls and floor. A small stage rose one step higher than the main floor and spanned the far end of the space, with an oaken podium as its single adornment. About halfway down, the central aisle parted around a cast-iron stove. Its black flue rose like a slender column up into the dark between the trusses. Instead of open pews like my father's church in Texas, the congregants who had already arrived sat in wooden boxes, about three feet tall, with doors that opened on the central and side aisles.

"My place is in the front," said the old woman. "I share it with the Widow Gillcrest and her sons. We got no room, but you'll be fine back here." She indicated an open bench along the back wall.

I took a seat beside the doors. Soon those who had been socializing out front began to enter the sanctuary. I recognized one of them as Zeke, the short bald man with the strange rolling gait who had so rudely refused to offer me directions to Bleak Beach. He passed swaying down the aisle, greeting people here and there. When he got to the front, another man rose and stepped out of his box to meet him. This was the powerfully built fellow I had met within minutes of my arrival on the island, the darkly bearded man who had reminded me of Paul Bunyan and who had accepted the island's mail from Steady Wallis as we walked from the landing to the packing shed. Nathaniel was his name, if I remembered correctly, husband of Rebecca, she of the wildly windswept hair who had offered to pray for my grief.

Nathaniel spoke with Zeke until the man in the coat and tie, Mr. Honeycutt, took his place behind the podium.

Mr. Honeycutt said, "Let us pray."

Almost everybody bowed their heads, but I watched as Nathaniel gripped the bald man's shirtsleeve and pulled him close, whispering urgently. After listening a moment, the bald man nodded solemnly and moved on. Then, as the two men stepped into their respective boxes, I saw each of them cast surreptitious glances toward the rear of the little church. I had a strong impression they were glancing back at me.

I pondered this as Mr. Honeycutt led the congregation in prayer and as he asked for announcements. I considered it as the service seemed to dissolve into a town meeting, with people rising to their feet to speak of everything from the whereabouts of lost lobster traps—which the man called "pots"—to a request for help to build a porch.

Surely those two backward glances were coincidental. I should not assume I was the center of attention all the time. Still, I could have sworn . . .

The man in the coat and tie led us all in a hymn. There was no piano or organ, or any other musical instrument. The man sang with great enthusiasm, but his vocal range was limited to approximately three notes, and the congregation seemed to disagree about the key. The resulting chaos soon distracted me from curiosity about the two men glancing my way. I thought of coyotes howling in the field behind my father's house in Texas. I laughed, surprising myself and offending an elderly man in the box ahead of me, who turned to glare.

Just then the door beside me opened, and Evan Frost stepped in.

I tried to pretend it did not matter, but that was hopeless. My spirit soared merely at the sight of him. He held a Bible in one strong hand. He wore a pair of gray slacks and a navy blazer with a crisp white dress shirt open at the collar, the quality and stylishness of his clothing unexpected, as if he was a banker instead of a hardworking mariner. Evan saw me right away, and I was almost certain the pleasure in his eyes was real.

Bending close to me, he whispered, "Enjoying the music?"

I giggled.

"Hey," he said, "see my shoes?"

I glanced down. He lifted a foot about six inches off the wooden floor. On it was a casual brown leather slip-on kind of shoe with a white rubber sole. His lips almost brushed against my ear as he whispered, "Topsiders."

In my attempt to avoid laughing out loud, I snorted. Appalled, I pressed both hands over my mouth. The old man in the box before me turned around again. He raised a crooked index finger over wrinkled lips. "Shhh!"

Ignoring him, Evan's lips were at my ear again. "Wanna have a picnic tomorrow?"

I stared at him, eyes wide above my hands, and nodded.

Evan grinned and touched my shoulder. "Meet you at the landing around ten."

Cautious happiness rose within me as I watched him take a seat in a box up near the front. Then, across the aisle and up three rows, I saw Steady Wallis watching me. My brief happiness vanished at the man's expression. What kind of thoughts might mold a face that way? Was Steady Wallis feeling pity? Worry? Fear? Suddenly he seemed to realize I had noticed him. He smiled and nodded before turning toward the front again, but I had seen what I had seen, and no smile could disguise what lay behind his eyes.

fourteen

ERCIFULLY, THE MUSCULAR MAN in the awkward coat and
tie brought the congregation's singing to an end. On
my uncomfortable pew at the rear wall, I settled in to listen to
him speak of miracles. Mr. Honeycutt began in ancient Egypt,
the plagues and Passover, the bloody Nile, the parting waters.
He said miracles would never cease, everything around us was
a miracle, and we could count on God to grant the miracles
we needed to get by. It reminded me of my father's constant
exhortation, *"You can have a miracle today!"* It had the same
naïve assumption of safety. Like my father, the preacher said
nothing about the dangers of a miracle.

I thought about the bitter cost to Egyptian firstborn children,
and a firstborn son miraculously awash upon a beach. "Miracles
are blessin's," said the Winter Haven man, and I could not
stop the memory of my mother's prayer each Sunday morning. *"Please don't make him stand before the people again. Please
don't make a spectacle of him. Let him be our little boy, not some
circus sideshow freak."* Unnoticed at the back of the small sanctuary, I fought the undertow. I would not listen to the sermon
anymore. I would resist the arguments my parents thought
they held in private, my father certain Siggy was a holy gift,

my mother begging him to let Siggy be, her fierce protection battling the will of God.

God's will had always persevered of course, at least my father's version of it had, with Sunday after Sunday of my brother standing at the podium, my mother watching from a pew, squeezing my hand too hard as greedy crowds demanded chapter and verse, prophecy and testimony from our precious Siggy.

I heard the island preacher say, "Some families got three hundred years of history here, but no one remembers a time when the sea stopped givin' what we need, till now. Some can make their livin' away, but the rest of us got to get by on Winter Haven. It's that or leave this place our people chose.

"Now the good Lord has answered our prayers. Showed us what was in the soil beneath us since before the Pilgrim times, a blessin' no one knew about till our need was greatest. Think about the timin' of it, friends. Miracles *do* happen, and them that don't believe it ought to look what God Almighty done for us through Cap'n Frost."

At the sound of Evan's name, my danger passed. Fully in the present again, I saw Evan's head bow down, as if he too had tempting memories to resist.

The man at the podium continued. "Barren sea or no, now we got a chance again. People from away will come to visit. They're gonna bring their money. They're gonna need places to sleep and food to eat and things to do. It might not be the old way, but it's a way to keep our homes. The Lord let his people go, way back in the Bible times. Now he's gonna let us stay, and we oughta call it what it is, a miracle by the grace of God, and I say God bless Cap'n Frost for findin' it right below our feet."

At that, a weather-beaten man near the front rose and turned toward Evan. He began to clap. One by one the others did the same, until the entire congregation stood in Evan's honor. Then Mr. Honeycutt offered a parting prayer, and everybody started filing out.

I lingered beside the church doors, hoping I would have a chance to talk to Evan, but Steady Wallis reached me first and said, "Miss Gamble, could I speak with ya a moment?" The man steered me through the door, down the steps and across the front lawn, until we stood in the shade of a mighty pine some distance from the others. As villagers filed out behind us and chatted in small groups on the sunny lawn, Steady Wallis said, "Seen ya with our Cap'n Frost in there." The man passed a palm over his mouth. "Did ya talk about your brother?"

"Why would we do that?" I said.

I saw Evan emerge from the church surrounded by a little crowd of people who patted his back and spoke to him in jolly tones. Meanwhile, Winter Haven's storekeeper, postmaster, harbormaster, and constable said, "Ya heard about them Vikin' things the cap'n found?"

"What Viking things?"

"Jewelry, tools, and whatnot."

Remembering the strange bronze brooch in my brother's pocket, I faced Steady Wallis. "Like Siggy's little ship?"

"Could be. See that fella over there, come on the boat with ya?" I turned to see the owlish man who had been my fellow passenger. He stood apart from the churchgoers, looking completely out of place in his khaki safari jacket with its epaulets and loops for elephant-gun shells. Like me, he seemed to be watching Evan from a distance. Steady Wallis continued, "That there fella's from the university. A doctor of archaeology. Says them Vikin' things of Cap'n Frost's is real. A thousand years old or more. Calls it proof the Vikin's come to Maine back then."

Remembering the preacher's words, I said, "That's the miracle Mr. Honeycutt was talking about? The thing they think is going to bring a lot of tourists?"

" 'Fraid so."

"Doesn't sound like you're a fan of miracles."

"I like breakfast in the mornin' and dinner every night. A warm house in the winter. Them kinda little miracles is fine. Far as the big ones go . . ." He shrugged. "I like things quiet and predictable."

I nodded. "You have to be careful what you ask for."

"Sounds like the voice of experience."

"I know a little bit about it."

"How's that?"

"It's kind of personal."

He peered closely at my face. "Are we talkin' 'bout your brother, Miss Gamble?"

"It's nothing."

" 'Cause if we're talkin' 'bout your brother, the more I know 'bout him, the sooner we can get this whole thing figured out, and the sooner ya can take him home."

"What do you want me to say?"

"Anythin' that comes to mind."

I thought for a moment, then said, "Siggy had this amazing silky hair, almost pure gold. It was light and fine and moved in the air when he walked. He had this funny laugh, like a donkey. It cracked me up every time. He loved to draw with Crayolas. He used to leave his drawings on my bed sometimes, his favorite drawings, the ones that took him longer than the others.

He never gave them to me, exactly. They were just there on my bed. He didn't show affection the way you or I might, but I knew what it meant. Sometimes he washed the dishes in the middle of the night. We'd walk into the kitchen in the morning, the place would be a wreck, water everywhere, dishes piled in weird places, but my parents and me, we knew what that meant, too. Is this the kind of thing you need?"

"It helps."

"I don't see how."

"What about that miracle ya mentioned? The thing to be careful of?"

I sighed. "You remember I told you he had savant syndrome?"

"Ayuh."

"Well, my father was a healer."

"A doctor?"

"No, a faith healer."

"That's the miracle? I thought it had somethin' to do with your brother."

"It did. It caused problems with Siggy."

" 'Fraid I don't follow."

"My father couldn't heal him."

"Ah. That'd be a problem for a faith healer, I expect."

"It embarrassed him. Made him look bad."

Steady Wallis let that hang in the air a moment; then, "I still don't see what ya meant by bein' careful what ya ask for."

I did not want to speak of that. I dared not take the risk. I said, "It's really not important."

"I'd like to hear it anyway."

My hands started shaking. I slipped them in my pockets. I said nothing.

"Miss Gamble, ya mustn't keep things from me. I'm askin' ya officially, ya understand? I need to know everythin' I can about your brother."

I inhaled a ragged breath. Against my will I told the man about the first time my father stood Siggy up beside the podium and proclaimed he was an anointed wonderment from God. I spoke of this, remembering my mother squeezing my hand too tightly, hurting me without knowing as we sat side by side on the first pew in front. I remembered the moistness in my mother's eyes, and the sight of people all around us, watching my dear Siggy. I had known there was trouble coming, but I was young and did not understand exactly what, or why. To me, Siggy was indeed a wonderment from God, my constant companion, my closest friend, who had somehow found a way to reach me through the shroud of his profound infirmity. He was breakfast, dinner, and a warm house in the winter to me. But up onstage the shepherd of the flock had wanted something bigger.

Trying to explain all this to Steady Wallis, I did not quote the words my father used that Sunday morning, but they came to me anyway, as if I were sitting in my father's church that very moment as he stalked across the stage, shouting, "I know y'all been murmuring 'bout my boy! Murmuring like a bunch of stiff-necked Israelites! Asking why this boy ain't healed! Wonderin' why my gift has failed my own family! Well, let me ask you something. . . ." My father had paused then, his voice dropping nearly to a whisper, a trick he often used to keep his congregation interested. "Should I heal a miracle?"

I remembered a woman calling out, "No!"

And a little louder, my father asking, "*Could* I heal a miracle?"

"No!"

"Could any *man* wash away the Holy Ghost's anointing?"

More people shouted "No!" this time, and even in my youth I understood. Some miracles could not be healed.

"This boy has a *gift*!" hollered the perspiring man onstage, the gray old man who was my father under other circumstances. "It has been given for the common good, as all of God's gifts are! It's good for you! It's good for me! Do you really think I'm fool enough to try to heal a Holy Spirit *gift*?"

Beside me on the church lawn, Steady Wallis cleared his throat and said, "So your father thought that syndrome thing your brother had, he thought that was a miracle?"

I nodded. "He thought Siggy was a prophet."

In explaining it to Steady Wallis, I thought about the very words my father used. "Come on, people, ask this boy a question! Come on, somebody! Ask him for a holy word! You can have a miracle today!"

I remembered a woman asking in a quiet voice, "My Andy's awful sick. Got his operation this next Tuesday. How's he gonna do?"

The congregation stared at my brother, but he did not reply. For at least one long empty minute, his reclusive eyes explored the floor between his feet. The urge to fill the silence nearly overwhelmed me. I almost shouted, *Leave him alone!* Then suddenly Siggy said, " 'Is any sick among you? Let him call for the elders of the church; and let them pray over him, anointing him with oil in the name of the Lord.' "

"Praise God!" cried the woman, and all the people clapped and shouted and threw up hands to heaven.

I knew I must have missed something. This must have been a grown-up cause for celebration, because it seemed to me my

Siggy made no promises to the woman. But then more people shouted questions. What does God want me to do about my pickup truck? Should I plant corn or alfalfa this year? Is it right for me to marry Charlie? And Siggy quoted Bible passage after Bible passage, sometimes going on for ten or fifteen minutes before he paused to take another question, a tireless fount of holy words.

Next had come a kind of parting in the congregation's flood of praise, the waters rolling back to leave a dry and empty moment, and a dark-complexioned man in the midst of it, leaping to his feet to shout, "*¿Es usted un profeta?*"

All eyes turned from him to Siggy, who convulsed beneath their scrutiny like a puppet twitched by strings. When another silent minute passed and my brother did not speak, the preacher, the healer, my sometimes father, leaned in toward the microphone and said, "There are different kinds of gifts of course. He doesn't speak in tongues. He—"

"'*Tú lo has dicho . . .*'"

In my mind's eye I saw my father look at Siggy in surprise, and heard my brother going on to say, "'*Y además os digo, que desde ahora veréis al Hijo del Hombre sentado a la diestra del poder de Dios, y viniendo en las nubes del cielo.*'" And the dark-skinned man stood up to shout, "*¡Gloria al Dios!*" and again the sanctuary erupted. "Praise God! Praise God! Praise God!"

Steady Wallis interrupted my description of these things. "You're sayin' he really was a prophet?"

"I'm saying it turned out Siggy could quote the whole Bible in seven different languages. I'm not sure if that made him a prophet, but it did make him seem like one, and that's what my father needed him to be."

"'Cause it explained why your father couldn't heal him? Got him off the hook with his congregation?"

"Something like that."

"What do ya think yourself? Was he a prophet?"

"I'm not sure."

Steady Wallis spoke as if he were alone. "If a person thought your brother might see somethin' private in the past or future . . . a secret they didn't want told . . ."

I looked at him with new respect. "It would be a motive for what happened here."

"I'm just thinkin' out loud."

"Most of what Siggy quoted when they asked him questions wasn't the kind of thing you could come back later and say, 'Yeah, that happened,' you know? I mean, they weren't clear predictions. He was always pretty vague."

"Okay." Steady Wallis nodded. "Let's talk about how he learned all those languages. That's not the same as memorizing books, right? That syndrome thing and all?"

"I think maybe it is the same. There was a library in Mount Sinai where we used to go a lot. They had a Spanish Bible. And my father had Greek and Hebrew Bibles in his study at home. He might've just read them and memorized the sounds. So people asked him something in a language, and he heard the sounds and quoted something back that sounded the same, just sounds he couldn't forget, without understanding what they meant. I used to get the feeling people would take anything he quoted and find a way to make it fit their situation. He didn't even pronounce the foreign words right half the time. He spoke them the way you would if they were written in English, you know?"

Steady Wallis nodded. "You're saying he was like a human tape recorder. He didn't have to know what it meant. He just repeated it."

"I think so. Maybe."

"Still, some folks might not want certain things recorded."

"You think he memorized something he shouldn't have?"

"Could be."

"What could be so important in a place like this?"

"I don't know, Miss Gamble. Like I said, I'm just thinkin' out loud."

Lost in thought, I turned back toward Evan Frost, who remained surrounded by a small crowd of well-wishers on the church lawn.

After a few silent moments, Steady Wallis continued, "I'm also wonderin' how that little Vikin' ship got in your brother's pocket."

"Siggy found it somewhere, obviously."

"No, miss. Him and the cap'n both findin' things like that at the same time independent-like? Odds of that are pretty slim. 'Course, could be the cap'n gave it to him."

"Evan didn't even know Siggy."

"How do ya know?"

"Well, I think he would have mentioned . . ." I fell silent, suddenly realizing I had never asked Evan if he knew my brother, and he had said nothing about it, one way or the other. "You really think Evan gave that pin to him?"

"Hard tellin' not knowin'. There's other ways. Your brother coulda just taken it. That would explain why somebody might get angry at him."

"You think Siggy *stole* that pin?"

Over in the midst of the crowd by the church's entrance, Evan glanced our way. Steady Wallis said, "Keep your voice down, if ya would."

"Why should I, when you're accusing Siggy like this? He's the *victim* here!"

"Might be somebody else did the stealin', instead of your brother. Or maybe it was your brother rightly found the Vikin' things and somebody else stole 'em from him. Or maybe your brother and somebody else dug up them things together and they had a fallin' out."

"You keep saying 'somebody else,' but you're talking about Evan." I shook my head. "He wouldn't hurt a flea."

"Know him pretty well, do ya?"

I felt myself begin to blush. "Not as well as you, obviously."

"Look. I ain't sayin' the cap'n's done wrong. But there has to be some connection between two fellas findin' them rare Vikin' things at the same time in a little place like Winter Haven. We got to consider all the facts." The man extended his callused hand and began ticking off his points, finger by finger. "Two bodies, found a week apart in the same place, so accidental death looks real unlikely. An' your brother had that Vikin' thing in his pocket. An' Cap'n Frost claims he dug up a whole lot more Vikin' things like it. An' your brother had a photographic memory. An' even in a place like this, there's always somebody's got somethin' they don't want remembered."

I said, "There's something else."

"Ayuh?"

"My brother was fascinated by Vikings way before he came here. He drew pictures of them and read about them all the time."

"How come ya didn't tell me this before?"

"I didn't know it mattered till now."

The man's expression went blank, as if his mind were suddenly a long way off.

I interrupted his thoughts. "None of this explains how Siggy could still look the same after all these years."

"I figure that's one of two things. Either your brother died a long time ago and somebody preserved his body somehow for some reason. Got no idea why anybody would do that, but I guess there's no explainin' what some folks will do. Or else maybe your brother wasn't as young as he looked. Doc Belamy says that's possible. When he looked your brother over, the doc had no reason to think he was anythin' but a teenaged boy, so he just focused on the cause of death and didn't pay much attention to the body's . . . I mean, your brother's, age. He ain't a real coroner, ya know."

"So you think Siggy could be twenty-eight and still look like he did when he ran away from home?"

"Ain't no stranger than a fella memorizin' the Bible in seven languages, if ya ask me. I've heard of people passin' as teenagers for different reasons, all the way up into their thirties."

Remembering news stories of exactly that, I said, "Shouldn't you search the place where Evan found the Viking things? Siggy could've been there. Maybe he left something behind that will explain all this."

"Cap'n Frost won't tell nobody where he found them things."

"But why?"

"That fella from the university come here kinda pushy, talkin' 'bout the state of Maine sendin' people out, makin' the site a national landmark and whatnot. Cap'n heard all that an' just clammed up. Says he don't want no government bureaucrats messin' with his land. Can't say as I blame him, neither."

Over by the church steps Evan Frost stood talking with his fellow churchgoers. Watching him, I put a finger in my mouth and bit down on the nail. From out of nowhere a large raven swooped to within a few feet of the handsome man's head. I followed its flight to see it rise and perch upon the church roof, where at least a dozen other ravens had already settled. The ravens started cawing as if to mock the pleasant chatter of the Christians below.

I said, "Couldn't you just get a bunch of people and go search until you find the site?"

"Got no reason for a search warrant. Plus it's a lot of ground to cover, seein' as how the cap'n owns half the island."

"Half the island!"

"More or less. And there's only two or three fellas here would go along with me to search it, not countin' that university man, of course. Everybody else on Winter Haven's either part of Cap'n Frost's crew, or related to one of 'em, or else a fisherman or lobsterman on tough times and lookin' to profit from this Vikin' thing some kinda way. With the fishin' and lobsterin' played out around Winter Haven, their homes and livelihood is at stake. Don't nobody want no scandal to put a bad light on things."

"It's a little late to worry about scandals. My brother's dead!"

"Ayuh, and I'm gonna find out what happened. Promise ya that."

"I don't see how, when everyone's against you."

Steady Wallis had no reply. We stood side by side watching the Winter Haven people on the far side of the lawn, who would not lift a hand to help us learn the truth about my brother. My thoughts sank from one uncharitable accusation to another, becoming more and more malicious, until suddenly I realized the venom was as much outside my ears as in my mind. A low corruption had arisen in the air, an ugly sound, the same hissing I had heard before at Gin Gap Cove and along the village path. Surely it had been there all along, just below the edge of my awareness like the omnipresent hum of insects on a summer night in Texas. Swelling slowly louder it began to ebb and flow like acid waves upon a sulfur shore, yet still the Winter Haven children chased each other gleefully, the adults laughed and smiled, and even Steady Wallis showed no sign that anything was wrong.

Could it be that no one heard the awful sound but me?

A raven cawed loudly. I looked up at the roof beside the steeple. The newly arrived bird had cocked its head to watch me with a single shining eye as black as flint. It cawed again, demanding my attention. I forced myself to speak normally. "What about that man we found on the beach? Did you learn anything from his body?"

"I'm followin' up on some things. But he was a lot worse off than your brother, like ya seen. Looks like he got beat up pretty bad. Broken legs, broken arm, a lot of broken ribs."

The hissing seemed to feast upon this recitation of violence, becoming louder still, competing with the mocking raven on the roof. Had it been called up by my memories of Siggy, that prophet wonder on my father's stage? As I told Siggy's story to the man beside me, I had felt no clutching at my mind, nothing pulling me outside myself. But what if I had gone beyond the feeling of it? What if I was in it all the time now, so immersed I could not tell the difference between freedom and possession?

I tried to speak normally. "The man we found was beaten? That's what killed him?"

"Maybe it was just the surf and rocks. I'll get a proper coroner over from the mainland this time instead of ol' Doc Belamy. We'll know the truth of things soon enough."

Across the lawn, the archaeologist approached Evan and began to speak, gesturing dramatically with his arms. Evan replied, shaking his head. The owlish man waved his hands more urgently. The stubborn expression on Evan's face slowly changed. I had seen the handsome man aloof, amused, compassionate, and sad, but now his features filled with menace. The archaeologist must have been too caught up in his argument to notice. He continued talking. Evan Frost leaned very close to the man's ear. His lips moved, and whatever he said made the archaeologist take a quick step back, as if he had been slapped.

I remembered the alarming argument I had heard while lying in the guest bedroom at Evan's decrepit mansion, the sound of locusts, the rising rage beyond the door that had driven me to bolt it shut and kept me wide awake most of the night. I said, "I just want to get my brother off this island."

"Oh, miss. We been over that, and nothin's changed."

I watched as the owlish man hurried away, glancing fearfully over his shoulder at Evan Frost. I looked at Evan too and found him staring straight at me. He bared his teeth across the space between us. Had I not seen his words' effect upon the archaeologist, I would not have guessed the truth behind his comely smile.

Determined to ignore the hissing imprecations in the air, I gave the man a little wave, even as I spoke to Steady Wallis. "Evan asked me to a picnic tomorrow. I'll try to get him to tell me where he found those Viking things."

"Ya can't do that!"

A pair of children approached Evan Frost. I saw the natural way he knelt down to their level. One of them, a little girl, pointed at the church steeple and said something. Or maybe she was pointing at the ravens. Evan laughed, and in his easy way with them I realized all the man had needed was one candlelit dinner and one morning walk along the beach to disarm me with false hopes. Had he bewitched poor Siggy, too?

I said, "I have to go with him. I have to know what happened to my brother."

"It's too risky, Miss Gamble. There's no way I can let ya do it."

"What are you going to do, throw me in jail?"

"Look, Miss Gamble . . . Vera." At his use of my first name, I turned toward him. There was worry in his eyes. His obvious concern made me uncomfortable. It placed a burden on me, a sense of obligation I did not wish to bear. Steady Wallis said, "I don't want to see ya in the same condition as your brother.

Ya must give me your word ya won't go nowhere alone with Cap'n Frost. Ya must."

As village life went on oblivious to the hissing in my ears, I said, "All right, I promise." And in the moment that I spoke that lie, the awful hissing stopped.

fifteen

ENCIRCLED BY ADMIRERS, Evan Frost gestured for me to wait. I forced myself to smile. But the hissing might resume at any moment. I could not bear it anymore, knowing I alone could hear. What did that mean? How was it possible? Remembering my brother's state of mind and my father's empty eyes, I knew the answer. Autism. Alzheimer's. Completely different, of course, yet mine was a family of mental frailty all the same, and I was hearing things again. The punishment I had hoped to elude with years of dogged apathy was upon me now.

I raised my arm and tapped my wristwatch, although it was ridiculous to imply I had an appointment in a place like Winter Haven. Evan frowned as if disappointed, then shrugged and nodded. I set out walking toward the harbor, striding quickly, hoping to outpace the wicked whispers in my head.

Shells crackled underneath my shoes as I passed several houses and the ramshackle boatyard. A pair of fishing vessels lay propped on metal stands like accident victims in traction, waiting to be mended. One large wooden boat languished on its side, abandoned to its fate. The wheelhouse windows glinted cheerfully in the midday sun, even as a horde of greedy vines and underbrush clutched at the hull's naked ribs, drawing it down into the soil.

I went by Steady's store, then the meeting hall, and beyond I saw the packing shed where Siggy's strangely unchanged body lay beside the other corpse. What would the autopsy reveal about the unknown man? And what about Siggy's real age? Might Steady Wallis also ask the coroner to conduct another autopsy on my brother? The thought was hateful to me. It meant knives piercing my Siggy's skin, strange hands inside his chest, uncaring eyes upon his naked flesh.

For one instant I considered stealing him, somehow getting him on a boat and leaving this island to seek sanity. But of course it was impossible. I could not imagine wrestling Siggy's stiffened body down the dock and rowing with him to someone's boat, heading out of the harbor and braving the Gulf of Maine alone. With my landlubber's stomach and total ignorance of navigation, I would only add myself to the Winter Haven body count.

I reached the harbor's edge near the town dock. On the water a pair of seals chased round and round a lobster float, like village children around grown-ups on the church lawn. Five black cormorants drifted watchfully nearby, and seven fishing vessels floated on their moorings. Near the harbor's center were two boats side by side. A man transferred green wire cages from one boat to the other. I supposed the cages were lobster traps. He stacked them five high, which placed the top of the upper trap above his head. Unconsciously I estimated the number of columns he could arrange across the deck, and the number of rows from front to back. I did the math and figured he could carry seventy traps out to sea.

I might be hearing things, but at least I could still use my mind.

It did not matter.

I was the daughter of a healer and the sister of a prophet. I knew some kinds of calculations—the ones that mattered most—would never yield an answer. Sometimes you could add one complaint to another and multiply by every form of misery there was and divide by all the heartache in the world, and even if you reached infinity the sum of all your questions would still be met with nothing but an evil whisper, a vacant stare, or else a silence like the taste of lukewarm water, the feel of empty air, a vision of the color white. When it comes to evil, God does not explain.

Such things were unwise to contemplate. I should have turned to other calculations or forced myself to take some pleasure in the lovely evergreen-and-granite-bounded harbor. I should have fought more bravely against such self-indulgent thoughts. But fatigue and fear had weakened me. I felt overwhelmed by solitude, futility, and divine neglect. I felt I had already fallen. In my shameful frailty I flirted with temptation. I allowed myself to think of sitting on the front pew at my father's church, my mother's place beside me empty, my brother missing from the stage, which bore only my father's charismatic presence, his congregation shouting, dancing, lifting hands to heaven, and in the midst of it another of my sinful episodes arising.

Always before I had been immobile in my delusions, paralyzed by the same whiteness that seemed to grope my brother, but that one time I followed. I ran after Siggy. I saw him fall to his knees, and rise and run again, his mouth wide open, shouting words I could not hear. I saw him step into the air and fly, arms wide like a bird, and I soared with him, dipping and rolling until he stopped, all of a sudden, as if something had ensnared him. I saw him lying motionless in the whiteness of my vision, and in my vision somehow I knew the awful thing was coming.

"Siggy!" I had shouted. "Get up! We have to run away!"

Then from flat upon my back I saw the whiteness slowly fade, as grown-ups leaning over me materialized, and my father was there, angry or concerned, and up beyond the downward-looking circle of their faces, on the white church ceiling I could see a creeping stain.

The sudden rumble of an engine on the harbor brought me back to here and now, as if awakening. I had fallen to my knees like Siggy, the power in my legs no match for these re-newed hallucinations. My posture was appropriate. I clasped my hands and bowed my head and begged for mercy. I offered no excuse. I fully understood the danger; I was overwhelmed, and knew where it would lead, in spite of thirteen years of abstinence.

Fumes belched from an exhaust stack atop the lobsterman's boat. While I had wallowed in forbidden invocations, the man had shifted all his traps from one boat to the other. Now his vessel motored slowly toward the harbor mouth. The playful seals were out of sight. One by one the cormorants arose. Their wingtips left concentric circles where they touched the water for the first few flaps, and then they glided off an inch above the mirrored surface. For the first time I noticed Evan Frost's small motorboat tied up at the dock. Like the lobsterman and cormorants and seals, I had to get away. Evan might appear at any time. I could not face him now, not until I made some sense of these unwelcome illusions and sorted out the eerie hissing, these sights and sounds that came to me alone.

I decided to follow the harbor's curvature beyond the packing shed where Siggy's body lay. That route would avoid the path Evan would take when he left the church. I slipped behind the shed. A large raven stood upon the shingled ridge. Head cocked, it kept one unblinking obsidian eye upon me as I passed. I did not understand how these malevolent creatures had appeared on Winter Haven, so far from the mainland. They were not seabirds; I was sure of that. Might a breeding pair have come as stowaways on some long forgotten vessel? Might the cunning things descend from ancestors that survived the Pilgrim shipwreck?

Distracted by the raven, I stepped into a mud puddle. I muttered in frustration and wiped my shoe in the grass beside the path. Water trickled across the path and down into the harbor, the tiny stream appearing from beneath the packing shed's rear wall. It had carved a gully about three feet deep. I realized it must be runoff from the melting ice around my brother's body, and imagined Siggy lying in the weathered shed, only a few feet away, looking just as Evan Frost had found him, just as I had seen him thirteen years ago.

I remembered something Steady Wallis said. *"I been keepin' him good and cold."* I considered the villagers' strange behavior. From the start they had made it clear I was unwelcome. Steady's explanation for their rudeness seemed reasonable. With the end of lobstering and fishing around Winter Haven, maybe they really were desperate to avoid a scandal connected with the discovery of Viking artifacts, desperate to protect any benefits the artifacts might bring in treasure or in tourism. But as the melted runoff traced its way down to the harbor, I realized it had taken years for such a tiny stream to carve the gully in the soil, thousands and thousands of pounds of ice, melting in the packing shed.

How could I be certain all that ice had been for fish? How could I be certain Evan Frost had found Siggy on Bleak Beach? What if my brother lay exactly where he had always been? What if Siggy's body was part of some twisted ceremony, a symbol or an idol of some kind, a talisman to be preserved in ice? Could it be that Steady Wallis used the Viking artifacts to distract me from something else, something awful, something Winter Haven had concealed for thirteen years or more? Had that same unholy secret caused my sudden loss of discipline, my slide back to the nightmares of my childhood, the way these visions seemed to be alive and irresistible again?

What if Winter Haven was imposing itself on me, forcing me to dream these awful dreams? I thought of the hissing I alone could hear, the way Siggy overwhelmed me and possessed me. I thought of the fearsome thing in flowing black, the carvings on the boulders in the forest, the charred depression in the center of that huge circular stone, and the incantation written there.

O thou perfect goddess,
Receive mine heart,
An eternal offering to thee.

A sacrificial altar for a goddess, or a witch?

I told myself such things as possession and human sacrifice did not happen. Besides, Siggy's body was untouched. But there were other forms of sorcery. What if I had been drawn to Winter Haven because, somehow, Siggy drew me?

No, no, no! I had to stop this hysteria before it tempted me to slip forever back into the deceptions of my childhood.

Probably all was just as Steady Wallis had suggested: Siggy simply grew up to become one of those people who can pass for a teenager well into their twenties. He had somehow become involved in boating, and fallen from a passing vessel, and died in the Atlantic's frigid waters and washed ashore at Bleak Beach. And I was only weakened by a wound reopened. It was perfectly normal that the sight of Siggy in the packing shed might bring back memories so strong they sometimes seemed to happen in the here and now. After all, if the people of Winter Haven had preserved my brother all these years for some unholy reason, or if Siggy had somehow remained a child for thirteen years on this enchanted island, why produce my brother's body now? Why ask me to come to get him when they could have simply buried him or dropped him in the ocean?

I tried to remember what it had been like when the phone rang in my cubicle at the office, my mind on the Daimler depreciation schedule, not paying close attention until at last I understood what the man with the strong accent was saying. A kind of shock had taken over. My memory of his exact words was vague, but I was almost certain Steady Wallis had been the first to suggest I make the trip to Winter Haven. In my dazed inertia I had declined, asking if there was another way. He had no legal means to force me to come, and he had seemed very conscious of my grief, but he had used a subtle and effective kind of pressure to get me here. *"We'll have to bury him in a pauper's grave, miss."* What sister could resist the guilt of that? It was almost as if Steady Wallis knew exactly what to say to draw me there. What if he had also guessed I would not leave without my brother? What if he had used

Siggy to lure me to the island and was using Siggy still to keep me?

The ice inside the shed seemed to rise within my veins as I realized Winter Haven might be a kind of prison.

I heard another engine roar to life and looked down at the harbor. Evan Frost's motorboat came slowly around the dock's far side. Quickly I stepped out of sight behind the packing shed. But even as I acted on Steady Wallis's warning, it felt wrong to hide from Evan. He had found me when I was hopelessly lost, fed me like a queen, given me a place to sleep, guided me to the spot where Siggy's body had been found—according to him—and offered gentle comfort. And there was a final fact, a very important thing to keep in mind. My only reason to fear the handsome mariner was Steady Wallis's warning, yet I knew no more about Steady Wallis than I did about Evan Frost.

What if I was hiding from the wrong man?

Concealed behind the shed, I saw the windows of Steady Wallis's store across the grassy field. Although I spotted no one there, I had the sudden feeling I was being watched.

It was always possible that neither Evan Frost nor Steady Wallis had anything to do with Siggy's death or his body's strange condition, but *something* on Winter Haven held the secret to my brother's death. I considered the brooch in Siggy's pocket and the other Viking artifacts recently found on the island. Allegedly found. I had not laid eyes upon them, and I must remember even the discovery of those artifacts might be a lie or an illusion. Yet there had to be a connection to my brother's pet obsession, his precious comic books, *The Mighty Thor*, and his love of all things Viking. I remembered when Siggy had first seen the *National Geographic* article about Leif

Erickson in Greenland. For more than a week he refused to put the magazine down, clinging to it everywhere he went, sleeping with it, eating with it. The arrival of my brother and the discovery of Viking artifacts in a place like Winter Haven could not be coincidental.

For thirteen years I had assumed it was our mother's death and Siggy's fight with our father that drove my brother away from home, but what if he had somehow known about the Viking artifacts on Winter Haven? What if, somehow, that knowledge caused his death?

sixteen

PEEKING PAST THE CORNER of the packing shed, I watched Evan's motorboat move beyond the western point of the harbor mouth, out of sight. Then I cast a glance toward Steady Wallis's store. Seeing no one there, I set out to circle the harbor toward the Widow Abernathy's cottage. Several times I stopped abruptly to look back, sensing eyes upon me, yet as I traversed the little village I saw no one whatsoever. This seemed very strange.

Where were all the people who had loitered on the church lawn? Why was I the only one still outside on such a fine day? Might the Winter Haven people know some reason to remain indoors, something that explained my sense of being spied upon? Crossing a clearing between two old shingled houses, I looked back again, certain I would catch somebody following, but still I was alone. It occurred to me this was ridiculous, frightened one moment because I was alone outside, frightened the next because someone might be with me there. I told myself to pick one worry at a time, and continued on toward the widow's cottage.

Then I rounded the harbor's north end, and the hissing came again.

As before, I sensed it had been in my ears long before I noticed, welling up among the omnipresent sounds of nature in the background, the surf, the gulls, the wind high in the trees. Could it be the reason no one else was out?

Somehow I knew not to run. I must show no fear, even as the hideous whisper rose to surround me. Hurrying while attempting to avoid all outward signs of haste, I no longer stopped to look behind. I did not want to know what might be following. I only wished to reach the widow's cottage safely.

The sound was indefinable. One moment it seemed like a form of speech. The next moment I felt sure it was incoherent madness. I thought of the strange black shape I had glimpsed along these paths just yesterday. Surely it had been a trick of the light. Yet there was the widow's warning.

"She kills and kills and comes again to kill."

What if that story was true? What if I had really offended something that had lived four hundred years on Winter Haven, the remnant of a soul whose flirtation with a seaman caused the Pilgrim ship to flounder on the rocks that bore her name? Could this truly be a phantom who had stranded a whole colony, who saw to it that they would disappear into the looming forest, their moldering essence drawn up from the soil to be enslaved forever in the timeless flow of crenulated bark?

The awful whispers seemed much closer now, hissing like the greedy inward sucking of a raging fire intent on tasting all the oxygen within my lungs.

Without betraying my intentions in advance I turned sharply into the front yard of an old house and climbed the steps and banged a fist against the paneled door. I pressed my face against a distorted pane of antique glass, staring at a gloomy entry hall, the scene through the rippled window like something out of picture books of old Salem: wide wooden floor planks, no furniture, an unlit candle in a pewter fixture on the wall. I thought of scarlet letters, stocks, and gallows. Though it must have been only ten seconds, I felt an hour pass before an aged woman hobbled into view, a gray shawl around her head as if it were a shroud. I rapped upon the door again. The old woman stopped in the center of the entry hall and cocked her ear. The awful hissing rose. I saw nothing of the woman's face beyond the shawl. I pounded on the door with all my might. "Can't you hear me?" I shouted. "Help me! Let me in!"

At my desperate plea for sanctuary the old woman limped toward the front door, stopping just on the other side of the glass. With a deformed arthritic claw she lifted the gray shawl to reveal a face carved deep by time, and eyes blinded by a film of perfect white. Crying out, I recoiled from her grotesque countenance. The woman laughed with naked gums.

I stumbled down the steps, followed by the whiteness in the old crone's eyes, pursued by her mocking laughter, which seemed to weave a pattern in the air, merging with the hissing, the two horrific sounds attracting something new: a distant chop, chop, chopping, a slow and uncoordinated echo of the brutal blows of axes thrown against the evergreens by Pilgrim spirits doomed to try and try again for all eternity, doomed to linger on amongst the trees they had so foolishly attacked to save their lives.

Trembling, I set out on the village path again. Just beyond the houses on my left the giant pines and spruces silently bore witness to my flight. The awful whispers never stopped. The distant chopping cleaved my mind. I imagined Siggy, his head in constant motion, his eyes on something well beyond my world. I imagined my father, staring blankly at the back side of the whiteness in his corneas. Was it in my blood, this awful thing? I heard the widow's words again.

"Now look at what you've done."

Desperate for help I looked left and right at every house and yard I passed. Where were all the people? Were they watching from the safety of their homes as the sacrificial lamb rushed by, relieved it was not one of them, glad a stranger had been lured to Winter Haven for this purpose? I called for help. I heard nothing in reply but chopping axes and the mocking hiss. I saw nothing but the ominous antique buildings. I remembered how the story went, how they came to rescue the shipwrecked colonists and found no hint of anything alive.

A black stone struck the trail beside me, then another and another. Covering my head with my hands, I broke into a run. *The animals had fled for fear of what they'd seen.* With each blow of polished stone upon the shells around my feet I heard an axe fall in the forest. The granite island and the trees it bore allied themselves together, with me as their victim. As the sky rained rocks, the axes beat a mad, disjointed cadence, an image overwhelmed me, a vision perhaps, of Pilgrim souls in humble black, weak from famine, pitiful beneath the ancient canopy, their dead in shallow soil beneath their buckled shoes, their tattered faith a sacrifice to new religion, newly pagans in their desperation, sacrificing at the clearing filled with boulders, trusting only in the ancient ones around them, the Viking gods, a bargain with the devil.

I reached the Widow Abernathy's cottage.

Running in, I slammed the door and threw my weight against it. Stones flew against the other side like hail upon a roof. I bolted the door and hurried down the hall, calling for the widow. I threw open her bedroom door, and saw nothing but a narrow bed, an old-fashioned washstand, and a black dress hanging on a wooden peg. The stones rattled on the cottage walls. I went to the kitchen, calling Mrs. Abernathy, but she was not there. I saw the cellar door. I remembered the stern admonition. *"Do not open this door, ever."* I hesitated. Then a stone crashed through the window at the sink, spraying glass across the floor. Desperate to escape, I opened the forbidden door.

Beyond it lay a set of wooden stairs descending to pitch-blackness. I saw no light fixture. I went down anyway. In the darkness near the bottom, I slid my hand along the wall of granite and found a switch. I flipped it. A dim red bulb glowed above my head. I saw a narrow table along one wall, which bore three metal trays. A deep sink stood beside it, and shelves with jars of chemicals and boxes of photographic paper. It was a darkroom, just as the widow had said.

Behind the stairs I saw another door. From the gap beneath it spilled a bit of yellow light.

"Mrs. Abernathy?" I could hear the stones above, tapping at the cottage. In the faint red light I walked to the door. "Mrs. Abernathy, are you there?"

Only stones replied.

I tried the knob. It turned. I pushed, and the door swung open. Beyond it another cellar room with walls of granite and a single light bulb burning brightly. Several lengths of cord or heavy string ran along the walls. From the cords hung dozens of black-and-white photographs. I stepped into the room and peered at the closest photos.

Every photograph contained a scene from Winter Haven—the village, the forest, the harbor. In each one was a creature clothed in solid black, with pale hands and raven hair that seemed to crawl in lumps upon its head. In every shot the thing ignored the camera. In every shot it seemed slightly blurred, as did the scenery around it, as if that part of the photograph was out of focus. Words had been inscribed along the lower edge of every photograph.

Murderess.

Witch.

Demon.

Devil.

I moved along the wall, examining the images, reading the words, filled with a strange compulsion. I needed to see this creature's face. But again and again it had been photographed while looking away. As I neared the far end of the room, the inscriptions on the photos changed. Now they read like curses.

Die forever.

Suffer slowly.

Be damned.

These words were written in a lovely hand, almost like calligraphy, the beauty of the writing in stark contrast to the ugly meaning. The sound of falling stones was muted now from where I stood, deep below the widow's cottage. I might have doubted their existence had I not been looking at proof of their source. I continued searching for the creature's face, until finally, on the back wall of the cellar room, I found it.

She hovered beside a mammoth tree, staring at the camera, her pallid features out of focus, her eyes twin holes of black, her mouth an open pit, her entire face askew as if the hand of Satan had rubbed across it sideways. Below her molten image the lovely handwriting spelled a string of words I did not understand, words that did not fit with the others.

Next to die.

This was not a curse, and not an insult. It seemed more like a prediction. I examined the photograph more carefully. As in the others, I saw the way the creature and the space around it seemed out of focus and yet all else in the image was perfectly rendered: the trees of Winter Haven's great forest, the branches, and something in the background, a lighter object in the shadows, a large rock perhaps. I leaned closer to the photo. It took my eyes a moment to adjust, but then I recognized the thing that loitered deeper in the woods, beyond the appalling creature.

That thing was me.

I backed away, out the door and across the darkroom. At the stairs, I turned and charged up to the widow's kitchen. There I stopped. Those images . . . What had I seen? Those words . . . What did they mean? As I stood at the cellar door, trying to understand, I heard the hail of stones again. Or was it the tapping of the widow's heels upon the cottage floor? My thoughts drifted to the heavy buckled shoes and black clothing of the Pilgrims. I thought about their loss on Winter Haven, and . . . the widow! She was coming, and there I stood as if in a trance. Frantic lest she realize I had found her secret, I slammed the cellar door. Only then did I recall the red light I had left glowing down below.

I trembled as the old woman came into the kitchen from the hallway, holding her Bible with a bony finger in the pages to mark her place. At a glance she saw through me. She cocked her head and asked, "What kinda foolishness is this now on a Sabbath afternoon?"

I remembered the clicking I had heard while lost in Winter Haven's forest, the sound I thought had been a squirrel. It was the widow's camera shutter, of course. She had watched in secret as I panicked, lost and alone, or so I thought. I fell into a chair beside the table. I felt my eyes too wide, too wild, betraying too much whiteness.

The widow came closer. "What's got into ya, child?"

I tried to form the words I wished to use, but only heard a keening sound emerge. The Widow Abernathy bent down, grasped me by my shoulders, and gave me a hard shake. "Stop your foolishness!" she snapped. "Tell me what's the matter!"

Pointing to the outside door, I said, "That thing!"

"Thing? What thing?"

"That awful voice. Whispering. Or hissing. I don't know! All around me, and . . . those axes chopping. Don't you hear it? You must hear it! Look outside! It's raining rocks!"

"Raining rocks, is it?" The widow gazed at me disdainfully.

I looked away, unable to return her stare.

Another pane of glass above the sink suddenly shattered as a black stone flew into the room. The old woman stared down at the rock, then up at the broken window, and then she slammed her Bible on the kitchen table, shoving me aside. "Get outta my way!" she snapped. Instantly she was outdoors, charging down her back steps. I heard the haunting corruption in the air, part whisper and part hiss. I dared to peer out through the open door and saw another stone come sailing toward the cottage. Moving absolutely nothing but her arm, the widow plucked it from the air. She held the polished stone aloft and shouted, "You're not to harm my house! Do ya hear? I should not have to tell ya that!"

As I cowered in the cottage, the widow stood defiantly in her backyard, hands on her hips. The hissing slowly faded. When I heard the sounds no more, the widow turned and came inside.

"You're not afraid?" I said.

"Of what?"

"Evangeline." I heard my voice pronounce the name, giving substance to it.

"Bah! That witch already done her worst to me."

I saw the widow watching through the window, sunlight slipping through the woman's parchment skin to reflect upon her bones. How many bones were in the human body? I wished to know the exact number, because surely witches could not exist in the same universe as numbers. Or could a dark form with hair that writhed like snakes around a face as pale as moonlight, could such a soul as that subdue the numbers in my mind? And if it could, if even numbers made no difference, how could the widow be so brave in the presence of . . . of . . .

The Widow Abernathy gestured toward the broken glass on her kitchen floor. "You're the reason for that, so I expect ya won't mind the cleanin' of it. And don't be bringin' her back here again, or I'll lock my door against ya."

Like the chopping of the axes and the clatter of the stones, the old woman's heels beat a fearsome rhythm as she strode from the room. Slowly, obediently, I went to kneel beside the shattered glass. One by one I picked up the larger pieces. I kept a careful count of them. Leaving many tiny slivers, I rose to my feet. I saw a single drop of red impact the floor. Delicate tendrils shot out from the spot, radiating from the center of the drop, trailing through the tiny bits of glass remaining. All of this was nearly microscopic, but I saw every detail. I saw a little stream of blood across the broken glass in my left hand. I saw a sliver pressed into the soft padding of my thumb, saw exactly where it pierced the flesh, and wondered why I felt no pain.

I raised my hand to study the crimson rivulet, turning the glass this way and that. Was this how it had been with Siggy? Had his mind been elsewhere all the time, watching from a distance? And my father, reliving his childhood from a bed in the Mount Sinai rest home, did he see this through the whiteness in his eyes, did he feel this space weighed down with nothing?

I should not have left my numbers. I had sailed through clouds upon the water to reach a place where time stood still, where little boys went decades without changing, where trees rose up forever and dying houses had a hundred empty rooms, where whispers chased me down into the freezing valley of the shadow, along the face of lofty cliffs and across a million shattered shells, where memories of prophecies pursued me and the polished bits of stone beneath my feet could rain down from the sky. Autism. Alzheimer's. A savant in a burning heaven, a husband with a dying wife who would not let God send a doctor. Widows. Witches. What weakness of the mind had I inherited, and what had I imposed upon myself? Pilgrims lost. Vikings found. Handsome eyes that wandered and a misplaced boy who looked at everything and nothing, saying, " 'I go to prepare a place.' "

I had been enticed to leave my refuge of numbers, and without them I was lost. But I could not bleed forever. I would go to my room, lie upon the bed and sleep. I saw myself set out across the kitchen. I heard glass crack like shells beneath my feet. Gently, gently, I put the bloody bits upon the table by the widow's Bible. I touched the leather cover of the Holy Book. I left a stain behind.

seventeen

A TAPPING ON THE WINDOW. Surely not the stones again. The widow had forbidden it. So this was my imagination, probably. I resolved to trust in nothing, especially my senses.

Curled up on my side atop the bedcovers, fully clothed, I believed I might be in my apartment back in Dallas, or in my room in Mount Sinai. I might be twenty-four years old. I might be eleven. Maybe Siggy was asleep right down the hall, with my mother in the kitchen fixing breakfast. I saw a brown stain on the bedcover. I saw blood clotted on my thumb. I put it in my mouth, closed my eyes, and sucked.

The tapping again. I opened my eyes. There beside the bed was a window. It would be a simple thing to play along. Still lying on my side, I reached to part the sheer white curtain. Sunshine struck my eyes.

Blinding whiteness rent my mind, an interior explosion flinging bits of Siggy up into my consciousness. As before, he came without preamble. I had no chance to choose, no temptation to resist. He seized me as his own, for I had slipped from willing creature into slavery, just as it had been before, all those years ago.

The glowing bedroom curtain became Mrs. Thomson's pure white choir robe. From my place on the front pew, with no mother at my side, the little girl I used to be saw Mrs. Thompson's fat, wiggling arms thrown out wide, and her smiling face thrust up toward heaven. Then white emptiness came as it always had, always in the midst of praising God, always in my father's church on Sunday morning, never in a profane place or time. Mrs. Thomson became Siggy, her white robe the empty place, my brother spinning like the fat saint on the stage, his arms flung out, a dove of peace in flight through nothingness. I saw him dip and roll and soar. I saw him stop, all of a sudden, as if he had hit a solid kind of whiteness, and I knew the awful thing was coming, as I had seen it come before.

"Siggy, I'm so scared."

Siggy's smile was brilliant. "'And Jesus answering saith unto them, Have faith in God.'"

"I *do* have faith!"

In the white absence of everything, his head wavered.

I said, "Why did you leave me? I'm here all alone."

Siggy raised his eyes toward heaven, directly toward the face of God. "'It is good for me that I have been afflicted; that I might learn thy statutes. The law of thy mouth is better unto me than thousands of gold and silver.'"

I did not understand. Did he mean it was good to be autistic, a savant, because it let him memorize God's Word? But why say that to me? It was not a comfort. I had no amazing memory, no special gift like Siggy to explain my suffering.

Then the greatest miracle occurred.

Siggy laid his eyes on me.

In all our time together, it was the one and only time, a miracle within a vision, a vision within a miracle. But Siggy robbed it of its glory, saying, "'Fear not them which kill the body, but are not able to kill the soul: but rather fear him which is able to destroy both soul and body in hell.'"

I was lost inside his eyes, fascinated by red flecks in green irises, immersed in wondrous colors he had hidden from me all his life. But the import of his words profaned my reverie. "What?" I asked. "No, I don't have to be afraid. Why are you saying that?"

Still looking straight at me, still transfixing me with mystery, Siggy said, "'For all have sinned, and come short of the glory of God.'"

"I know that!"

"'For God so loved the world, that he gave his only begotten Son, that whosoever believeth in him should not perish, but have everlasting life.'"

"I *know* that! You know I believe in Jesus! Stop this, Siggy! Stop it!"

But he would not stop. "'For by grace are ye saved through faith; and that not of yourselves: it is the gift of God.'"

Heartbroken, I wept. This was not the Siggy I had loved in life, not the boy who tried heroically to reach me through his omnipresent membrane of infirmity. This was not the steady friend who always showed up at my side when needed, even if he could not comfort through his touch or through his eyes. This was not that boy. This was an aloof prophet, remote and imposing. He gave my heart's desire, and then he mocked it. He offered me his eyes, but even as I searched for wisdom in those windows to his soul, he shrouded truth in mysteries that I already knew. My brother preached to me as if I were among the damned.

Why would he do that?

In a halfway place I came back into a little girl upon the floor of her father's church again, and I came back into a woman on an antique bed again, once more the center of attention, all alone while worried grown-ups knelt to lay their hands on me, praying for me, using words like *epilepsy* as my father stared in helpless fury at another loved one beyond healing. I held the curtain parted, and the sunshine in my eyes became the fuzzy form of someone standing just beyond the glass. I stirred, determined to escape hallucinations. I would waste no time on guilt. If I could not halt the devil's progress, if he must come for me again through these forbidden memories, at least I would live in my right mind within the time remaining. Rising on one elbow, I lifted the window a few inches. Outside, the fuzzy person stooped a little closer to the opening.

I heard Evan Frost speak quietly. "Happy birthday."

Pondering these words, I did not reply at first. Eventually I said, "It's not until tomorrow."

"I thought you said Monday."

"That's right."

"Well then, happy birthday."

I rolled over, felt around the nightstand for my eyeglasses, put them on and squinted at the alarm clock. It was ten-thirty. My mind rebelled at this. I had gone to sleep early Sunday afternoon, yet the clock now read ten-thirty, and it was not ten-thirty Sunday night, obviously, since the sun was shining outside, so . . . I did the math. I must have slept for twenty hours! But surely that was impossible.

"Come on, come on," said Evan from outside the window. "I can't stand out here all day."

"So why are you standing there?"

He glanced left and right. "The widow hates me."

I thought of the message written in the widow's flowing hand on my photograph—her curse, or her desire. *"Next to die."*

I said, "She hates everyone. So what?"

"So I can't knock on the front door like a normal person—that's so what."

"You're here to wish me a happy birthday?"

"Oh." The good-looking man frowned. "You forgot."

"Forgot what?"

"The picnic."

"No," I lied. "Just teasing. Can you give me a few minutes?"

I almost believed the relief on his face was real. I almost believed it really mattered to him that I had not forgotten. He said, "Sure. But I can't wait out here. How's about we meet over at the landing like we planned?"

"Fifteen minutes?"

"Hope I can hold out that long."

At first I thought the man was rushing me, but then I saw he meant it as a compliment. Closing the window, I did my best to smile.

I faced disaster in the bathroom. I had not bathed properly since leaving the mainland. There was no time to wash my hair, but throwing punctuality to the wind, I filled the claw-foot tub and stepped in. The hot water felt delicious. Soon I was out again and doing my best with the widow's talcum powder since there was no deodorant or perfume. I could only hope the chemical odor of the house had not settled into my unwashed clothes. I brushed my teeth. Rummaging around in my backpack, I found an alligator clip and arranged my hair into something I hoped might approach a French twist, all loose ends and waves. I had no lipstick, but a little lip balm for a moist look never hurt. After I applied it, I pursed my lips to the mirror, vamping just a little. Then I frowned as I thought of Steady Wallis's warning about Evan Frost, the bitter argument I had heard in Evan's house, and the furious look on Evan's face when he spoke to the archaeologist. I felt my hereditary weakness rising, the thing that made me sleep almost an entire day. I felt a self-defending dullness doing battle with my dread. Staring at my own reflection, at the moistness of my lips, I said, "Don't be ridiculous." I wiped my lips and left the room.

Mindful of a world where pebbles rained from clear blue skies, I rushed across the widow's unkempt yard. It was another bizarre, hot day. The high temperature in Maine that time of year should have been in the fifties, but I was sweating in Steady Wallis's loaner sweatshirt before I got a hundred feet from the widow's cottage. Farther down along the trail I saw two piles of branches, pruned apparently from the trees beyond the clearing. Approaching them, I wondered why this had been done. The piles were large, and lined both sides of the trail for about fifty feet. To cut and carry so many branches all the way across the clearing and to pile them up that way seemed a lot of useless work.

The branches were not there the day before; I would have noticed on the walk to church or on my headlong flight back to the widow's cottage. Drawing closer, I realized the deep green color of the needles still looked fresh—not brittle and faded like a Christmas tree in February, but freshly cut and full of sap. So this had been done while I was sleeping almost a whole day away.

I had nearly reached the branches when I heard the chopping sound again. I stared up along the gentle slope toward the towering forest, seeing no one, yet the sound must be coming from there, unless it was inside my mind. I set out again, walking faster. I passed between the piles of branches, which stood like tangled hedges at the entrance of a maze. Mostly the stacks stood higher than my head, but here and there I could see the ancient trees beyond. I glanced anxiously at the distant giants as the chopping rhythm quickened. I ignored the nearby branches.

Then I saw dark sap dripping from the cut end of one limb. Sunlight sparkled in the fluid slickness. In my preoccupation with the chopping from the ageless forest, at first I had not recognized the horror right before my eyes, the bright red color of the sap, the bleeding branches everywhere throughout the piles, the splatters and spots and rivulets covering the needles and the bark and the trail where I was walking, the bloody amputated limbs. I stopped dead in my tracks. I stared. I thought of bloodred flecks in emerald eyes. I told myself it was not true. I was not seeing what I saw.

Tree branches did not bleed.

I blinked in hopes the vision would vanish. When the hemorrhaging pile of limbs remained, I set out again, walking at a normal pace through a numbing mental whiteness. I passed beyond the branches. I passed through the quiet village. Sweating in the heat, I reached the landing.

"Hey." Evan met me with a perfect smile. "The birthday girl."

I did not reply.

"What's the matter? You don't like birthdays?"

From a distant place I answered, "Can we just go?"

He led me down the ramp toward his motorboat. "Seriously, what's the matter? I thought you'd be glad to get away from here for a while."

"I'm okay."

"You sure?"

"I said so, didn't I?"

"Okay . . ."

Down on the dock, I let him help me into the boat. He said, "How come you ran off after church yesterday? I was hoping we could talk a little."

"I had, uh, a thing."

"A thing?"

"Listen, are the waves big today? 'Cause I get seasick."

"No, it's almost like a mirror. You'll be fine."

Moments later we were idling out of the harbor, the engines sputtering and coughing loudly. I saw that Evan was right; the ocean was completely calm. He said, "Have a seat, will you?" and just as my bottom hit the cushion, he pushed the throttles forward.

The engines thundered, driving the sleek motorboat up onto a plane effortlessly, pressing my back against the seat as we flew around the rocks off the western point, leaving a long V-shaped wake behind. The wind played havoc with my hair, but I did not mind, not when the sun commanded such a perfect cloudless sky, and the ultramarine water winked like diamond pavement, and I had escaped from Winter Haven's horrors, if only for a little while. I saw hundreds of giant conifers standing guard along the ramparts of the passing ebony cliffs. I saw no other boats, no buildings on the shoreline, no hint of humanity. From the ocean, from a distance, Winter Haven might be paradise. Or hell. They said the devil was a charmer. Lucifer. Light Bringer. Morning Star. Beautiful.

In that pure and treacherous moment, I laughed.

The rushing wind snatched away my unexpected outburst, but not before Evan heard it and turned my way. "Feeling better?"

Not exactly, I thought, but I could only nod.

"Excellent!" The attractive man grinned widely as he pressed the throttles further forward. The boat responded as if it had been waiting for the chance.

I glanced at his instruments. We were doing fifty-five knots. I might yet escape. I asked, "What if we hit a rock or something?"

He said, "We're goners!"

I laughed again and turned back toward Winter Haven, letting my eyes run along the passing shore. The Atlantic Ocean was a prolific artist. Hundreds of granite formations along the coast had been carved and polished smooth, the coast an endless sculpture with no two boulders alike, no two even similar unless one only thought in superficial terms. I considered clouds, and snowflakes, and human fingerprints. God had endless creativity. I wondered why he could not find a way to create some kind of lasting peace out of my family's suffering.

The answer was, of course he could. He simply did not choose to do it.

Lest I laugh some more and never stop, I embarked on calculations. The guidebook claimed the isle of Winter Haven was about ten square miles in size. Assume it was a circle. The square root of ten square miles was about three and one eighth. Double that and multiply by the square root of pi for the circumference. I did the math with eyes fixed on ageless evergreens, timeless granite, endless ocean. I ignored irregularities of coves and peninsulas, much as God ignored the warp of human minds. I determined Winter Haven's coastline would stretch nineteen and three quarter miles in a world where imperfections did not signify. I might have gone on taking comfort from my calculations, imitating God's aloof considerations, but we rounded a point and I lost my train of thought, distracted by the sight of Evan's mansion rambling along the rocky precipice.

I had seen the house from across the clearing on the landward side, but from the ocean it was even more imposing. Evan pulled back on the throttles and turned toward land. A few minutes later we idled up to the small floating dock behind the granite jetty. The engines vibrated powerfully behind my seat, no longer sputtering but rumbling with self-satisfaction. I thought of tigers purring after a good run. Then Evan shut them off, and in the relative quiet I heard gulls protesting and the gentle lapping of the waves.

He led me up steps carved into the old rock of the cliff. At the top, we crossed the grass toward one of many doors into his house. Beneath a columned portico he pointed to a pair of Adirondack chairs placed side by side on a mossy pavement of red bricks. "Want to wait there while I get the goodies?"

I did as he suggested, sitting just inside the shade provided by the overhang. To my left and right the mansion's woebegone façade followed the edge of a narrow lawn, which filled the level ground between the house and cliff. I saw other overhangs, porches, pavements, and balconies. Obviously the old building had been planned for entertaining on a massive scale, back in the golden days, when privileged guests of robber barons might linger for entire summers. So much space, so many wonderful vantage points from which to view the grand Atlantic, yet the chair where I sat and its one companion were the only signs of life remaining outside a building dying of neglect.

I turned toward the ocean. High aloft, the angular black silhouette of a single bird soared on stationary wings—a hawk, or perhaps an osprey. Dozens of gulls circled above the shoreline at a much lower altitude, sometimes dipping out of sight below the cliff top, sometimes rising, wheeling, flapping. Constantly complaining.

The lone soaring bird reminded me of Evan, the way he lived so far from all the others on the island, so solitary. The gulls were villagers, self-centered and rude. No wonder Evan chose to keep his distance.

Then I thought of Siggy, and the other man who had washed up on Bleak Beach—I was assuming for the moment that he had not been put there on purpose—and I remembered Steady Wallis's warning, and I realized Evan's solitude might have other motivations. It might be just the thing for gruesome work.

eighteen

"WANT TO CHANGE out of that sweatshirt? You look a little hot."

Turning, I saw Evan Frost with a classic wicker picnic basket in one hand and a man's white dress shirt in the other.

"That would be nice," I said. "Thanks."

He handed me the dress shirt. "Why don't I wait here while you go put that on? You can just step inside that door."

Moments later I was back, with Evan's shirttails nearly to my knees and the sleeves rolled to my elbows. The light cotton was delightfully cool compared to the heavy sweatshirt I now held in my hand. Folding the sweatshirt, I laid it on the seat of the Adirondack chair. Evan stooped to lift it up.

"I thought I'd leave it there until we come back," I said, tying the shirttails at my waist.

"Probably be better to take it along. In case you get cold."

"I won't get cold. I love cool weather."

"Then how come you live in Texas?"

A good question. There was my father, although he no longer even knew me. There was fear of change. Inertia. Masochism. Pondering these poor explanations, I did not realize Evan still carried the sweatshirt until we had rounded the house and crossed the landward clearing. He stuffed it between the picnic basket handles. I wondered why he had not left the sweatshirt on the chair. I did not think he really believed it would get cold. Something about that shirt . . . He had asked about it over dinner, and so had the widow when I returned from Bleak Beach. *"Ya went across the island. Ya went across while ya was dressed like that!"*

This was a distraction. I must focus on the reason I had come. I said, "So, I heard you found some Viking things. Jewelry and artifacts and things."

"Who told you that?"

"The preacher said so in his sermon."

"No, he didn't."

"Sure he did. All that talk about the miracle that's going to save Winter Haven."

"He never mentioned what it was."

"No? Then I guess somebody must have told me. It's all over the island."

He said nothing. I walked half a step behind him, afraid he might guess I had learned of this from Steady Wallis, afraid he might guess the reason for my question, might guess my suspicions. My heart raced and my hands felt shaky, but I had to keep on pressing. After a few minutes, I said, "Are they worth a lot of money?"

"That's what I hear."

"Where'd you find them?" I held my breath. I had meant to build up to the question, put it to him slyly, not just blurt it out that way. Would my transparency make him angry? I was acutely aware of my isolation, six miles from the nearest Winter Haven resident across a bewildering forest maze. He could do anything he wished with me, absolutely anything. No one would ever know.

Evan Frost paused at the forest edge with his back to me. "Maybe I'll show you the spot one of these days."

"How about today?"

"No. Today there's something better."

"Better than thousand-year-old Viking stuff?"

He turned and smiled. I hated how I loved the way his laugh lines crinkled.

"Way better," he said.

I saw his wandering eye take off again, aiming for something to the right while his good eye searched my face. I had to look away.

We stepped into the endless twilight beneath the ancient trees of Winter Haven. Deep in darkness I heard the steady crack of branches slapping branches two hundred feet above my head, and wondered if it was some kind of language among giants, a way to spread the news of our intrusion. I wondered if the trees were watching me. Glancing up, I saw no motion in the canopy, no wind to explain the sound. But Evan did not seem to notice as he strode along the path, swinging the picnic basket in time to his confident gait. A burl the size of a coffin protruded from a massive trunk beside the path. I saw an old man's face in the gnarled bark: the chin, the nose, the eyes, everything. Warily I passed, saying, "Someone told me you own half of Winter Haven."

The old man in the tree watched me with a pitiless glare. Evan said, "Don't believe everything you hear, Vera."

"So you don't own half the island?"

"Not half, no."

"More?"

"Less."

"A lot less?"

He laughed. "What are you, some kind of gold digger?"

"Of course not! I don't care how much money you have. Why would I? I don't care about anything like that, I mean, anything about you."

He stopped to look back, his random eye refusing to cooperate. "You don't?"

"I didn't mean it that way. Of course I care. I mean, I don't *care*—not the way that sounds—but I do care. Just not, you know, that way."

"What way?"

"Well, you know, like . . . like the way some women care about some men. I mean, I don't want you thinking I care about your money, or your house or all this land—however much land you have, or anything—because I'm not like that. Really."

"Hey." He smiled. "Relax a little, will you?"

Blood rose like sap behind my cheeks. Rooted in my paranoia, I felt the old burl's eyes upon my back. "Could we just keep going?"

"Sure." He set out again. I focused on his back as we threaded through the massive trees. I tried not to think about the sense of danger in the forest, or the cracking sound the branches made without apparent movement, or the fool I had just made of myself. I started counting my own footsteps.

"I'm not rich," said Evan from in front of me.

"I don't care, one way or the other."

He laughed, and then, "I'm just saying, I'm not rich. In case you're interested."

"Well, I'm not. Interested, I mean. And I'm not rich either—just so you know."

He laughed again. "Glad we have that out of the way."

We walked in shadows. My shoes pressed into the forest floor, my weight compressing the loose layer of needles, compacting the trail, defining it just a bit more clearly, reinforcing the unwelcome presence of humanity upon this primordial place, much to the rising anger of the trees.

No. Trees felt no emotions, just as trees did not bleed.

I saw Siggy in the surf, our mother's written plea adrift beside him. *I am not dangerous.* How untrue it was.

I continued counting giants, reducing them to numbers, but the cracking overhead grew louder. It began to sound like axes, as if the trees wished to make their accusation with a reenactment of the crime, as if they wished to say, "This is what you did to us." I knew it was no use to speak to them of four hundred years gone by, to claim the distance of twenty generations. For these timeless ones, the outrage that began with English axes had gone on to cut across a continent in moments. The Vikings and the Pilgrims might as well have been yesterday. I cast another furtive glance up into the canopy. Behemoth branches hung above my head, thousands of them. Any one of them could break away, drop at any moment to drive me deep into the earth to decompose and rise again within the bloody sap of roots and ancient trunks and mix my mortal residue with that of Pilgrims and of Vikings. I remembered what the widow warned:

"Folks has died there since the olden days. Died and disappeared into the soil."

I closed the distance between Evan and myself. I nearly gave voice to my anxiety. But what could I say? The trees are threatening us? They're talking to each other? We have to get away, get out from underneath them? We ought to run back to your boat as fast as we can? Evan seemed oblivious. I wondered if the man could even hear the cracking, chopping sound. He appeared to be so comfortable, so confident. Could he be in league with the forest? Could the trees be using him somehow?

Madness.

This strange, forgotten island, these horrible, aloof people, and Siggy lying dead on ice—everything conspired to make me lose my mind. I must regain control. I had to focus on reality. I needed to keep the conversation going, pretend I was normal.

"So, you're telling me you're not rich, but you have this mansion and all this land. How does that work?"

"Maybe I am kind of rich if you look at the property. But I don't have much money. And you can't eat land and houses."

I nodded. "My father used to say there's dirt poor and there's land poor and the two look just alike."

"He sounds pretty smart."

"Why don't you sell it?"

"The land?" Walking in front of me, he waved his free hand toward the giant evergreens. "Could you sell this? Knowing some developer would cut these trees for timber? Replace them with vacation houses for rich people from Boston and New York?"

"What about your house? I'm sure you could get a lot for that."

"It's not just a house. It's like part of the family. It even has a name. My great-grandfather named it Weatherly. That's a boat that sails close to the wind and doesn't drift to leeward. It's what Weatherly has been for my family—a place that doesn't drift."

My father's pipe tobacco-scented house came to mind, empty for three years in Mount Sinai because I could not bring myself to let go of the last room where I saw my mother living, or the front porch where I did not lift my voice to stop dear Siggy from his final walk into the whiteness as the church bells tolled four-fifteen exactly. I said, "I think I understand."

"I'm glad."

"How'd you come to own all this, anyway?"

"Remember I told you I'm a captain? I work for FHL?"

"On a ship that does things for oil platforms. Sure."

"It's a family business, I guess you'd say. My dad was an oilman. He was the son and grandson of oilmen, too."

"They all worked on ships?"

"No, they owned them. My great-grandfather was the 'F' in FHL."

"Wow."

"Before you get too impressed, you should know this house and land are all that's left. My father didn't inherit the business gene or whatever. He lost money faster than my grandfather and great-grandfather made it, so he had to sell off his shares of the company."

"That's why the house is kind of . . ."

"Falling apart? Yeah. I can barely afford the property taxes, much less the upkeep."

"I understand it means a lot to you, but if it's such a burden, I mean, it's not going to repair itself. Wouldn't it be better for the house if you sold it?"

"I already sold pretty much everything else to pay off the old man's debts, along with all my parents' other properties and what was left of their stock portfolio and whatnot. These last few years it's come down to pawning off the furniture and art in Weatherly. But the house has too many memories. Besides, a man has to live someplace when he's ashore."

"A hundred people could live there."

"Let's hope you're right."

Before I could ask what he meant, I saw sunlight up ahead. I broke into a run without a thought, leaving Evan in my headlong flight to escape the canopy of wrathful trees. But there was no relief as I emerged beneath the open sky. I only heard the chopping sound more clearly. Languishing in the sunshine, I watched Evan catch up, and searched for a sign that he could also hear the battering of axes. It was all that I could do to keep from covering my ears.

Evan reached my side. He wiped his brow and smiled. "Not much further now."

Obviously he heard nothing. I could not let him guess how close I was to losing control. If he knew my thoughts, he might think in terms of hospitals. I imagined padded rooms and burly men in white. I shuddered. If that kind of help was necessary, I would get it back in Texas, at a time and place of my own choosing. Besides, the chopping might be real, maybe not as sound waves traveling through air, but real, nevertheless. It might exist on a plane beyond the realm of mathematics, an alternate reality that only I could hear, and yet reality. If so, it would change nothing. Everyone would still think me insane—everyone except perhaps the widow, who believed in witches.

Evan Frost raised his face toward the sky, shading his eyes. "Come on," he said. "We can't be late."

I walked beside him as if moving underwater. The path dipped into the surface of the land, declining between two low hills, which were dressed in purple underbrush. "Blueberries," said Evan. "They're going to yield awful early this year, I think. Maybe even before June."

I felt cold. I was sweating. I barely listened to his words. How could he remain uncut by the pounding axes in the distance, immune to the watchful forest's animosity?

A few yards farther, a tiny stream came trickling down the hill on our left, emerging from under a fragile sheet of ice to meet the path and turn alongside us. Suddenly I realized where we were. I said, "This trail leads to Gin Gap Cove."

He nodded. "You have a good memory. This is how we went to my house the other night."

"Do we have to go this way?" I could not get the terrifying whisper out of my mind, the hissing I first heard high above the cove, or my flight down the narrow granite ledge along the cliff, the opaque fog where no such fog should be, and the inexplicable bone-chilling cold. "Can we have our picnic here?"

"What? Right here on the path?"

"It's a beautiful spot."

He looked at me, his brow wrinkled. "What's wrong, Vera?"

"I'm a little tired of walking."

He checked his watch. "It's only been twenty minutes since we left the house. You feeling okay?"

Twenty minutes? How could that be? Surely we had been walking in those dreadful woods for hours. I did my best to give him a bright smile. "I'm fine," I said.

"It'll be worth the effort. I promise."

We continued on. The little stream gurgled on the left, bouncing over small rocks and under overhanging ferns, which had uncoiled prematurely. Suddenly I saw the malignant gouge in Winter Haven's shoreline that was Gin Gap Cove. The gap lay ahead of us just as I recalled, a deep insult carved into the coast, laying Winter Haven open on the left and right, exposing looming granite cliffs. Beyond the cove the menace of Evangeline's Folly crouched low in the ocean like black salt on a wound. Incredibly, the dense fog still sprawled flat and motionless between the cliffs, obscuring any view of the water in the cove.

I tried to understand how this fog was possible. We had circled half the island in Evan's motorboat and I had seen no hint of mist, either ashore or on the ocean. A sun so hot and high would have burned off ground fog hours ago. So how could Gin Gap Cove alone on all of Winter Haven be so thickly veiled?

As the path dipped closer to the mist, I felt the air begin to cool. The temperature seemed to drop a full degree with every step I took. I shivered in the sunshine. I clutched myself for warmth and cast a glance at Evan's profile. He looked at me and smiled. I almost believed he was unaware of the cold, the dreadful obscurity, the menacing axe blows. Perhaps whatever he had planned would make him happy. I did not think it would have the same effect on me.

We did not descend into the enigmatic veil of fog. We merely touched its hem and turned aside. Ascending on another path, we soon reached the lofty margin of the cliff. Ahead, I saw the monumental fallen tree that had barred my escape three nights ago, lying as it did across the path, its lower trunk and huge ball of roots far back on the shadowed forest floor, its upper trunk and long-dead branches soaring out a hundred feet beyond the cliff edge, a bridge to nowhere, ending in midair above the eerie fog.

Evan turned at the tree trunk, walking next to it straight into the darkness of the forest. I followed. Even on its side, the tree was nearly twice my height. I felt shrunken, insignificant, distant from my surroundings and myself.

Our walk through the malicious shadows was much briefer this time. We reached the mangled roots of the mighty fallen giant. They clutched a granite boulder twice my size, holding it fifteen feet aloft, having drawn it out of Winter Haven in the final instant of the tree's long life, gripping the boulder like a druid's fingers around a sacrificial victim's heart.

I saw a clearing just beyond.

"Here we are," said Evan Frost.

He led me out into the sunshine yet again, but this time I stepped from underneath the canopy with dread, for I had seen that evil place before. There in the clearing's center was the circle of low stones around a broad flat rock charred black in the center, and a pair of taller boulders looming over all. It was the ruins I had stumbled upon while lost in this eternal forest, the roughhewn temple clearly meant for dreadful offerings. Before, this place was overrun with vines and half-buried in fallen branches. Now it was well manicured, the underbrush trimmed back, the broken limbs removed, a temple fit for profane liturgy again. I saw the altar as if from a far-flung place. Following Evan, I approached it with a strangely willing mind, even as a small voice begged the rest of me to flee.

Evan walked directly to the stone that squatted before the dreadful inscription on the altar.

O thou perfect goddess,
Receive mine heart,
An eternal offering to thee.

Shading his eyes, he looked up toward the sun. "We're just in time."

I heard a voice come from my lips, although it did not sound like mine. "Just in time for what?"

"You'll see. Come sit down." He pointed to the low stone before the inscription. Of all the stones that circled the sacrificial altar, it alone languished in the baneful shadow of the pair of boulders standing on the altar's other side. That shadow was the one place in the clearing where I least desired to be. Again I remembered the widow's prophecy beneath her photograph of me. *Next to die.* I knew I ought to run. If indeed I had been lured to Winter Haven for this very purpose, if I had been a prisoner on this island from the start, this might be my final chance. But even if I could escape, every hope of learning what had happened to my brother would be lost, and that knowledge had become my only hope of sanity.

This man claimed he had found poor Siggy's body. He claimed to possess the Viking artifacts that had drawn my brother to the island, or at least he pretended to possess them. Evan Frost and Winter Haven's mysteries were somehow bound together. I had to know the secret of this island. I had to know my brother's fate. I had to know what had been done to Siggy, or else the suffering I had endured for thirteen years might go on for eternity. I had to *know*, even if it meant my brother's fate was also mine.

I walked to the low stone beside the man, and sat.

Opening the wicker basket, Evan Frost removed a pure white cloth, which he laid over the inscription on the flat boulder before me. Next from the basket came a long serrated knife. Clutching the knife, Evan Frost looked toward the sky. "Any second now."

"Did you bring Siggy here?"

His eyebrows came together. "What?"

"My brother. Did you bring him here like this?"

"What are you talking about?"

"I know what this place is."

"How could you know that?"

"It's written right there underneath that cloth."

He stared at me. His face was somehow darker. "What do you think that means?"

I refused to play his game any longer. If I must sacrifice my life to find the peace that had been stolen long ago, at least I would meet my death with dignity. I looked away. I felt his eyes upon me, felt him raising the knife, felt it drawing closer. I closed my eyes and said a little prayer, but not to God.

Siggy, wait for me. I'm coming.

nineteen

"LOOK!" SAID EVAN FROST.

"Just finish it." I was quite prepared to die.

"Will you please look? Quick! Before it's over."

Opening my eyes, I turned and saw him pointing to my feet with the knife. Looking down into the shadow of the twin boulders, I saw a miracle.

From the narrow gap between the tall boulders a sliver of sunshine had escaped, a strip of light no wider than an inch that streamed across the altar top to strike the very stone on which I sat. The bright sliver widened all around me, spreading out to form an unmistakable shape within the shadow. Bathed in the miraculous pool of light, I said, "I don't understand."

"Happy birthday," said the handsome man.

"It's . . . it's a heart."

He waved the knife at the twin boulders on the other side. "My grandfather set this up for my grandmother. Remember I told you she had the same birthday as you?"

"This . . . this is a birthday present?"

"Happens only once a year, on my grandmother's birthday and yours."

I looked at the ground around myself in amazement. The perfect heart-shaped patch of sunshine piercing the shadow was straight out of a valentine, and just large enough to encompass me completely. Then, as quickly as it came, the sun moved on and it was gone.

"Oh, Evan."

"Did you like it?"

"It was wonderful!"

"I'm glad. Since my grandma passed, it's always made me kind of sad to see it falling on an empty seat."

"This is a seat? All these little stones are seats around this . . . this table?"

"I thought you said you knew that."

"And your grandmother, she used to come here on her birthday?"

"The whole family had a picnic here every year. We'd all walk over from Weatherly and sit around this table. Grandpa would build a big fire. See that dark place in the middle of the table rock? Us kids would get up there and roast marshmallows."

I watched him arrange a simple feast on the tablecloth. From the basket came a golden loaf of bread, smoked salmon, mustard in a stoneware crock, cheese, a jar of olives, and fresh carrots and broccoli with a tin of creamy sauce to dip them in. Then came a corkscrew, a bottle of red wine, a bottle of Perrier, and a pair of long-stemmed glasses. It would have been a fine last meal, if that was what he had in mind.

"Do you like wine?" he asked, applying the corkscrew to the bottle.

"I don't drink."

"Nothing?"

I heard my father's fury from the pulpit. "Not alcohol."

"That's a pity." He pulled the cork out with a pop. "This is the good stuff."

Evan poured a glass of wine for himself and a glass of sparkling water for me. He picked up the knife and carved pieces of cheese and salmon for us both. Sitting on the stone stool beside me, he began to eat.

After a moment he spoke around a mouthful of bread and cheese. "How come you asked that about your brother? Me bringing him here?"

I had to think of what to say, some reasonable explanation. "I just thought, since he was over on this side of the island and you're the one who found him, maybe you guys knew each other."

"I would of told you that by now." Evan took another bite and considered me as he chewed. "You sure that's what you meant? Because you seemed kind of . . . I don't know, scared or something."

I knew I had to deny it. I needed to offer innocent explanations. But watching him, I found I could not bear the thought of lying anymore. I was so tired of being lonely in the midst of crowded places, so tired of my own self-denigrating inner voice, so weary of the doubts and questions plaguing me. How I longed for an ally, a friend, someone I could trust. How I wished I could just speak the truth aloud, just say, "Sometimes I think I'm losing my mind." But it was too risky. I could never find the courage to admit my fears. What if they were true? What if—

"Why?"

Evan's voice broke into my thoughts. I said, "Excuse me?"

Still chewing, he said, "Why do you think you're losing your mind?"

Had I said those words aloud? Surely not. I had not meant to do it. Yet apparently he had heard me speak them. Could he read my mind?

"Did I say that out loud?"

"You sure did."

"Well, I guess that proves it. I'm saying things without even knowing it."

"Sometimes I think I'm saying things when I'm really not, and I'm no more nuts than you are."

"That's not very comforting."

He laughed. "I guess not."

I reached out for a small piece of cheese. I raised it to my mouth and nibbled on it, like a mouse. A mousy girl, who did not know enough to wear mascara, a mouse beside a dashing prince who had the power to chase darkness from this storybook picnic place with a magical touch of light. Might he also chase the curse from me? If I simply spoke of the dark things in my heart, might he hear, and understand, and shed light on my burden? Moments ago I had been prepared to die. How could honesty be worse than that?

Hiding behind the little block of cheese, I said, "My brother was autistic, remember? And I don't know if I told you about my dad. He has Alzheimer's."

"You told me. Are you having problems with your memory?"

I almost smiled. "No," I said. "Not that."

"Well, you're obviously not autistic, so I don't get the connection."

"I guess it's just, having two people with mental problems in your family, it makes you more aware of how fragile the mind can be, you know?"

"Yes, I do."

Something in the way he put it, something in his tone, made me look at him more closely. I said, "When we were on the beach the other day, I was talking about my brother and it seemed like you were kind of sad." I left it there, not daring to ask outright if he would share his sorrow with me, hoping he would speak of it without more prompting. He did not. After a few moments, I asked, "Are you okay?"

"Let's talk about me later. Right now I want to know why you think your mind is going."

I took a deep breath. "When I was little, I had these . . . day-dreams. Not like a kid looking out a window at school or any-thing. They were more like seizures."

"Yeah?"

"Uh-huh. I'd be sitting there and all of a sudden it would be like I was someplace else, seeing other things. Like I was really in that other place, you know? Then I'd wake up, and I'd be down on the floor as if I'd passed out or something."

"Did you go to a doctor?"

I heard the men in suits. *"Why didn't you call a doctor? Why didn't you take your wife to the hospital?"* Avoiding Evan's eyes I said, "No. You remember how my father felt about that, right?"

"Oh, yeah. So, when you say you're losing your mind, are you talking about those seizures? You still have them?"

I considered his question. Were they seizures? Daydreams? Visions? Hallucinations? Memories? How was I to know the difference? Whatever was at work within my mind, for thir-teen years I had beat it back with discipline and numbers. Yet ever since I first set foot on Winter Haven, the prophet Siggy in his empty whiteness had assailed me with an independent will. Was he the boy I loved, or a dreadful prophet? If I could not even tell the difference, how could I explain this warring in my mind?

I said, "They're not seizures, exactly. More like, I don't know . . . really bad memories, I guess."

He laid a hand on my shoulder. "We all have those. Doesn't mean you're crazy."

"They overwhelm me. They make me lose myself."

"I know what you mean."

"Do you?"

"Sure. Sometimes when I think of certain things I get sad, even though I don't want to. It's like I can't help myself. You shouldn't worry about it so much. Just let the grief wash over and away. It's something you have to live through."

His words enticed me. I longed for simple grief. I leaned toward him a little, suddenly awash with wishing he would take me in his arms. Yet just moments ago I had thought this man would murder me. Was this part of my insanity as well? And if so, did the real imbalance lie in fear or in desire? Shrugging off those thoughts, I resolved to explain further, to risk the distance that would bring. It was not fair to let him think I only dealt with sadness. I said, "I'm also hearing things."

"Like what?"

"Well, right now I hear the sound of axes. Sometimes I think it's those missing Pilgrims and they're in some kind of hell or something, like they're cursed for cutting down the trees to build their raft."

He laughed.

I said, "I told you I was going crazy."

"No, no, no." He touched my shoulder lightly. "You're not crazy. It's just some of the fellas doing a little work around my place."

I turned and looked into his face, searching his eyes. "You hear the axes, too?"

"Have to be deaf not to, with those guys whacking away over there."

"So that sound, it's just some people chopping wood or something?"

"A few guys from my crew, earning extra money while the *Albert Murray* is in dry dock."

"What are they doing?" An image came to me of bleeding branches. I felt a sudden jolt of fear. "They're not cutting down the trees?"

"No, I'd never let anyone do that. They . . . Uh, can you keep a secret?"

I nodded.

"You know those Viking things I found? I'm hoping when word gets out about them, they'll bring more tourists to the island. So I had this thought. About turning the house into a hotel."

"A hotel? That's a wonderful idea!"

He grinned. "It is, isn't it?"

"You can save Weatherly."

"I hope so. And maybe after we're done fixing up the old place, we'll have a need for housekeepers, maintenance guys, tour guides and all that, so some of the Winter Haven people can have steady jobs right here on the island."

I thought a moment. "I hear axes in the village, too."

"Well . . . lots of folks use wood to heat their houses over there, you know. Some even use it for their cookstoves."

It was true. The widow had a wood stove in her kitchen. "You think that's all it is? Someone chopping firewood?"

"Sure."

"But that's not all." In a rush I told him of polished stones falling from the sky and the hissing in the forest and the village, of my certainty that the trees were bent upon revenge, the bleeding branches, the old man's face I had just seen in the gnarled tree trunk, the remains of Pilgrims and Vikings drawn up into roots, and my ridiculous belief that the very place where we were sitting had once been used for human sacrifice. I said, "I know it's all in my head. I know I shouldn't let my imagination run away with me like that, but I just keep hearing things and seeing things and thinking awful things, and I can't seem to stop."

I waited for his response, afraid he would laugh again, or distance himself some other way. I knew from bitter experience how frightened people were of mental illness. But when he spoke, there was no fear in his voice, and certainly no humor. He said, "In spite of all this, you still came here with me?"

"I have to find out about Siggy."

He gazed at me, and both his eyes were true. "That's the bravest thing I've ever heard."

I felt myself blushing.

He stood. He walked to the edge of the clearing, then turned and strode back, then did it again, striding back and forth, casting glances at the circular tree line all around us. I watched him closely, like a child observing a lion as it paced in its cage. "These rocks that fell," he said. "And the bleeding branches. Tell me about that again."

I repeated every word. He interrupted several times, asking questions, drawing details from me. He never stopped moving

as I spoke, the sudden welling up of energy in him uncontain-
able. When I had repeated everything, he said, "The widow told
you it was Evangeline?"

Nervous at the forceful way he asked the question, I said,
"She went outside and yelled that name."

He paced some more. I thought to mention the photographs
in the widow's cellar, and the hateful words written on those
frightful images, but then I saw darkness entering his expression, the same fury he had shown the archaeologist in the
churchyard. His anger pressed me back against the table as he
stalked the clearing, kicking at the ground, muttering under
his breath. What a fool I'd been to open up to him. I heard his
quiet curses, felt his every imprecation as if it were a slap. I
began to tremble. I did not dare to watch him. I looked everywhere else, gauging my chances of escape. But he knew these
woods too well. I could not get away. I cast a secret glance his
way. He had ceased his pacing and stood staring at the trees,
in the direction of the distant chopping axes. Then he turned
abruptly toward me. Quickly I looked down. He said, "You said
this all started when you saw your brother's body again. Why
would you say that?"

"Why are you so angry, Evan?"

"Please just answer!"

"You're scaring me!"

He charged across the clearing straight at me. I pressed back
against the stone and closed my eyes, certain that the end had
come. But then I felt his hands on mine, and looked to find
him kneeling at my feet, gazing up at me, entreating me with
both his eyes. "Please don't be afraid of me, Vera. I couldn't
stand that."

"You're so angry."

"For you! I'm angry at the things they put you through!"

"They? Who are 'they'?"

"Don't ask me that. Not until I know some things for sure."

"Why not? What are you hiding?"

"Look. You came out here with me in spite of everything. I'm asking you to keep on being brave. Trust me just a little longer."

All the anger had dissolved into a perfect picture of a pleading man, a man who might be holding secrets but made no secret of his heart. He cared for me; he really did. Any fool could see it. In that moment I had no doubt of him. "All right," I said.

"I just need to understand a little more."

"Okay."

"You said these weird things, they started when you saw your brother?"

"Well, Siggy was the first thing that was, you know . . . really strange."

"Strange? You mean because he was dead?"

"No. Because he hasn't changed."

"Hasn't changed? What does that mean?"

"The way he looks just the same."

"The same as what, Vera? Tell me what you're talking about."

"He looks just like he did when he disappeared."

"Why would you expect him to look different?"

"Well, it has been thirteen years since I last saw him, so—"

"What did you just say?"

"I said it's been thirteen years."

"Since he ran away from home?"

"I thought you knew that."

He released my hands, stood and began pacing again. "But the boy I saw, the one I found, he couldn't have been much older than thirteen."

"He was fifteen, actually. The last time I saw him."

Evan made a fist and slammed it into the palm of his other hand. "The fools!"

"What fools?" I asked. "Would you please just tell me what's going on?"

Pacing to the chopping rhythm of the axes, muttering, he ignored my questions. I stared at him, waiting. At last he turned to face me. "Listen," he said. "I think I know what's happening here."

"You think it's real? I'm not going crazy?"

"No." He shook his head. "You're not going crazy. And I can fix it, if you'll trust me."

I had no reason for the words that I next spoke, yet I had never said a truer thing. "I do trust you."

He smiled, and it was like daylight breaking through a thunderhead. "I'm so glad."

We lingered in the clearing until the sun had dipped behind the branches of the awesome trees that stood in witness. We spoke of many things, unimportant things, perhaps, but still it seemed to me each word became another precious bond between us. Never had I felt this free to be myself with anyone. Oh, how could I have doubted him? Steady Wallis was a fool, or worse perhaps, and I myself a fool to listen to the man.

When the time came to return to Evan's boat, we walked beside each other through the trees. Evan took my hand to lead me past the chill and the unnatural fog of Gin Gap Cove, and up into the trees again, and it never crossed my mind to be afraid of anything. The only voice I heard was the one inside my head that cursed Evan's motorboat for its swiftness as we raced across the sleeping ocean toward Winter Haven harbor. The only dread I felt was of the coming time without his company.

Evan tied his boat up at the floating dock below the village landing and disembarked with me. Then to my amazement he drew me close and kissed me. It was a brief kiss, over in a second. But when he finished, I remained with my face upturned toward him. He only pulled away an inch or two. Both his eyes were searching mine, asking the obvious question.

"Do it again," I said.

At first I received his second kiss in absolute stillness. I savored the softness of his lips, accepting this tenderness as a gift, as something made for me, a glorious endearment demanding nothing in response. Then I felt the need to give to him as well, and although I had no practice in such things, I reached up and ran my fingers through his hair, holding him exactly where I wanted him as my own lips yielded and moved in closer.

He was the first to pull away. He said, "Don't worry about anything. I know what to do."

"All right," I replied, certain I had found my peace at last.

He smiled that bright smile of his, then bent down to untie his boat. "I can't wait to see you tomorrow."

"You will come back?"

"Of course. First thing in the morning."

"Promise?"

He frowned, teasing me with sudden gravity. "I thought you said you trust me."

"Oh yes," I said. "I do. I really do!"

I stood watching as he idled out between the fishing vessels at their moorings. He looked back just as his motorboat disappeared around the rocky point. I rose to my toes and waved. He waved too, and then he was gone.

Vacillating between sorrow at our parting and joy at what had risen to unite us, I turned to climb the ramp up to the village landing. It was only then that I saw Steady Wallis on the far side of the harbor, watching.

TWENTY

T HE FOLLOWING MORNING, for the first time in recent memory, I rose gladly from my bed. Evan filled my thoughts immediately, just as he had been the last thing on my mind the night before. Somehow that gentle man, that incredibly good-looking man, had feelings for me! Could it be that God had finally decided to be kind?

I found new joy in everything. The cold water on my face smelled of roses. My clothes, though stale from overuse, seemed to fit more comfortably. I saw myself in the bathroom mirror and believed I might be beautiful. At least to him.

In the kitchen, I even tried to greet the widow with good cheer. "Morning, Mrs. Abernathy!"

Seated at the table, the old woman sniffed. "I hear ya made a shameful exhibition of yourself down at the harbor yestidy."

"If you mean I kissed a man, you're absolutely right." I moved to the cupboard, searching for something to eat for breakfast.

"That kinda thing is not done here on Winter Haven."

"Oh, but it is! I did it myself." I bent to peer into the woman's antique refrigerator. "Do you have any blueberries?"

"They're not in season, girl."

I laughed. "I think they will be soon!"

"Nonsense. Sit down and let me make ya eggs and bacon."

Remembering the warning on the photograph down in the woman's cellar, I decided not to trust food prepared by her. "No thanks," I said. "I'll just fix myself some toast."

From the table, the old woman watched me carefully. "What's got into ya?"

"You were married once. Don't you know love when you see it?"

"Love, is it? And Captain Frost at that? Ha!"

In spite of my happy mood, I paused to look at the old woman. "What's that supposed to mean?"

"Child, ya need to sit down here beside me. Please."

It was the first time the old woman had asked for anything politely. My joy vanished at once. "Just say what's on your mind."

The widow sighed. "There's things ya need to know about him."

"I know everything that matters. He's kind. He cares about the people of this island. And he wants to help me when the rest of y'all won't give me the time of day."

"I'll admit there's some here could of been more friendly to ya. But that don't mean ya ought to put your trust in Evan Frost."

I spread strawberry jam on a piece of buttered toast. "I can trust him."

"Can ya now? And what if I told ya he's not as free as ya believe?"

I thought about the Spartan setting in his house. "Are you saying he's married? I know he's not married."

"Ayuh, that's right enough, though it's peculiar for a man of his years, ya must admit. And it don't mean he's got no woman in his life."

"If you have something to say, just say it plainly!"

Her eyes were strangely gentle, almost sorrowful, as she looked at me and spoke the name, "Evangeline."

I felt my confidence begin to waver. "Something strange is happening on this island, I'll admit. But Evan said there's an explanation for everything. He's going to work it out."

"Work it out? How could he do that when what's done is done? She took my husband! Steady and Abigail lost their boy to her! She's been the ruin of your Captain Frost. Nearly forty years old he is, and never married. Did ya think to ask him why? She's been the ruin of him, the ruin of this island, and now she's set her hooks in ya, and ya can't even see the danger!"

I had no doubt the widow knew much more than she was telling. I longed to ask about her photographs of the witch, especially the awful words that included me. *Next to die.* But even if there was some innocent explanation, how could I ask about it without admitting I had gone into her cellar? I remembered the woman's anger when I fed my breakfast to her dogs. I could not bring myself to face her rage again, so I said nothing, wrapped my toast in a paper napkin, and left through the back door. I had no destination in mind; I only knew I must escape the widow's superstitious poison.

The two Labradors rose from a patch of bare soil to plead for scraps with tenderhearted eyes. In my haste to get away I gave them nothing. Rounding the old woman's cottage, I set out for the village path. I took a bite of toast and wished I had brought along some coffee. My throat felt parched and dry, just as my heart had been for so many years. But Evan's affection promised an oasis. No more judgments, no more condescension, no more guilty fears; from this day on I would be nurtured by his love.

Oh, I could hear the widow's thoughts as if the horrible old woman were right there beside me on the path. *You barely know the man. You spend one evening with him at his house, two days total with him on this island, and already you think he's falling in love with you. You need to be realistic. You're acting like a foolish schoolgirl.*

"No!" I told myself, muttering as I stomped along. "No, no, no!"

A Winter Haven woman just a little farther up the trail paused to stare.

I turned off the path and crossed an open meadow toward the pines and spruces rising up behind the village. I did not fear them anymore. Evan Frost would stand for me against the horrors of the place. I need have no further fear of anything, not even Siggy's prophecies.

Love at first sight was a fantasy for little girls, and Evan had not said the word aloud, but I had seen him say it with his eyes. Not true love certainly, not yet, but a seed of love to come— something I had seen in no one's eyes for years. My father had once felt love for me. He was older than a father ought to be, and filled with other passions, but he had been my father, after all. And Siggy always held me dear; I had no doubt of that. But the only time Siggy ever showed his eyes to me, they had held no love. His were the cruel eyes of a prophet in my wild delusions. And my father's love had always been a matter of obedience, something to be earned and not the tenderhearted kind of love I craved. Then came Evan Frost. Evan had laid eyes on me while I was at my worst—defensive, hysterical, weak, and fearful—and still he cared. Surely that was at least the start of love. What else could it be?

Approaching the tree line, I turned to stride through knee-high grass along the wooded edge. Eternal shadows stretched beneath the towering forest on my right. A loose accumulation of houses and other village buildings lay at the far side of the meadow on the left. I cried out when a pair of pheasants erupted from the tall brush just ahead, their wings slapping the air in panic. I stood still as my heartbeat slowed to normal. Yet I told myself quite forcefully that I was not afraid.

I continued on, heading for the ocean in the distance. Soon enough I reached the shore, the meadow still on my left, the forest on my right. The coast here was not lined with cliffs like Gin Gap Cove or Winter Haven harbor or the landing behind Evan's house. Here the ground sloped gently down to greet the wild Atlantic, the ocean restrained from the meadow only by a low and crumbling fringe of rocks. To my left I saw the harbor in the distance, the fishing boats unmoved on glassy water ringed by shingled sheds and houses. To my right, the seacoast seemed to curve away forever, the skyscraping trees just a few feet back from shore. Between the trees and the coastal band of exposed granite I saw only one sign of human presence: a narrow path, no doubt worn into the earth through centuries of use by villagers who had fished along the rocks.

I turned my back on the meadow and the distant village and set out on the shoreline path. My intention was to find a place—a peaceful place—where I could sit and wait for Evan. I did not wish to wait back at the harbor, where Winter Haven people could confront me with their stares and sour judgments. I would not let them spoil what Evan had begun in me. So I walked along the narrow path, the breeze caressing lofty trees on one side and the ocean gently lapping on the other, until I found a soft bed of needles atop a little earthen ledge at the base of a mighty spruce. Behind the ledge was a slight depression in the tree trunk, which offered to support my back most comfortably. I settled down to watch the ocean.

I had a broad view of the Atlantic. Evan would appear in his motorboat far to my right, giving me plenty of time to walk back along the path and across the meadow to meet him at the landing as he docked. Filled with eager expectation, I waited.

The omnipresent gulls amused me with their selfishness, endlessly debating ownership of mussels down among the rocks. The sun rose higher. The deep blue morning sky began to pale. I waited.

Awake at midmorning for some reason, a raccoon emerged from the forest just twenty feet away, sniffed the air, saw me, and stared long and hard with beady eyes. When I did not move, the creature waddled across the narrow strip of land between the trees and waves to disappear down into the rocks. I assumed the gulls would now have competition. And still I waited.

When the sun had passed its zenith, I saw a boat leave Winter Haven harbor on the left. As it cruised past my position, I saw Steady Wallis standing on the stern deck. I sat very still and willed him not to notice me. His boat passed out of sight around the island to my right. My stomach growled. I wished I had brought more food, not just a piece of toast with strawberry jam but something more substantial. I had not expected to be watching for so long a time. I could have sworn Evan promised he would come in the morning. Apparently, my mind had failed me on the details, but Evan had convinced me there was no need to fear. The basic facts remained true. My mind was sound. Evan would return for me, and so I waited.

Sometimes I rose to walk along the path a little way, or to throw pebbles in the water, but never did I lose sight of the ocean. I saw Steady Wallis's boat returning toward the harbor. I checked my watch. It was four-fifteen exactly, the moment I let Siggy leave me standing on the porch with the bells of Father's church ringing in my ears. "*'I go to prepare a place for you.'*" But why go at all? Why leave me standing there, alone? The questions came before I could throw up defenses. "Why" could only lead to madness. But the love of Evan gave me strength. I shook my head. I tried to drive the questions out. I tried to blank out my mind. I fought the awful thing.

Later, as the sun sank to the horizon far beyond the harbor, as darkness overwhelmed the gloaming and the nighttime came without a sign of Evan, taunting words returned inside my head. But the voice was not the widow's anymore. It was now my own, asking a new set of vicious questions. What makes you think a man like that would care for you? You're nothing but a bookkeeper. You have nothing interesting to say. Your hair is dull and frizzy. Your eyes are small. Your hips are big. Your skin is blotchy. He's fascinating. He's gorgeous. What makes you think a man like that would love someone like you?

"No," I whispered as I gazed at stars and sea. "No. Please. No."

I stood upon the shore of Winter Haven, bathed in moonlight, lost between the ancient forest and the timeless ocean, thinking of my birthday—that selfish day when I was too consumed with my own sorrow to stop Siggy from walking away, the day that lured me out of hiding with a heart of sunshine in a clearing, and a heartfelt conversation with Evan, the perfection of each moment, his hands upon my face, his lips upon my lips, his eyes now wandering, now searching mine with authentic tenderness.

Lies, of course. All lies.

He had only wanted information. I tried to remember what I had revealed to him beside that stone table with its secret heart of light. We had spoken of so many things, of work and families, hopes for the future, of children, home, and faith. I had mentioned my delusions, but what else? I did not remember speaking about Steady Wallis's suspicions, but maybe Evan drew it from me cleverly, in a way I did not notice. I replayed the conversation and saw in my imagination the dark cast of Evan's anger on the churchyard, at the stone table, the way rage sometimes seemed to overshadow him. I now knew darkness was his natural state, and tenderness a sham. Rolling doubts and bittersweet memories broke with violence on the shoreline of my mind, eroding me like waters crashing on the nearby rocks and rushing back to sea, wearing hope away with every ebb and flow.

Looking up, I saw the lunar whiteness grow, filling the periphery of my vision. I did not try to stop it. My fantasy of Evan's love was just another form of condemnation, one last test that I had failed. I had reached the outer edge of sanity at last, and Evan's falseness left me naked to the dread temptation of it. In the end, I did not fall into that absence of all color; I was pushed.

What did Siggy see in me that one and only time he looked? A timid girl, unremarkable, and wrongly convinced of her salvation? A child even less fortunate than he? Sinking through the nightmare, I remembered well what I myself had seen in him: the emerald within his eyes, sprinkled with disturbing flecks of red, as if the blood of Christ had seeped into his irises, tinting everything on which he gazed. I should have known his secret eyes would be unlike all others.

There was so much to fear. Dementia. Damnation. The dreadful specter at the center of my childhood hallucinations, the prophet, the boy who was not Siggy. I had only myself to blame. I summoned him with evil doubts. If God was good, if God loved me, why had he required my brother's absence? Why must my mother die? Why this evil in a world God claimed to love? With these effronteries the little girl I used to be now conjured up a boy who was not Siggy, and he offered up his eyes and spoke gospel verses to me as if I was a pagan, saying, " 'The truth will make you free.' "

I cried, "I know the truth! I'm already free! I love Jesus, Siggy! I do! I do!"

Then Siggy said the last words I would ever hear from him, the words that robbed me of all hope of answers, for they were spoken in a foreign tongue: " 'Vera, *liberabit vos.*' "

My brother slowly blended with the whiteness as I tried to make him stay, crying in my desperation, "What does that mean? What does it *mean*?" Siggy faded, leaving me no colors, nothing of comfort in the blinding white, nothing but one last pronouncement, booming godlike in its depth and volume, one parting condemnation I might not survive, the judgment I had dreaded most since opening the door to it that one weak moment on the mail boat bound for Winter Haven, a voice I had been fighting not to hear, a booming shout that seemed to come from everywhere.

"THIS IS WRONG."

As it had so long ago, again the power of that voice dumbfounded me. The little girl I used to be came back into herself, and back into the woman I was now. Somehow she and I had fallen to the floor of my father's church, carpeted with pine needles upon a distant island. Charismatic Christians stared down with concern for me, or her. I stared up at the stained ceiling in my father's church, at the moon and stars in Maine. Gasping on my back, I—she—wondered who had spoken, and who had heard.

"*THIS IS WRONG.*"

What did it mean? Had I survived the voice of God replying to my wicked questions, passing judgment on my doubts? Was I that little girl again forever, awakening upon the center aisle, or was I a woman in her right mind on the edge of Winter Haven? Were these nightmares still inside of me, or was I now inside of them?

Even that, it seemed a sin to ask.

I heard a different sound. From the place where I had tumbled I lifted up my head. My eyeglasses had fallen from my face. I saw only a blurred figure. Although I longed to see it clearly, I dared not move to find my glasses. I watched as the unfocused form came gliding into moonlight. It crossed the narrow strip of open land. At the water's edge it hovered for a moment, giving me a cloudy glimpse of something dark from top to bottom except for extreme paleness where the face and hands should be. This pallor seemed to absorb light rather than reflect it. Long tendrils whipped around the creature's head, angered by the onshore breeze, utterly black and writhing like snakes. Something filmy wrapped the form and wafted back into the air like a bride's train flowing in a breeze, yet it had no wedding lightness; it was a funereal thing, a thing of shadows. Mesmerized by this waking vision, I remained perfectly still. It was Evangeline, of course, there before the weakness of my eyes.

Shadows rose from it like arms, reaching for the ocean. It threw back its head. From its open mouth I heard the hissing sound, which started low but rose until at last it overwhelmed the gentle lapping of the surf and the whispers of the wind among the trees. The sound went on and on as it had before. She hissed, and suddenly I realized there was meaning in it. Even in my terror of the witch I felt a kind of joy to know I had returned into myself again; this thing was there outside of me and not a phantom in my mind, for the meaning in her horrid call could not have come from me.

Issssssaac . . .

This was no curse. It was instead a mourner's cry. The creature seemed to suffer as I did. I stood from my fallen place, drawn toward the ancient soul, summoned without thought for caution by the irresistible attraction of our common misery. I took a step, and paused, and then took another, but these movements were not mine. I was animated by a force I did not understand. Undisturbed, the awful thing still gestured toward the waves, as if beseeching Neptune for the blessing of escape. I walked more steadily, closing the distance, closer, closer. I was quite near when at last the figure turned.

Its mouth yawned wide, the ceaseless hiss still flowing from that broad black maw, and then the creature drifted back across the narrow open strip of land to disappear into the forest's darkness.

My limbs became as water. I collapsed again, all in a pile, poured out on the soil of Winter Haven. Wave after wave approached me, the Atlantic's inky surface undulating at the prompting of a boundless hidden energy. I watched as trees that once saw Caesar's time now clutched at passing stars. I lay and pondered all the things I did not know, how vast the universe, how insignificant my aching heart. An icy moon slid silently across the velvet dome of space.

Only when the morning's glow began to singe the eastern sky, only then, I stirred and rose, and in the dim new light I found my glasses lying on the sod and put them on, and I walked to the place where the grieving Pilgrim woman's spirit had strained toward the ocean, begging to escape the island that imprisoned her as it now imprisoned me. I looked down toward the joining place of land and sea, down among the rocks, and there I saw the crabs at work upon the body of a massive bear, which swayed gently in the surf and was the perfect white of my hallucinations.

twenty-one

T HEY HOISTED IT BESIDE the landing with a rusty crane, which I assumed was normally intended for less gruesome cargo. The motorized winch strained against the weight as the cable hummed with tension. Some of the Winter Haven people who had gathered on the dock backed away as if they feared the line would snap. Others crowded closer to gaze at the giant bear.

It hung suspended by a loop of cable around its chest. Driven upward by the cable's pressure, the bear's front legs and fearsome claws stretched toward the heavens like a rapturous charismatic. Water streamed into the harbor from its fur, and it was the fur that most astonished everyone.

The animal's tongue lolling from its gaping mouth, the vacant eyes, and the pale pink blood diluted by seawater all combined to turn my stomach. I looked away. I wished to see no more of death.

"Ya okay, Miss Gamble?" asked Steady Wallis at my side.

"No."

"Anythin' I can do for ya?"

I longed to beg for help, for some sense of normalcy without, if not within. But of course I knew the answer to his question. Again I said, "No."

"Wanna wait back at the store? I'll just look this thing over and be there in a jiffy."

Nodding, I set out walking. A man detached himself from the small crowd along the railing and fell in at my side. "Remember me?" he asked, adjusting the strap of a black canvas bag that hung from his shoulder.

I glanced at him—the owlish fellow passenger from my sickly crossing through the fog to Winter Haven—and said, "What do you want?"

"Just wondered if I could ask you a few questions."

I said nothing. We reached the main path and turned toward the village proper, crunching shells beneath our shoes. Steady Wallis's store lay just ahead on the left.

"I can't believe we haven't had a chance to talk," said the archaeologist, his eyes magnified through the thick lenses of his glasses. "It's such a small island, and we've both been here almost a week."

"What's your name?" I asked.

"Edward Thorndike. Call me Eddy."

"I'm not much in the mood for company, Eddy."

He said, "I see," but stayed beside me anyway, all the way to Steady's store.

It was one of the only buildings in the village with a covered front porch. The thick wooden steps were worn down in the middle where countless feet had trod. The windows by the door were made up of many little panes of glass, which reflected their surroundings with distorted waves as I passed, like the wind-swept surface of a pond. The doorknob was white porcelain. Below it was a lock made for a skeleton key.

"Allow me," said the archaeologist, Eddy, as he opened the old door. It squealed on rusting hinges. The upper portion struck a tiny bell, which tinkled in a lonely way. It made me think of the harbor buoy tolling in the fog on the day I met this man. I stepped into the store, a long, low room lined with shelves up to the ceiling. On the shelves were bolts of fabric, floats for lobster traps, motion pictures for rent, food in cans and bags and boxes, work gloves, hand tools, matches, mousetraps, and other items of all kinds. In the center a cast-iron heating stove squatted above a metal box filled with sooty-colored sand. Around the stove loitered several wooden chairs with ladder backs and cane seats concaved to the bottom shapes of countless occupants. I saw a pair of roughhewn tables near the window to my left. A refrigerated deli case hummed loudly, its sweating glass front covering a variety of cheeses, meats, and other perishables. Strangely, although I had only eaten one piece of toast since yesterday, I was not hungry. But I was thirsty, and inside the refrigerated case I saw a generous assortment of soft drinks. I walked behind the counter, slid open the rear door of the case and withdrew a cola.

The owlish man said, "Can I have one of those?"

Wordlessly, I took out another and carried it to him. I sat at the table by the front door. Through the window I saw the landing, where the bear now twisted slowly in the air as if the crane above it were a gallows. Eddy set his canvas bag upon the table and dropped onto the chair across from me. "You know Captain Frost pretty well, right?"

I turned my eyes to him. "Not really."

"No? I thought I heard you were, uh, kissing him down at the harbor."

"Doesn't mean I know him well."

"But you know him kind of, right?"

I looked out the window again. I thought about the way this man must see me: a woman who kissed relative strangers in public. But I was not that woman. It was just another way this island twisted what was real.

Outside, Steady Wallis stood close by the bear, examining it while the crowd of villagers stared. I watched the bear and realized it was a fellow stranger in this place.

I said, "Do you believe in witches?"

"I . . . uh . . . I was hoping we could talk about Captain Frost."

"Do you believe in them or not?"

"Well, sure. There's that religion where they call themselves witches, right?"

"I don't mean that. I mean real witches. Hundreds-of-years-old witches, who never die. You believe in them?"

"Of course not."

"Why not?"

"Are you serious?" He looked at me, and saw I was. "Well, I mean, there's no evidence. Nobody has any real data to support the idea. It's just stories."

"I've seen a witch."

"What did you see?"

"I just told you."

"No, I mean, what did the witch look like?"

Outside, Steady Wallis took photographs of the creature, walking around it, kneeling, getting it from every angle. I thought of the widow's photographs. I wondered if there was enough evidence in all the world. I sighed. "That's a polar bear."

Edward Thorndike twisted in his seat to follow my gaze out the window. "It appears so."

"Does Maine have polar bears?"

"No. They live much farther north."

"Why would you say a thing like that?"

The man frowned. "What?"

"We're here, and we're looking at that thing, so why would you say there are no polar bears in Maine?"

"Uh, I think I see what you mean."

"Do you?"

"Well, sure. I mean, obviously there's at least *one* of them here."

"How do you know? You have no data."

"We're looking at one now!"

"And I've seen a witch."

He leaned back. "Okay . . ."

"I'm not crazy. I'm not."

"Of course not."

"But I can't prove it."

He said, "It's hard to prove a negative."

I had never heard that before. Maybe I should have focused more on thinking about sanity instead of thinking about the negative. I sipped my soft drink silently as the deli case behind us hummed.

Finally the man said, "You know about the artifacts your friend found, right?" When I did not reply, he went on. "He finally let me see some of the things. They're amazing. Incredible. Up to now there was just one Norse artifact, a coin, found this far south. People call it the Maine penny, and most everybody assumes it was brought here by indigenous people from Labrador or Newfoundland to trade."

Through the window I watched Steady Wallis speaking to the villagers, waving his hand at the suspended polar bear. A few people had walked away from the landing, heading into the village. I found it interesting that this man claimed he had seen the Viking artifacts. In what way was I supposed to believe they were real? Like that bear? Or like the witch?

The archaeologist continued, "The captain has a comb, pendants, a brooch, a small blade, and who knows what else. One or two of those kinds of artifacts might have been brought here to trade, like the Maine penny, but not so many different items."

When I gave him no reaction, the man turned to his canvas bag. Unzipping it, he rummaged around and withdrew a pair of small plastic sacks.

"Look at these." He laid them on the table. "Captain Frost loaned these to me. You know what they are?"

I glanced at them and then away.

"This is a needle made from a walrus tusk. A sewing needle. And this . . ." He lifted the other bag. "This is a tool used by pre-Columbian Nordic women for spinning wool. See that little pattern there? That's a hammer pattern etched into the bone. Thor's hammer."

I betrayed an interest.

"These are essential tools. No one would trade these things away. They're the kinds of things you only find in settlements. They must have been lost or left behind in some sort of disaster."

I stared at them. "Did you say 'Thor's hammer'?"

"Yeah. That right there." He pointed to the spindle through the plastic. "You understand what it means? It means they must have been *living* here."

I looked away again, seeing Steady Wallis disperse the crowd. I risked a thought of Siggy and *The Mighty Thor*.

Eddy the archaeologist said, "Captain Frost won't tell me where he found them. If I could just see the site, I'd know for sure. I mean, after a little excavation. Nothing too invasive."

I saw Steady Wallis coming toward the store, alone.

Carefully, the owlish man placed the plastic sacks back into his canvas bag. "I guess the captain's worried about giving up part of his property, but it doesn't have to be like that. The university could get a letter if he wants one, from Maine's attorney general, something to reassure him."

Steady was almost to the store's front porch. I saw his hands, red to the wrists with blood. I recalled a sliver of broken glass slicing my thumb, a pile of ancient branches flowing red, and flecks of Christly blood in emerald eyes.

"Would you talk to the captain for me?" asked the archaeologist. "Tell him about the letter?"

I turned to him. "Why me?"

"I guess I made him a little angry the other day."

The door opened. The bell tinkled. Steady Wallis entered.

"Sorry," I said. "I can't help you."

Steady Wallis turned toward us. "What's that?"

Eddy shifted in his chair.

I said, "We were just talking. It doesn't matter."

Steady Wallis crossed behind the deli case. I heard the sound of running water as he washed the bear's blood from his hands. Looking over at us he said, "Doc, I hope ya ain't been askin' what I think ya been askin'."

The man lifted his chin. "She can do whatever she wants."

"Thought I was pretty clear about that."

"Have y'all been talking about me?" I asked.

Steady Wallis answered. "Not you so much as Cap'n Frost."

"What about him?"

Eddy said, "He's sitting on the most important American archaeological discovery of the decade, maybe the century, and he won't let anybody near it. That's what."

The older man said, "I ain't half as interested in Vikin's as I am in bodies washin' up on my island. Makin' sure there ain't no more."

"You still think Evan has something to do with that?" I asked.

Steady Wallis came around the counter drying his hands on a dish towel. "I got no idea. But I wish you'd listen to me 'bout keepin' your distance from him."

"I'll keep my distance from now on. You can count on that."

"Don't know as I can believe ya, seein' as ya was a good ways down the trail to his place when ya found that bear."

So the trail along the shoreline led to Weatherly. I tucked that fact away as Steady joined us at the table. He said, "I'm serious, miss. I seen ya with him day before yestidy down at the harbor. Maybe ya can get the truth out of him that way, but you're playin' with fire."

"You think that's why I kissed him?" I focused on my hands, which lay clasped together in my lap. "I wouldn't do that."

The two men sat in awkward silence a few moments, then Steady Wallis stood all of a sudden, scraping the legs of his chair across the wooden floor. "Lemme get you folks some ice for them there pops."

"That's okay," said Eddy Thorndike. "Mine's pretty cold."

"Naw, they's always better on the rocks." The man was already walking to the back of the store. The archaeologist and I remained silent at the table until Steady Wallis came back with two glasses filled with ice. He also had a piece of paper tucked under his arm. "Here ya go," he said, putting the glasses before us.

"What do we owe you?" asked the archaeologist.

"Don't worry about it." The older man sat down and laid the paper on the table. "Uh, Miss Gamble, I got a little information for ya."

"Something new?"

"Ayuh. And we got Dr. Thorndike here to thank for it."

I glanced back and forth between the men. "Well?"

Steady Wallis cleared his throat. "That fella ya found on Bleak Beach. Turns out his name was engraved on the back of his wristwatch. Some kinda gift, I guess it was. Ya ever heard of Aden Sean McAllister?"

"That's the man's name?"

"Ayuh." Steady Wallis slid the paper across the table. I saw it was a photograph of three men wearing heavy winter clothing and standing in front of what appeared to be some kind of tent. All three smiled at the camera. "The one on the left. Recognize him?"

Staring at the picture, I said, "I don't think so. . . ."

"Ya don't sound too sure."

"Well, he does look kind of familiar."

"Think hard, miss. It's important."

I searched the smiling face—a two-day growth of beard, bushy hair sticking out around the edges of a knit cap, straight teeth, a slightly crooked nose—and I was almost certain I had seen the man before, but where? I slipped the photo back across to Steady Wallis. "I'm sorry. He has an average face."

"Ayuh. Guess he does."

"So, who was he?"

"A very famous archaeologist," said Eddy Thorndike. "Until he disappeared in Greenland thirteen years ago."

"Thirteen years ago? But that's . . ."

"When your brother ran away from home," said Steady Wallis. "Ayuh. I remembered that."

"So you think, what? This man kidnapped Siggy?"

"No, no, no," said Dr. Thorndike. "Nothing like that."

"What then?"

The younger man drew a breath. "He was last seen in Greenland, like I said. Working the Björnsson site. That's a very rich Viking site, a village, on the west coast."

Something about that name, Björnsson, brought a memory to the surface. I said, "Could I see that picture again?" Steady Wallis gave it back to me. Staring hard at the man's face, I was almost certain. "Was this guy in a *National Geographic* story?"

"Yes," replied the archaeologist. "I believe they did an article about Dr. McAllister's work at Björnsson about a year before he disappeared. He discovered some very rare written material there, about Leif Erickson."

Holding the photo, I saw the magazine cover in my mind. I saw Siggy clutching it as he bathed, as he ate, as he slept. "So this Dr. McAllister, how did he disappear?"

"They say he stayed late at the site while everybody else went back to their camp. A freak storm blew in, a blizzard basically, although it wasn't the season for them. Apparently it was quite severe, a total whiteout. He was separated from the rest of the party, and never seen again."

"What's a 'total whiteout'?"

"Remember she's from Texas, Doc," said Steady Wallis.

"Sorry," said the younger man. "A whiteout is when it's snowing so hard you can't see anything at all but white."

The hair on my arms and neck rose up. I closed my eyes and watched as the delusions whirled around me, with the harsh and dreadful prophet Siggy as the only form of color. I opened my eyes again, and saw the face in the photograph. "It really snows that hard somewhere? Somewhere real?"

"In Greenland, certainly."

"Here too, sometimes," said Steady Wallis.

"You just see white? Nothing but white?"

The two men exchanged a glance. "Miss Gamble," said Steady Wallis, "how come you're so interested in that?"

I remembered the last time I had spoken of the details of my visions, my confession to Evan at the stone table, and the lies my revelations had engendered. I did not know these men. I would not make that same mistake again. I said nothing.

The older man's face darkened at my silence. "If there's things ya know about this situation, ya need to tell me. I'm the law here, remember."

"I don't know anything. Not really."

"Ya recognized Dr. McAllister, and ya seem awful interested in the way he disappeared."

"I just remembered that my brother had a copy of that magazine, is all."

Steady stared at me a while; then he looked at Eddy Thorndike. "Tell her the rest of it, Doc."

The archaeologist said, "The party took a seaplane over from Newfoundland. The plane had already landed in Greenland and taken off again before they found a stowaway among their equipment. A young boy, about twelve or thirteen—"

I saw Siggy walk away from me, passing underneath the trees, his backpack filled with precious Viking comics. I saw myself refuse to stop him. I said, "My brother was older than that." I did not tell them he had looked younger than his years.

"Well, the survivors didn't know for sure because the boy never said a word to anyone. They assumed he had a mental health problem."

"You're trying to make it sound like Siggy went to Greenland. There's no way he could have done that."

"How can ya be so sure?" asked Steady Wallis. "He managed to come here."

I stared down at my glass of cola on the table, saying nothing. After an awkward moment, the younger man continued. "Okay . . . the, uh, the story I heard was, the boy seemed fascinated by the archaeology. He pitched in wherever he could, and actually was kind of helpful. I guess money was tight—it always is—so they decided not to send him back until the plane's regularly scheduled return, two weeks later. Unfortunately, the boy stayed late on site with Dr. McAllister the day the blizzard came, and . . . you know."

How could Siggy possibly have found his way from Texas to Newfoundland, much less to Greenland? I tried to imagine him, crossing half a continent alone, feeding himself, taking care of himself. It was impossible, utterly impossible. Yet what if Siggy had somehow done it anyway? What if Siggy chased his dream all the way to where the Vikings really lived? Wretched, warped, and tortured though he was, might my dear, sweet Siggy somehow have brought his dreams to life?

I allowed myself to think it might be possible, and hopefulness arose within me. But this was surely just another delusion, another trap, my fickle conscience longing to escape the shame of letting Siggy walk away at four-fifteen exactly by the tolling of my father's steeple bells.

Desperate to be convinced, I said, "Why should I believe you know all this?"

The man smiled as if being patient with my ignorance. "Everybody knows about it, Vera. Everybody in my line of work, at least. To archaeologists, Aden McAllister is a legend, especially for those of us who specialize in the Viking culture. So there was a lot of interest in the story when he disappeared, an all-out search, everybody hoping for the best."

"Where is this place they disappeared, this man and the boy?"

"On the southwest coast of Greenland, like I said, between Ilulissat and the Sermeq Kujalleq glacier. It was only discovered fifteen years ago. Ever since then there's always been—"

"What happened to the village?"

"Well, it's the Björnsson site, you know? Incredibly rich. They had to keep working it, of course. They couldn't just—"

"I mean before, when the Vikings lived there."

"Oh, sorry. Uh, nobody knows for sure. But that's true for all the Viking settlements in Greenland. Would you like me to give you a little historical background?"

"Please."

So I took it in, learning more of Vikings in five minutes from Dr. Edward Thorndike than I had learned in all my years with Siggy. But my brother had known all these things; I was sure of that.

I learned the Greenland Vikings had been Christians. It was a surprise. I had always thought of Vikings only in terms of Thor and Oden, their pagan mythology, a rustic version of the ancient Greeks. But that religion was already nearly dead before they came to Greenland. A Viking noblewoman built Greenland's first church in about 990. Over the next two centuries they established a bishop's see with sixteen other churches. There was active trade with Iceland, and on through Scandinavia, with around two hundred eighty farms scattered along the southern Greenland coast, and a population of three thousand. From Greenland's shores these Viking Christians ventured farther west, establishing a short-lived settlement at a place in New-foundland now called L'Anse aux Meadows, the one and only pre-Columbian settlement by Europeans on the North American continent—one and only, that is, until Evan Frost's discovery on Winter Haven.

"That's why I need your help with Captain Frost," repeated the archaeologist. "Can't you see how important this site could be? I have to see it!"

Steady Wallis interrupted. "Doc, I thought we agreed ya wouldn't bring that up."

"It's a free country. She can do what she wants."

"You're gonna get her hurt."

"I don't see how."

Steady turned my way. "Ya need to take me serious on this, Miss Gamble. There's somethin' bad wrong on the far side of this island."

"Come on, Mr. Wallis," said the archaeologist. "So a couple of people washed up on the beach. They probably came from some boat that sank a hundred miles from here."

"What about that bear?"

"Are you saying the bear killed Dr. McAllister and the boy?"

"I'm sayin' somebody killed the bear!"

"So someone shot a bear. That doesn't have anything to do with Vera's brother."

"It wasn't shot. It looks like somethin' broke its neck."

"That's impossible! You're talking about the largest carnivore on land."

"I'm just tellin' ya how it looks. And that ain't the worst of it. Ya seen them wounds along its legs and stomach? Them bite marks?"

"A shark . . ."

"I'm gonna tell ya somethin' I ain't said out loud to nobody, and I don't wanna hear about either of ya spreadin' it around, all right?"

I nodded.

The owlish man said, "Yes."

"Some a them bites, I'm pretty sure they's human."

After a pause, the younger man said, "You're saying someone killed that bear and ate the carcass raw?"

"That's the way it looks. Wanna come and see yourself? Maybe I'm wrong. I hope I am."

"All right." The archaeologist stood. "Let's go."

Steady Wallis also rose.

"Hang on," I said, still seated at the table. "You never told me what happened to the Vikings."

The archaeologist looked down on me. "What difference does that make?"

"I'm not sure. But I think it matters."

"Well, it's a mystery, actually. They just fell out of contact. They stopped sailing to Europe, and there's no record of anyone from the European world visiting Greenland between 1408, when we know the Nordic Christians were still there, and 1721, when a Danish missionary named Hans Egede arrived to find only the Inuit people. No one knows what happened. Most authorities think their disappearance had to do with a phenomenon called the Little Ice Age. The growing season probably became too short. And there was probably warfare with the Inuits who descended from the north as the planet cooled."

I felt there was something important in his words, a half-formed possibility. I said, "These people, they were colonists, and they just disappeared?"

"What ya thinkin', Miss Gamble?" asked Steady Wallis.

"This Aden McAllister person obviously survived. He must have followed some connection from Greenland to here. I mean, there must be a connection. Polar bears come from Greenland, right? And you say all the Viking colonies in Greenland were lost. The Vikings here on Winter Haven were lost too, right? Nobody knew they were even here until just now. And what about those Pilgrims? They were lost, too."

Steady Wallis said, "Them Pilgrims is just an old wives' tale."

"I wouldn't be so sure," said the archaeologist.

Steady Wallis said something in reply, and the men continued talking, but I paid no attention. My mind ran wildly back and forth among the possibilities. It was as if I had been lost within a dreamlike, bleeding maze, but now the pattern was becoming clear if only I could glimpse one last missing connection. So many lost people, so many disappearances. Surely there was one secret at the center.

I thought of my hallucinations, of the harsh, prophetic Siggy running for his life. I heard dreadful hissing in the forest, felt the unnatural chill of Gin Gap Cove, saw the fog that never lifted. I heard Evan speaking of himself, his parents, his job as he strolled among the polished pebbles and the human flotsam of Bleak Beach. I pondered ancient giants, the last creations of their kind below the great north woods, and a house too massive for repairs. I saw cold stone become a glowing heart, and Siggy's unchanged face within the packing shed, and a little Nordic brooch of bronze, and the polar bear suspended in midair. It was there, just behind all that, where the answer lay, so obvious if only I could see. Yet I could not see.

A more clever person might have reasoned her way down into the truth beneath the patterns, but I could only sigh, and as I sighed, my breath blew onto the beverage just before me, a minor gust of warm air across the ice, causing a tiny cloud of mist to rise and linger, captured by the rim of the glass. I saw this, and considered it, remembering something the archaeologist had explained about the fog when I first met him on my agonizing passage from the mainland. Then, at last, I began to understand.

twenty-two

I ROSE FROM THE TABLE in Steady's store and crossed the island. Following the trail along the shore, I passed the place where the witch had brooded over the polar bear. I continued on the path as it slipped into eternal darkness underneath the evergreens. I descended into the malignant fog and chill of Gin Gap Cove, and I rose up again. Arriving at the forest edge, I stopped to stare out from the shadows at the decomposing mansion far across the field. Weatherly lounged along the cliff top like an aged courtesan at ease upon a threadbare chaise, her heavy-lidded windows peering back at me, disinterested. I checked my watch. I had stormed across the island in just two hours, across the very wilderness where I had spent a full day lost and searching fruitlessly before, and not once had I felt fear. I had one instinct only. Evan Frost must pay.

I now knew what he had done—not every detail, but enough—and to disrespect my Siggy as he had, to fling him out into the sea as an unnecessary byproduct, to make no attempt to find out who he was, who loved him, where he belonged . . . my hands balled into fists, my filthy fingernails dug deep into my palms. Tight-lipped in my fury I stared at Evan's decadent mansion and thought of Siggy, not the dreadful prophet in my hallucinations, but the precious boy who once had been my brother. I thought of the promise hung around his neck.

I am not dangerous.

I set out across the open field, running hard. I reached the empty concrete pool, the silent fountain and then the house itself. I stopped to catch my breath, pressed against the stone veneer below a rotting portico. Had I been seen? I listened, hearing nothing but the distant surf, a meadowlark, and the pounding of my heart. It did not matter much if Evan was at home. I was going in, no matter what the risk. I must gather proof. I must have my justice.

I climbed the steps to try the door. It was unlocked. I slipped into the soaring entry hall. I saw the chandelier with only a few light bulbs working, the strangely incomplete painting of heaven on the ceiling, and the sweeping stairs ahead. The room where I had slept was upstairs on the right. The voices I heard arguing had come from farther down that hall. I might as well start there.

I tiptoed to the stairs. About halfway up, a tread creaked. The sound reverberated loudly in the empty space, bouncing back and forth between the wood and marble. I stopped, my right hand on the oaken banister. The echoes faded. I heard no hint of footsteps coming. I continued.

From the large landing at the top of the stairs, hallways ran both right and left. The view along them faded into distant darkness. Turning right, I soon reached the room where I had slept. I touched the door in passing. It had kept me safe. My eyes adjusted to the shadows, revealing many other doors just like it farther down the hall. I resolved to learn the mysteries behind them all.

At the next door I paused. Placing my ear to the paneled wood, I heard nothing. I tried the latch. The door opened easily. I peered into the room. It was almost as gloomy as the hallway. Thick curtains dressed two tall windows on the far wall, allowing very little light to enter. I saw a dusty wooden floor and cobwebs draped along the corners, no furniture at all, and no sign that this room had been used for months, or maybe years. I moved on.

The next three rooms were much the same, empty and unused. But in the fourth I found a set of bedroom furniture. After glancing up and down the hall, I stepped into the room.

On a dresser near the doorway I saw a hairbrush, hand lotion, and a silver tray filled with earrings and bracelets. Also on the dresser were a pair of photographs in silver frames, one of Evan laughing at the helm of a sailboat, another of a very beautiful woman smiling toward the camera from a wicker chair. I moved around the room. Heaped upon the unmade bed, I saw a small pile of underwear, several pairs of men's boxers mixed together with a few black slips and bras. On a bedside table I saw a leather wallet. I opened it. Evan's face stared up at me from his Maine driver's license. My hand trembled as I put the wallet back onto the table. I stared at the bed, imagining Evan in it, holding the beautiful woman in the photograph. I remembered the widow's mocking words, *"What if I told ya he's not as free as ya believe?"* How could I have been so foolish? The woman in the photograph had the looks to be a fashion model or a movie star. Why would Evan settle for someone like me? I wiped my eyes, hating my tears.

At least I had explained the argument the other night, even if I still could not explain the voice that had come so strangely to my ears, mechanical, like a buzzing plague of locusts. Of course the woman would be angry with Evan for bringing me to their home to dine by candlelight and sleep just down the hall. I almost heard the droning echo of her outrage ringing from the bedroom walls. And although I had not understood Evan's words in reply, I could guess what he had said. *I had to find out what she knows. I only wanted information. She means nothing to me.*

I left their bedroom.

I tried two more rooms without success, both empty. Then I found another, much smaller than the rest, with built-in cabinets and shelves and countertops all around the walls. It seemed to be some kind of hobby room, or sewing room, a place where a lady of great means might have passed her days constructively back in the Gilded Age. I entered. Quietly I closed the door. I locked it, wincing as the latch went home with a loud *click*.

Through a tall window on the room's far side I looked down upon the Atlantic Ocean, stretched to the horizon from the shallow cove where Evan's motorboat rocked gently at its mooring. Since his boat was there, he was probably close by. It meant I must be very quiet. I must hurry.

I moved toward a counter on my left. There I saw about a dozen objects laid out in neat rows. I did not recognize most of them, but to my untrained eye they looked ancient. One item was a comb, cleverly carved from some kind of bone or shell, with an intricately interwoven pattern etched into the surface. Next to it I saw a long knife made of darkly corroded metal, much damaged by time with deep pits and holes. Although I assumed everything arranged upon the countertop was precious, most of the other items looked like trash to me. Decayed bits of leather bound by twine. Crumbling chunks of wood. I saw only two other things I recognized: a silver ring and a small silver cross. It seemed Evan Frost had told the truth about the Viking artifacts, at least.

I felt an eerie connection with the ring and cross. Although worn by people who had died a thousand years ago, the jewelry was familiar. Had some Viking man twisted that ring on his finger unconsciously while he worried, as I sometimes did? Had some woman touched that cross in earnest prayer as it hung around her neck? I owned a simple silver cross much like it. I sometimes touched it when I prayed. So many years had trod across the earth, and yet the earth was little changed. As I had before among the trees that guarded Winter Haven, I sensed the utter insignificance of time. I saw Siggy, lying unaffected in the packing shed. His image warned me not to linger in that room, warned me I must hurry, yet how could I move on? Gingerly I touched the ring. I verged upon a secret that might draw the curtain back from thirteen years of misery, might remove the weight of so much time gone by if only God permitted questions.

The mere idea of taking such a risk unleashed a final raging memory. It was by far the worst of all. It left me lying in the aisle at church again. I heard the congregation's ugly doubts. Stiff-necked in the wilderness they murmured, asking why my father could not heal his daughter of these fits. Even then I had been old enough to understand the danger in that question. What kind of healer cannot heal his own wife, his son, his daughter?

The few times I had tried to speak in his defense, to protest I was not sick, to affirm that I had only suffered visions from the Lord, my father quickly silenced me. Within the bounds of his theology this was even worse. No woman was to speak in church, and certainly no girl. My gift had been given—he himself had received the word from God, and my gift was not prophecy. I had been blessed to bear the Holy Spirit's gift of service, like my mother. All else was wicked pride and blasphemous delusion.

But on that Sunday long ago the final words of my hallucination would not leave my ears—that booming, godlike voice which had spoken words of judgment.

THIS IS WRONG.

What was wrong? The little girl I used to be could not stop herself from wondering. It must have been the things I saw, as my father said. I could think of no alternatives, yet in my childish ignorance I rebelled at this interpretation.

I tried to rouse myself from memories. Six miles distanced me from help if I was caught. I should focus on my quest, gather evidence against Evan Frost and leave his house as quickly as I could. Yet I did not move. Lightly, my fingers rested on the Viking ring. I recalled a silent lunch at the kitchen table with my father. My seizure at the church that morning was not mentioned. Afterward I wandered through my father's house as I now wandered Evan Frost's, adrift and filled with questions. I heard the springs and hinges creak as I pulled down the attic ladder. I ascended.

The light bulb burned so brightly in the heat. I smelled the baking shingles. I tried to gather courage, seeking inspiration from my vanished brother's paradise, surrounded by his multicolored Viking drawings, dozens of them hanging from the rafters, tribal banners all around his tabernacle.

THIS IS WRONG.

Alone in Siggy's attic, rebellion rose within the little girl I used to be. If anything was wrong, it was to lose your mother, to lose your brother, to have to watch your father change into a holy man who thought of nothing but his God and congregation. In my heart I felt that everything was wrong, *except* my visions. And yet these feelings shamed me. With knees drawn to my chin, rocking to and fro like Siggy up in paradise, I struggled to be faithful. I must accept God's will, just as my father said.

THIS IS WRONG.

But why had Siggy testified to me of Jesus on a cross? I was a believer, baptized at the age of seven. Siggy knew that very well. Why had he proclaimed the gospel to me, turned his emerald eyes on me, let me see the bloody flecks that God had sprinkled there, and spoken as if I were bound for hell? Why would Siggy hurt me that way, leave me that way? Was it just revenge because I let him go without a protest?

"Vera, are you there?"

It was Father underneath me in the hall. As the foul aroma of his pipe arose to taint the attic, I clutched my knees more tightly, determined to be silent, hoping he would go before I sinned and spoke my mind.

"Honey, are you all right?"

His tenderness broke my resolve. Weeping openly, I leaned to look down along the folding ladder. How I yearned to tell my father everything, to share my visions with him, to ask him what they meant. I did not think they were hallucinations. I believed the Lord had given me the answer, the reason why my mother had to die, why Siggy had to go, if only I could understand. But I remembered Siggy in this very place, Siggy's eyes on everything but me.

"'Between us and you there is a great gulf fixed. . . .'"

"What's the matter, honey?" asked my father, looking up.

In my desperation I told him of the things I had seen. I could not look his way. I stared at Siggy's Vikings as I spoke, at the shingles, at the rafters, at everything but him. I told my father every detail of dear Siggy in the whiteness, of his foolish joy in spite of our mother's passing—"*'I go to prepare a place'*"—and my terror as he fled the awful thing. I told my father of dear Siggy's arms thrown wide just like a dove as he dipped and rolled and soared through perfect white. "*'The mighty are afraid! The arrow cannot make him flee!'*" Looking everywhere but at my father, I spoke of Siggy's final visitation, the gospel on his lips unnecessarily, and then the final insult, the booming godlike words.

THIS IS WRONG.

Weeping, I begged my father for an explanation.

His reply was weak and distant. He was an old man, after all. "These daydreams of yours, I told you they're not of the Spirit. You don't have that gift."

"But I *see* Siggy there! It's the only time I feel like I might understand what happened to him and Momma."

"Things like that are not ours to understand."

"But I need to know why this happened! Everything was so much better before. I need to know why God took them away."

"No, sugar. You need to accept the Lord's will, just like you need to accept your gift. The Bible says God gives us gifts for the common good. There's no good to anybody in these foolish fantasies of yours. You've got the gift of service, sugar. You have to stop this other nonsense."

"It's not nonsense, Daddy! It's God, trying to tell me why he took Siggy."

"Oh, Vera . . ."

I sniffled. "I know if you could just pray about it for me, God would tell you what it means."

"Sugar, you have to accept God's will."

"What *is* his will? Please, Daddy. I want to know why God did this to us."

"Vera, that's enough!"

"But, Daddy—"

My father's upturned face had turned from gray to red. "That's *enough*, I said! You have no right to ask such things! The Lord has no interest in your questions! Even if he answered, do you think you'd understand? You're just a little girl! You could never understand Almighty God!"

"But why would God let Siggy come to me if he doesn't want me to understand?"

My father's mouth worked strangely. He breathed in deeply. He exhaled. In a calmer voice he said, "I told you a long time ago your gift is service. You're not a prophet, and these foolish dreams are *not* from God. They're of the devil!" His voice had begun to rise again. He stopped. He passed his hand over his face. He sighed. "Sugar, do you remember Job?"

I nodded fearfully, for I did indeed remember.

"The Lord is testing us just like he let Lucifer tempt Job. He's letting these seizures come to warn you about where you could end up. If you keep asking prideful questions and doubting God this way, one day he won't let you come back. He'll keep your mind trapped in that bad place where you've been going. You'll be lost to me forever, just like Siggy was." He drew a ragged breath. He said, "Please, sugar. *Please*. No more questions about your mother or your brother. This does no good for anybody. Please don't let your mind go to that place again. I couldn't stand it if I lost you, too. God has done what God has done. That's all we need to know."

"But I need to know—"

"SHUT UP! Do you *want* to bring more curses on us? Is that why you're so stubborn?"

I watched in shock as Father bowed his head and spoke with his big pulpit voice, the booming one he used in church. "Dear Lord, forgive me for allowing this child to become so proud. I've done my best with her, but I have failed. I beg you not to punish her as she deserves. Please have pity. Please show me how to make her learn your ways!"

I dared not speak. I waited on my father as my father waited on the Lord, and after several minutes, when he looked up again, I saw a strange light in his eyes. "The Lord has spoken, Vera. You must be punished. Your sanity depends on it. I must raise the ladder and close the door. You must turn out that light." He stared beyond me. "They're not visions. They are madness. *Madness*, Vera. If you keep talking about them this way, asking questions, the Lord will take your mind. You'll be worse off than Siggy. You'll be cursed like Siggy was, but you will never have his gift. This is your last chance. Turn out that light. Sit and think of what you've done. Your pride. Your blasphemy. Beg the Lord's forgiveness, and maybe he won't take your mind away."

He folded up the ladder, closed the door, and left me in the darkly burning crucible of paradise. In the awful attic heat that built without the open ladder door, baptized in my pouring sweat, I begged God for forgiveness. Blind to everything but pin-spot sunbeams streaming through the baking shingles, I asked the Lord to overlook my sin. I confessed it was my fault that Siggy left. I was thinking only of myself that day and never tried to stop him. I confessed I had no right to ask the Lord for answers, no right to understand my so-called visions, which were only lies and lunacy, after all. I promised to repent. The sunbeams faded, and my clothes became so drenched I might well have been drowning. I could not rid my mind of Siggy's words as he had crouched above the ladder in his hellish heaven, banished there as I had been. " *'They which would pass from hence to you cannot.'* " I prayed until I heard nothing, saw nothing, felt nothing. Only then did I emerge into the world of sanity again.

In my terror of the punishment so narrowly avoided, I vowed to leave my wicked dreams up in that burning attic. I would not think of Siggy's heaven or his visions. Throughout all the years between that moment and the day I rode a mail boat in the fog to find my brother unchanged on the isle of Winter Haven, I had kept my vow. Then, just once on that lonely boat, I had indulged a memory of Siggy in the whiteness. It was one memory only, yet there was no forgiveness for it this time, no way to stop the chaos creeping through the fissure I reopened.

In the decaying Winter Haven mansion, in Weatherly, with my fingers resting lightly on a ring some Viking Christian surely wore while challenging the great unknown, I recalled the maze I had traveled on the island's shore the night before. I recalled the in-between time when I was unsure if I had awakened as a little girl upon the aisle of my father's church, or if I had returned into a woman here and now. How hard it was to come back to myself. How easily I could have stayed within the whiteness. I wondered if I would survive my next involuntary memory, or if I would ebb back through the fissure and see my doom forever sealed. I wondered if—

A footstep, just outside in the hall.

I turned. I saw the doorknob shake. I heard a man's deep voice beyond. "It's locked."

Something replied, something emotionless and unnatural, like a million locust wings pulsing at the pleasure of a dreadful common mind. Then I heard the creature say the words that threatened hell itself.

"This is wrong."

twenty-three

I TURNED TOWARD THE WINDOW. There was no other way out. In three strides I was there against the glass, looking down. Because of how the land fell toward the ocean outside this wing of Weatherly, the bay window stood at least forty feet above the ground, and just a little farther out, the cliffs fell another fifty feet to the crashing breakers. This way would be suicide.

They tried the doorknob again.

I glanced around for a place to hide. The cabinets looked too small, but I knelt to open the one closest to me anyway. Inside I found a backpack. My breathing caught. I had not seen the pack in thirteen years. I pulled it from the cabinet and pressed it to my face. Instantly it was thirteen years ago and four-fifteen exactly by the distant tolling of the church bells as my brother walked away from home with this very pack upon his back. I inhaled deeply. There was no scent of Siggy left, but it was the proof I sought that Evan Frost had stolen from my brother, and not the other way around.

The doorknob rattled again.

Startled from my reverie, I rose to my feet. My only choices were the window or discovery by that horrid thing out in the hall. If I let it get to me, if I ended up awash on Bleak Beach like the others, that would finish everything, not just for me, but for my brother, and somehow also for my mother and my father. I had to live for all of us, to find some kind of justice.

I slipped on my brother's backpack. I opened the tall window.

The glass slid up, the lower half opening while the upper half remained fixed in place. At the window's base was a ledge, perhaps six inches wide. Leaning out, I saw the ledge continue as a piece of trim along the outside wall until it reached a corner. It seemed the room where I was standing filled a large dormer. Beyond the dormer lay a section of steep roof. I believed perhaps I could walk across the roof if only I could get there. I glanced back at the neatly arranged rows of artifacts. Surely they were Siggy's property, if anyone's. I should take them—they would easily fit in Siggy's backpack—but even as the idea crossed my mind, I heard the man's voice in the hallway calling out to someone.

I had to risk the window. Gripping the frame, I threw my right leg out over the sill. I paused, one foot still inside on the floor, the other outside dangling in midair. Surf slammed into rocks along the cliff a hundred feet below. I vowed not to look down. The onshore breeze assailed my face, much as air might rush against a falling body before it hit the ground. I considered turning back. Then I heard that horrible, buzzing voice reply to the man beyond the door, and without another thought I put both hands on the window jambs, pulled my other leg through, and stood up on the sill outside the glass.

On Weatherly's exterior, balanced high above the rocks, I pressed my cheek against the windowpane and teetered on my toes with both heels in midair. I willed myself to lean in toward the house. With just the slightest backward motion I would topple to the breakers far below. Desperately I gripped the mullions of the upper window. Through the glass I saw the door across the room. I would be the first thing they saw upon entering, and a child could push me to my death.

I slid my right shoe along the sill and moved my right hand to the next mullion in that direction. Slowly, I shifted my weight sideways, inching toward the edge of the window to get myself out of sight. At last I reached the shingled siding. Here was my greatest challenge. The windowsill at my feet continued on along the solid wall as a protruding piece of wooden trim. Would the trim support my weight as the windowsill had done? It was probably attached with only a few nails. How I wished I could count the nails! If I knew the number, I might calculate the possibility of survival. But while I longed to escape into that sanctuary, no reassuring math could save me if I fell.

I turned back.

Then I heard the horrid locust voice spew through the open window. In my imagination I saw the awful thing crash through the white, and Siggy, terrified. *"'The mighty are afraid! The arrow cannot make him flee! He laugheth at the shaking of a spear!'"* Whatever fate might have in store when I stepped on the narrow trim, trusting it with all my weight, I knew the evil thing inside the house was worse. I slid my right foot a little farther out.

Weatherly's shingles were very old. Many of them curled enough to let me get a fingerhold. But after so much time exposed to the extreme Maine weather, they were surely loose. It did not matter. I had to trust them, gripping with my fingertips as the moment came when I must shift my full weight off the window ledge, the moment when the trim would fail. I drew a breath and held it, as if that would somehow help. I rolled my hips and put my weight out on the narrow strip of wood.

It held. Releasing my breath, I slid my left foot along and transferred the grip of my left hand. Finally I was completely off the windowsill, out of sight from inside the room. But I was also clinging to the shingles like a cat burglar, all my weight supported by my toes and fingertips alone. Only then did it occur to me that I had left the window open. Surely they would notice that. Would the awful thing or its companion realize what had happened, lean outside to look, and find me where I was, in this utterly exposed position?

My calves began to burn. I must hurry or my own legs would betray me. I slid my right foot out along the trim again, on and on until I reached the corner. There, just as I moved my right foot to place it on the sloping roof, the trim at last gave way.

I slipped.

Clawing at the shingles, driving a splinter underneath a fingernail, I cried out in pain. But I got one foot onto the roof. With the other in midair, I somehow managed to hang on as the wooden trim on which I had been standing fell to the rocks below. Pulling with all my might, I drew myself back up and got both feet on the roof.

I scrambled up the incline to get out of sight around the corner, in case they did lean out through the open window. I paused, propped against the dormer's side wall, wincing as I pulled the splinter from my fingernail. I looked around for my next move.

The roof spanned about fifty feet to meet another part of the house, which rose another story. There, at the second floor level where I was, a balcony projected. I had no idea what or who might be inside the room beyond that balcony, but it was my best chance to get inside the house and then safely to the ground. I set out across the roof toward the balcony. Bending over the steeply inclined shingles with all my weight on hands and feet, I moved sideways like a crab. Compared to what I had just done, this seemed perfectly safe, but the motion quickly winded me. I paused to catch my breath halfway across. Looking down between my legs along the slope from that steep angle, I saw the ocean beyond the eaves of Weatherly, with Evan's motorboat bobbing on its mooring far below. I remembered my delight at the boat's powerful leaps across the waves, the way the wind had whipped my hair, and Winter Haven's deceptive beauty from a quarter mile offshore. I had wanted to be at Evan's side like that forever. What a fool I was to think it might be possible. I continued on across the roof.

At last I stood upon the balcony, peering in through a French door. The room beyond was one of those I had examined earlier, dark and empty. The French door was unlocked. I entered. Crossing quickly, I reached the hallway door. Carefully I opened it a few inches and peeked out to see a large man standing in the shadows down the hall. Apparently the awful thing had gone. The man's back was to me, but I was almost sure he was Nathaniel Miller, the broad-shouldered fellow I had met in my first few minutes on the island, the darkly bearded man who made me think of Paul Bunyan, who took the mail from Steady Wallis, and promised with his wife to pray for my grief.

I closed the door and considered my options. I could wait where I was and hope Nathaniel and his fearsome companion suspected nothing when they entered that room and found the window open, but after an unexpectedly locked door, surely they would be on guard. The open window would confirm their suspicions, and they might even notice Siggy's backpack missing. They were bound to search the house. I had to keep moving.

I bent down and removed my shoes. I opened the door again. Nathaniel remained standing with his back to me. I went right down the hallway toward the entry hall and stairs. All he had to do was turn around to see me. As quickly as I could, I padded along the marble floor, feeling the cold stone through my socks, counting footsteps, keeping calm. Near the entry hall with its grand staircase I heard a voice below. I stepped into the lofty space. Outlined in gray charcoal, vaguely rendered cherubim hovered above me in a world of pale white plaster, banished from the brightly painted heavens on the far side of the ceiling. The voice grew louder. Listening, I paused on the landing.

"Honey," said Evan Frost from somewhere out of sight. "Why would I do that?"

I closed my eyes. There was softness in his voice, the same endearing tone he had used with me. I heard no reply. I knew the sight of her with him would cause me pain, but suddenly I had to see the beautiful woman in the photograph, the one for whom he truly cared.

Step by step I descended.

Evan's words below were models of love's patient kindness. It was "dear" this, and "honey" that. It was sharpened blades to pierce my heart, poison mixed with sugar, a gracious form of torture.

Safely at the bottom of the stairs, I paused. His voice came through a door below the landing. Gauzy fabric fell across the opening, glowing in the northern light and gently wafting in the ocean breeze. I could not stop myself. I approached the open door. Outside, Evan Frost's voice rose and fell with warmth and kindness. But drawing near at last, I heard the other sound, the one I should have known would be there all along. Still, I had to be certain. I watched from a strange distance as my own hand reached to draw the curtain back.

There, hovering beside the chair where Evan sat, looming over him, I saw it draped in filmy black, its raven hair alive like writhing snakes, its skin so pale it seemed to swallow up the light. Against my will, I cried in fear. It turned. It pointed straight at me. And from its gaping maw issued a ceaseless hiss.

I dropped the curtain back in place. I also dropped my shoes. I fled across the entry hall, fled the awful thing, my socks slipping on the marble, losing traction in a waking nightmare, struggling against the dying house that groped at me like mud. I reached Weatherly's towering front doors. I opened one—too slowly!—and in that instant I heard Evan Frost behind me shouting, "Bring her back to me, Evangeline!"

twenty-four

DOWN THE STEPS BELOW the portico and past the empty fountain pool outside of Weatherly I fled. Rocks and stubble bruised my feet, yet I ran until I reached the forest edge beyond the field. There, sucking at the air like something trapped inside a vacuum, I turned to see the witch, Evangeline, gliding after me without a hint of effort, as if gravity did not apply, black robe flowing back, ropy tendrils flying wildly from its head. This was my first clear look at the creature. Always before Evangeline had appeared in forest darkness, or moonlit night, or only for an instant as it passed behind a village corner, but now it came straight for me in full sunlight. I saw its ghostly forehead pale and smooth above a pair of darkly recessed eyes, its pallid hands groping for me in a strangely plaintive way. I watched it come, and although it made no sense whatsoever, I felt a kind of sympathy.

Mesmerized, I slowly backed into the shadowed region underneath the giant evergreens. Evangeline drew closer every second. I knew I had to flee, yet the apparition's face and gestures would not let me go. I felt her sap my will, filling me with inertia, rooting me to the earth as if I had been planted there among the trees. Fighting her with all my will, I took one more backwards step. Something struck my shoulder. I whirled to find only an ancient pine. But in that turning, Evangeline's spell was broken. They said the devil was a charmer. I must not believe his lies. I set out running hard again.

Siggy's empty pack slapped at my back with every stride. Of course Evan would have seen it on me just now and known that I had proof of his connection with my brother's death. He could not let me get away. He would hunt me clear across the island. He would set the entire village after me. There was no escape. But the instinct for survival kept me running anyway.

Soon I broke from the tree line into sunshine again. I careened along the path another hundred yards before my lungs gave out. I stopped, bent at the waist, hands on my knees, desperate to catch my wind. I straightened up and set out walking, although I still had trouble breathing. The path began descending between twin slopes clothed in blueberries. I dared to look back.

The witch had drifted from the forest shadows, pursuing at a strange, unhurried pace, as if it had eternity to do its work. Considering Siggy's unchanged body, the ageless trees, and the black creature from the past that came for me with open arms, I realized even time stalked me on Winter Haven.

I hobbled to the spot where the little brook flowed down beside the trail and trickled past the dormant blueberries. It meant I was close to Gin Gap Cove. I believed I knew the reason for the fog and frigid temperatures which never left that place. If I was correct, there was no need to fear the mist and cold; indeed, I hoped to enter it and hide. If I was wrong, the end would soon come anyway.

Deeper down the path I heard the sound of waves. Then Gin Gap Cove was dead ahead, the long black granite cliffs spreading on each side below me toward the ocean, opening to

Evangeline's Folly in the distance, those cursed offshore rocks, and between the pair of mirrored cliffs the eerie fog remained as always, motionless and flat. I glanced back. The evil thing had closed the distance by a hundred feet or more with its unchanging pace. The witch still reached for me with bloodless hands.

I staggered toward the cove.

The path descended. The air chilled. The fog appeared. I could not see ten feet ahead, which was just as I had hoped. The trail began to dip more steeply. Moving carefully, I tried to control my breath so I could listen for the sound of my pursuer. All I heard was distant surf and the dripping brook beside the path. The mist became much thicker. Then, down in the cove at last, I could barely see my own feet as I stepped onto the level plane of polished granite pebbles.

I had to find a place to hide in the translucent whiteness before the demon Evan Frost had set upon me came close enough to hear my footsteps on the stones. I stepped out boldly, eager to gain distance from the path. Immediately I set my heel down hard upon a pebble. I winced, barely restraining a cry of pain. I dropped into a crouch to inspect my foot. The sock was ripped and filthy and stained with blood. I must have cut myself in the field by Evan's house, or else somewhere along the path. Gritting my teeth, I forced myself to rise and keep on moving. My limping footsteps on the pebbles echoed from the cliff. I made my way along the beach until a pair of boulders appeared through the mist. With Siggy's pack still on my back, I could not fit between them. I took it off and flung it into the fog. Then, slipping between the boulders, I settled down to wait.

The nearby trickle of the brook as it dropped through the rocks to meet the cove, the salt water lapping at the beach, the distant crashing of the surf against Evangeline's Folly, and then . . . a clattering of pebbles.

The awful thing had come.

My body shook. I did not know if this was due to fear or the unholy cold. The mist had beaded on my eyeglasses, nearly blinding me, but I dared not move to wipe them off. Crouching in that frozen hell between the boulders as the fearsome creature paced within the fog, I tried to pray for help. But when I closed my eyes and bowed my head, I felt myself fly back instead to Siggy's searing heaven, with Father raging in the hall beneath me, his ever-present pipe spewing a different kind of haze, and me above, christened by my pouring sweat and dappled by the spots of brutal sunlight through the shingles, staring at my brother's Viking banners.

Oh, how fervently I begged God for forgiveness! Filled with terror at the thought of being given over to this lostness, I begged the Lord to grant me one more chance. Never again would I ask why he had inflicted suffering, withheld truth, locked me in that fiery heaven or this icy hell with these doubts and fears. Acknowledged only by the fury of a wrathful father pacing back and forth below, an evil creature pacing furiously upon the pebbled beach, with beads of frigid mist upon my glasses merging with the sweat that flowed like blood from all my pores, I begged the Lord for mercy, then and now, with so much left I did not understand.

The awful thing kept pacing, invisible upon the gravel beach. Many times it hissed, its poison drifting in the mist. Yet it could not seem to find me.

An hour might have passed. A strange sense of distance dulled the terror that had driven me to Gin Gap Cove. In that dullness I could scheme again. Perhaps I would escape this evil, after all.

All I had to do was stay in hiding. I would trust the doctrine of my father. Somewhere between a Pilgrim witch and an angry preacher lay tempting questions, but asking was the very sin that led to madness. If I cleansed my mind of questions, the Lord might save me still. Questions equaled doubts. Doubts were sin. God was God, and I was not.

The sound of displaced pebbles faded. Silence entered in. The awful thing had stopped its pacing. Was it gone, or only waiting? I clutched my knees a little closer, huddled up for warmth in hell, hiding from the courage needed to expose the secret squatting in that desecrated cove. I stared wide-eyed into frozen fog. It was foolishness to step from hiding into whiteness. It led to less than nothing. In the silence of Gin Gap Cove, I returned to Siggy's burning paradise and the lesson I had learned: do not seek the truth, and you will find no evil.

Another hour passed, maybe two. The quality of light grew muted. Beyond the mist somewhere, a frigid sun sank toward ageless trees. My stomach growled. Soon it would be night. All I had to do was wait, do nothing, and survive.

Do nothing.

To my great surprise, a sob escaped my lips. Instantly I clasped a hand across my mouth. Waiting for the telltale sound of shifting pebbles, waiting for the awful thing to come, I tried to understand the impulse that had caused me to betray myself after such a long and perfect silence. Was it fear, erupting through the fissures of my self-control? No, I realized, it was not. Instead, what I found within myself was something unexpected.

Siggy shamed me.

In spite of his infirmity, my brother had gone out into the world to search for answers, but I had never dared to follow. In spite of death, he had worn a strange smile on his face. If I died in Gin Gap Cove, what would my expression be, the thing upon my face? I had shunned temptation, asking nothing, seeking nothing, accepting everything in silence. I had seen the answer back in Steady's store, in the mist within my drinking glass. I knew what lay within the whiteness Siggy dared to enter. I *knew* this, but remained in hiding. Would I really sit there meekly yet again, abandoning my questions yet again? Would I bow again before this mocking god of fear? Or like my Siggy, would I trust the truth enough to seek it out?

I thought of the promise he had worn around his neck. *I am not dangerous.*

Like Siggy, I might end my days condemned by God to live inside a formless world alone. But even at that cost I wished to be like Siggy.

I stood to follow him. All I had to do was cross the level beach, the pavement of black pebbles, without succumbing to the awful thing. I would seek. I would find. I took one step into a world that had no colors. This time I was not pushed. The whiteness did not come for me. This time I went in search of it.

I took another step.

My third step sent a pebble sliding off across the beach. The deafening crack of that one tiny stone echoed from the cliffs, expanded in the mist, and rose to fill the universe.

I broke into a run.

The pale fog hid the water until I was already in that frozen agony to the middle of my calves. A million needles pricked my feet and legs. Already I was shaking. This time there was no question of the cause. It was not fear that set me shuddering; it was evil's utter lack of warmth.

I took another step. Icy blades of water slashed my legs again, three inches higher. Another step, and the outrage reached my thighs. I knew my will would break beneath this torture. I must end it, one way or another. I could either turn back now or surrender altogether to my fate. I drew a shuddering breath and dove into the heartless pain of Gin Gap Cove.

Shock robbed my heart of rhythm. My underwater scream did surely reach the depths of the Atlantic. Then I found the surface, teeth chattering like heathens beating time with bones.

As I swam away from shore, my feet quickly lost sensation. My hands and fingers were the next to go. I knew numbness would devour my calves and thighs and forearms and then I would slip under. I tried to stand but could not find the bottom. I would not have felt the bottom even if it had been there. So I swam on, although in the nearly perfect whiteness of the atmosphere I knew not where I went. Was I heading out? Was I swimming in a circle? Had I turned back toward the shore, toward the witch that waited there?

In a few more minutes it would make no difference. Sensation in my legs began to fade. I focused on my larger muscles, willing them to move. When my arms began to go as well, I knew that I would die.

So this was what had waited all these years in Siggy's whiteness. This was the great mystery I had longed to know. It was not as I had imagined. It was simpler, and harder. As my nearly useless arms and legs went trembling through the water, I wondered for the last time why my brother, that harsh prophet of my visions, had believed I ought to hear the gospel. Was I damned for questions in my childhood, or damned for questions here and now? Either way, the damned had nothing left to lose, so I did my best with shaking jaw and deadened lips to whisper one last time, defiantly, "Why?"

I felt a kind of pressure, something I could not push farther, something I could not move beyond. I looked and saw it there, the wall of whiteness I expected, the ice before me in the mist, too smooth and high to offer any purchase. I saw blue and pale green veins within it. And, looking closer, yes, a smudge of brighter color, red and yellow. I tried swimming slowly to the right. I barely moved three feet, but that was far enough. I peered through lenses blurred with frozen crystals. Before me was the proof I sought, the proof in living color there beneath the whiteness, a comic-book god, *The Mighty Thor*, captured in an iceberg.

Here finally was an answer. How cruel to find it offered me no comfort. How sad that it did not explain. How ironic that it only left me numb.

I felt a blessed darkness coming. My mind began to wander. I lay back in the water, strangely buoyant, and wondered why I did not slip beneath the surface. I tried to speak a final prayer, to offer one last plea aloud for mercy, but words could not escape my quivering lips. So I resolved to sleep and let death take me in a dream. My dream did not bring angels or bright tunnels toward the light. As I drifted off to death, I saw instead the witch Evangeline, coming for me through the mist.

twenty-five

E VAN FROST BEGAN TO SNORE. From the blessed warmth beneath my blanket, I turned to see his profile in the moonlight. I sat on one Adirondack chair; he sat on the other. Side by side we had spent the evening watching stars above the sea behind his house.

I still had many questions, but they could wait until he woke.

I remembered bits and pieces. Evangeline pulling me into the tiny rowboat. Evangeline silently stripping off a black robe and wrapping it around me. Evangeline stepping from a flowing dress and wrapping that around me, too. Evangeline, merely human after all, nearly naked in the cold, shivering herself as she rubbed first one of my useless hands and then the other, and my surprise to find her pallid flesh could feel so warm and welcome.

I remembered waking to find Evangeline rowing through the fog, out beside the iceberg. I remembered watching as the towering ice went by, smoothly carved in dips and scoops along the waterline, laced by slender cracks of green and blue, but mostly white and hard to see within the whiteness. I remembered the creaking of the oars as we left Gin Gap Cove, inching out into the ocean, out toward the Folly, then around those cursed rocks that bore my savior's name, and on along the shore until we reached the floating dock at Weatherly. And Nathaniel waiting there, that big bearded man stooping down to bear me up within his arms, ascending steps cut in the granite cliff, with Evangeline behind us as he crossed the narrow grassy place between the ocean and the mansion, and Evangeline hovering nearby as Nathaniel gently lowered me onto the chair beside Evan Frost, saying, "Here ya are, Cap'n. Look who your sister brung to call."

Even in my numb condition, I remembered focusing on that one word, *sister*.

Evan and Evangeline.

I should have known it from the start.

The strange woman and Nathaniel had left us there in the Adirondack chairs. She had soon returned with blankets and a steaming cup of coffee. She had tucked me in. She had hovered at my side with a brooding look of worry on her pale, pale face. Throughout all this, Evan never took his eyes off me. It seemed he could not move, his leg propped on a wicker table, a bandage on it long and white. When he saw that I could listen, he mentioned an accident, a deep gash, a surging artery. He could not walk and dared not travel in his boat lest the motion open up his wound and let the lifeblood flow from him again. It was the only thing that could have kept him from returning to me, this weakness of the flesh.

How I wished it was the truth.

Time had passed so silently, the brother on my left immobile, the dark yet pallid sister sitting still upon the bricks. He stirred. He seemed to sense me watching, and turned. In the radiance of his attention I felt my own lifeblood begin to pound, but even as his left eye promised what I longed for, the other gazed at everything but me.

I sternly warned myself to have a care.

"Must of dozed off," said the handsome man.

I adjusted the blanket covering myself. Beneath it I wore something black, something dry, something of Evangeline's. I said, "There's a pile of clothes on a bed upstairs—underwear, yours and some woman's . . ."

Evangeline smiled at her brother.

"Laundry," said Evan. "Evangeline was sorting it up there."

"And on the dresser, I saw a woman's picture in a golden frame . . ."

"Our mother."

I soaked that in. "She was very beautiful."

"Inside and out," he said.

"You take after her, Evan. But, Evangeline, where did you get such lovely black hair?"

Evangeline looked away.

Evan said, "She has our father's hair."

Evangeline rose to her feet with remarkable grace. She touched her brother's shoulder lightly and left the veranda. As she glided out of sight into the house, I considered the strange black clothing, the wild, unruly hair, the way she roamed the island all alone, the awful hissing sounds she made. "Is Evangeline . . . is something wrong?"

"She has some problems, yeah."

I waited.

He looked out toward the ocean as if looking back in time. "We were here at Weatherly for a few days. Me and her, and Mom and Dad. The old place needed lots of work as usual, so

Dad hired Isaac Wallis to do a few odd jobs. And Mom had Mr. Abernathy working on the entry mural."

"Isaac Wallis . . . that's Steady's son, right? And the mural, you're talking about that painting on the ceiling? The widow's husband did that?" I remembered the watercolors on the widow's walls.

Evan nodded. "Dad wanted to spend the money on repairs, but Mom insisted. I guess Mr. Abernathy was an up-and-coming artist, and we got some kind of special deal. I used to sit in there on the stairs and watch him work. But not that day. That day we left him and Isaac here while we had a picnic lunch out at the stone table. It was my grandmother's birthday, and Dad always took us out to see the sunshine heart, in memory of her.

"It wasn't warm that spring like it is now. We had to build a fire in the middle of the table. But we had a great time, every-body laughing and all, telling stories about my grandparents. That afternoon Dad and I were supposed to ferry Isaac and Mr. Abernathy back to the village, and Evangeline wanted to go so she could be with Isaac, and my mom said she wanted to come too, so everybody went together. It got kinda foggy, and we never should of done it, but we let Isaac steer. My folks and I went down into the cuddy, and Mr. Abernathy, he was dozing on a bench back at the stern."

Evan paused. He lifted his eyes toward the stars. "Evangeline was sweet on Isaac Wallis, and Isaac felt the same about her. They'd probably be raising kids together now if I had just stayed topside. But Mom and Dad and me, we went down below, and Evangeline, she stayed up with Isaac, and he hit the rocks outside of Gin Gap Cove, going about twenty.

"I still don't know how I survived. I remember looking at my watch one second—it was seventeen-fifteen on the dot, and I was sitting on the vee-berth—and the next second I was slammed against the overhead, looking at a granite boulder sticking through the hull. I went on deck, but nobody was there. I shouted names and tried to find them in the water, but the surf out there was high and wicked loud, and it was foggy and the boat was already sliding off the rock and sinking, so I had to go over the side, too. I basically jumped out onto Evangeline. She was facedown and bleeding. I grabbed her and made for the shore. When I got her there, she wasn't breathing. I started CPR, but saw right off it wasn't working. I shoved my fingers down her throat and felt something. She inhaled a piece of wreckage with the water. I tried to pull it out. It wouldn't come. But she was dying, so I just pulled harder. That's how her throat got ruined."

"And the others?"

He looked toward the Atlantic. "After I had Evangeline breathing, I left her on the beach and swam back out for them, but it was way too late by then."

I understood too well what it was like to lose your family. In spite of everything this man had done, I felt a hint of sympathy. "That sound Evangeline makes, it's because of what you did?"

"I destroyed her vocal cords. She can use this little vibrator thing she holds up to her neck to form words if she wants to, but it makes her sound like a machine. She hates it. Gets embarrassed. Won't do it with anyone but me and Nathaniel and a few of the other guys."

I said, "The other night when I was lost in the forest, and a couple of times in the village, I heard a different kind of noise. Kind of a loud hiss, or a whisper . . ."

"Sometimes when she's excited or frightened, she tries to talk, and it comes out like that."

"She really scared me."

"I'm sure she didn't mean to. Everyone on Winter Haven is used to it, so she doesn't always understand the way she sounds to strangers."

Pondering this, I thought I understood a mystery. I said, "I heard her after church last Sunday, but it seemed like no one else did. It was really weird."

"I guess most folks on the island just ignore her. They're all used to it, you know."

I thought of Siggy, whose abnormalities had seemed so innocent to me, yet my mother saw the need for written reassurance.

I am not dangerous.

To get my thoughts on other things, I said, "One time I heard her try to say a word. It sounded like 'Isaac.'"

"You were wearing one of Isaac Wallis's old sweatshirts, re-member? He used to love that Texas Aggie stuff. They have a pretty famous marine sciences department down in Galveston from what I hear, and oceanography, that was Isaac's thing. Everything was always maroon and white with him. It was a big deal for the island when he got a scholarship to Texas A&M. He was all set to go right after that last summer."

"So it was the sweatshirt? That's why she followed me and made those noises?"

"Probably. I guess it kind of upset her."

I heard the sadness in his voice and recalled my premonitions about Evan at Bleak Beach and the stone table in the forest, the feeling that he truly understood my sorrow. I said, "Her mind isn't normal, is it?"

"She has good days and bad ones. The doctors say it has to do with going so long without oxygen, plus the psychological shock. Me, I think it's mostly guilt and grief."

"Guilt? For what?"

"She says she distracted Isaac. They were kissing when he hit the rocks."

"The rocks. You mean Evangeline's Folly?"

His head snapped around. His eyes narrowed, the lines beside them deepening. "Who told you to call it that?"

I tried to remember. "I think it was the widow. She said they named it after a woman named Evangeline who distracted a lookout when the Pilgrim ship was wrecked."

"Everybody on this island knows there were no Pilgrims, Vera. That's just an old story."

"But the widow said—"

"The widow hates me and Evangeline. She blames us for her husband's death. She made up that *folly* thing years ago and tells it every chance she gets, just to hurt my sister."

I thought about the widow's cellar filled with photographs of Evangeline. I told Evan Frost about it.

He nodded. "She follows Evangeline all over the island. Shoots pictures with a telephoto lens. She's been doing it for years. I have no idea why."

"She doctors the photos. She smears Evangeline's features and makes her look all out of focus and ugly. She writes things on the pictures."

"What does she write?"

"Horrible things."

"What exactly?"

I did not answer.

Evan said, "No, you're right. It's better not to know."

We sat in silence for a while.

He said, "Poor woman. She used to be quite an artist, you know. Her photographs sold for lots of money at galleries all over. But I don't think she's had a single show since the accident."

Evangeline emerged from the house behind us, wearing black as always. It occurred to me this was just the way the Widow Abernathy dressed, both of them in mourning all this time, the younger one turned inward, and the widow striking out with hate.

Evan's sister glided eerily across the patio to kneel beside her brother. Her eyes met Evan's. She made gestures with her hands.

Evan smiled at her and shook his head. "What?"

Frustrated, the woman gestured again.

This time Evan said, "I don't understand you, honey. Use the buzzer."

The woman turned darkly recessed eyes toward me.

"It's okay," I said. "Really."

She looked down. She withdrew a little plastic box from a pocket in her skirt. She placed it beside her throat and pressed a button. The buzzing started, like a distant swarm of locusts. Moving her lips, Evangeline shaped the steady sound into words.

"Do you know where Isaac is?" she asked.

Evan Frost said, "No."

She looked at me. "Isaac is my boyfriend."

Smiling, I said, "That's nice."

She frowned and shook her head violently. "I want him to come home."

"Honey," said Evan, "could I have some lemonade?"

The pale woman rose and glided back inside. I watched her go and thought of powerful hands reaching into freezing water, drawing me up, rubbing life back into my limbs, and a powerful back bent against the oars to fight the waves around the offshore rocks that had caused such pain on Winter Haven.

Evan said, "I can't believe she used the buzzer in front of you. She must think you're special."

"She's so strong. And graceful."

"Evangeline was a gymnast and a dancer, before. She was studying ballet at Juilliard. Still does her gym routines, even dances sometimes, when she thinks she's alone."

"Then maybe she'll improve. Mentally, I mean."

He ran a hand across his eyes. "She won't wear anything but black. She won't comb her hair. She has spent thirteen years standing on the shore and staring at those rocks."

"There must be something you can do. Some kind of therapy."

"It takes money. I make almost enough for our expenses, but there's nothing left over. This place costs a fortune to keep up."

"Sell it. She means more to you than Weatherly does."

"She'd come apart if I did that. I've tried to get her off the island before. She goes berserk."

"You did it all for her, didn't you?"

He stared at me, his eyes out of sync. "What are you talking about?"

"I knew about the iceberg, Evan. Before I swam out there. I figured it out this morning."

The truth had come with my breath across the ice within my glass of soda, like warm sea air across the iceberg in the cove, the mist that rose, the cold contained within the cliffs, the polar bear, my brother's unchanged body, the archaeologist's answer to my question about where the Viking site had been, beside some famous glacier, and Evan's description of his job, Evan telling me that icebergs are the broken ends of glaciers that have flowed down to the ocean. Icebergs begin on land, on Greenland, land of Vikings, where Siggy was last seen. As my warm breath blew on the ice back at Steady's store I also remembered something I had learned on the passage to the island, Dr. Thorndike's lecture on the fog, the damp warm air moving slowly over the cold sea causing a mist to rise. He had called it advection fog, but in my seasick misery I had thought it was more aptly named affliction fog, and so it was, in Gin Gap Cove.

I said, "You found it when you were working, right? Doing 'ice management.' Isn't that what you called it? You found it floating in the ocean and saw something in it that made you decide to tow it here."

He shifted his position to look more easily toward me, taking care with his leg. "It kept rolling. Some of them do that; they roll when you backwash them or hit them with the water cannon, so you have to get a line around them, tow them away from the oil platform that way." He paused. "You want to hear about this, right?"

"Yes."

"Okay. We circled the thing as usual—it's a pretty small iceberg, you know, but still big enough to cause some damage to an oil platform. So we circled it, paying out the line, and Nathaniel saw some color in it. You never see anything but white and a real pale bluish green, but this one had a red spot near the top. So we put a Zodiac inflatable in the water and went over. It's a crazy thing to do, landing on an iceberg. Especially when they're rollers, like this one was. But that red spot got us curious, so me and Nathaniel, we climbed on while Zeke stayed in the Zodiac.

"Anyways, we found a backpack poking out of the ice. It had all this stuff inside. Amazing stuff. You probably saw most of it upstairs, right?"

I could only nod.

"Well, we also noticed something deeper in the ice, too far down to tell what it was exactly, but obviously something there. We thought about digging for it on the spot, but the iceberg was just too unstable. We weren't in survival suits, and without them you only get a minute or two in the water up north, then you're dead. So we talked it over, me and Nathaniel. We were due to head in for repairs and maintenance anyway. I figured I could claim a mechanical problem slowed us down. Take the extra time to tow it home, wedge it up into the cove where it wouldn't have the room to roll, then go on up to Portland, leave the *Albert Murray* in dry dock, and come back down east."

I said, "You need to tell me about Siggy."

"I'll tell you what I can."

"Even if you did it for Evangeline, I'm not sure I can . . . live with that. I want to think it was a mistake or something, Evan." I was giving him excuses now, hoping he would use one, hoping I could believe him if he did. "Maybe one of your crew was responsible? Someone made you do it? I don't want to think you did it freely, or on purpose. I want to think the best of you. But I just . . . it's really hard."

His eyes widened, including the one that would not quite meet mine. "What is it that you think I did, exactly?"

"I know what it might be, but I'm hoping for something else."

"What *might* it be?"

He was going to make me say it. He would not use the way out I had given. My hopes would come to nothing now. I said,

"Obviously, Siggy was in the ice. How else could he still look like he does? So he was in the ice and you found him, or one of your men found him, and you just . . . you just threw him in the water. Then you let people think he washed up from the ocean. You let me think that. You lied to me and Mr. Wallis to keep your secret safe."

He straightened in his chair as if yanked upright by force. "But that's not it at all!"

"Good! Explain it to me. How did Siggy get on Bleak Beach?"

"He must have been somewhere further down, around the waterline or maybe underneath. Icebergs have a lot more mass than you can see, Vera. They're mostly hidden underwater. All I know is none of us saw him, or the other man, or that polar bear."

"If so much of the iceberg's underwater, how did you get it in the cove?"

"Remember those cliffs? Except for where the beach is, they keep right on going, straight down into the water. Gin Gap Cove is nearly fifty fathoms deep."

"So you're saying Siggy just floated away and you didn't even notice?"

"Of course! You've seen how thick the fog is in that cove, and the way the iceberg makes the mist. The cliffs hold it there. You can't see anything in the water because the fog never lets up."

Remembering the sides of the glass holding my warm breath on the ice cubes, I knew it was the truth. But it was not true enough. "You could have told me about Siggy when you found him on the beach."

"But I didn't know anything about him! Not until the other day at our picnic."

"How could you not know? You had Siggy's backpack upstairs in that room."

"How was I supposed to know that pack belonged to him?"

"It's obvious!"

"Only now, looking back on things. Come on, Vera, think about it. I found that backpack nearly eight hundred miles away across the ocean, and I sure wasn't thinking about backpacks when I found your brother's body on Bleak Beach two weeks later. Why would I?"

"But what else could it be? Siggy looks exactly like he did the last time I saw him years ago. Obviously he was frozen or something."

"I didn't *know* he looked the same! How could anybody know, unless they knew your brother back when he disappeared, or unless you told them how long ago that was? And you didn't tell me that, not until the picnic."

Was it really possible he was innocent? I thought about our conversations—in his kitchen, on Bleak Beach, at the stone table. I was almost sure that he was right. I never told him how long it had been since Siggy ran away from home, not until our picnic. So why should he assume Siggy disappeared years ago? How could he have known Siggy was unchanged? The light of hope began to dawn. But there were other insults Evan must explain.

I said, "At the stone table, you said you knew what was happening to me, those pebbles and the bleeding branches. Remember?"

"I'm so sorry about that. I was only guessing, but it turns out I was right. While we were still at sea, I called a maritime lawyer. He said he's pretty sure those Viking things are ours, but that was before the guys found out about your brother and you. We were just worried about the company back then, since we found the iceberg on the job. Then word got out around the village about your brother, his condition and all. Some of the guys figured out he must have been in the iceberg and that backpack was probably his. They figured maybe you'd try to claim the stuff, since your brother kind of found it first. They decided to try to scare you off."

"So your men threw those rocks and set out all those bloody branches and made those chopping sounds just to scare me?"

"I guess they thought with your brother's condition and all, you'd be kind of skittish. And they knew the widow would be filling your head with awful stories like she always does with everyone who stays there."

"I can't believe grown men would do things like that!"

"They're desperate. I'm not the only one who needs this, Vera. There's people here who can't hang on another season. Their families go back hundreds of years on Winter Haven, but unless they find some kind of way to make more money, they're gonna have to leave."

I shook my head. "I'm supposed to believe you didn't know about *any* of this? Siggy being in the iceberg? The plan to scare me off?"

"You know how isolated I am out here! All the guys live back in the village. They heard about your brother over there. They never said a word to me. I swear!"

"Oh, please. Of course they told you. You're their captain; they all think you're great. Last Sunday at church I saw how they feel about you."

"Yeah, and they also know I'd never go along with scaring you away like that. After our picnic, after you told me what was happening, I dropped you off at the landing and went straight to Gin Gap Cove to tell the guys to knock it off."

I had to look away. "I waited for you all day. You said you'd come back."

"I couldn't! Not with this leg. That's what I'm trying to tell you, Vera. I went to the cove and chewed out the guys, and things got kind of . . . well, a little agitated, and I slipped on the ice and fell on an axe blade."

"An axe?"

"It's how we were digging the stuff out of the ice."

"So that's the chopping sound I asked you about at the picnic? I *asked* you about it, Evan! You should have told me then."

"I told you some of it. I said the guys from my crew were working on my place, remember? Well, Gin Gap Cove is on my place." His good eye pleaded with me. "Look, I know that's lame. I know I didn't explain everything right when I should have, but I did do my best to protect you once I found out what they were doing. And I've never outright lied to you, Vera. Not once."

"You're lying to the whole world! You're telling everyone you found this stuff on Winter Haven."

Evan shook his head stubbornly. "I never said that. I just told that guy from the university that I found the artifacts. He assumed I meant they were on my land. But I never told him that. I never would."

"You're letting him believe it. What's the difference?"

"Why should I worry about what he believes?"

"Oh, I see. Why worry about leaving a few false impressions, when the price for all those things will be so much higher if people think they came from here."

"Price? What price? We're not going to sell the stuff. We're going to put it on display in the village, in the meeting hall or over here somewhere. Maybe build a little museum."

I stared at him. "You're not going to sell it?"

"No way! Then the stuff wouldn't be here anymore, would it? We want more people to come *here*. To Winter Haven, Vera. That's the whole point. People will be fascinated by these artifacts. We'll get lots of free publicity. If we can just get more tourists to come and see how wonderful our island is, maybe it'll build into something. The folks in the village can open a restaurant or two and some more bed-and-breakfasts. We already have a few summer visitors from New York and Massachusetts. Maybe we can attract more from other places. Who knows? We might even get a Texan to stay for a while." He grinned sheepishly, his teeth white and perfect. "And Evangeline and me, we can turn Weatherly into a hotel, and maybe then I can afford to get her some help."

"But people will come here thinking those things were found in Maine! The artifacts are interesting and valuable and all, but the idea they're *from* here, that's why they'll come. You'll be taking people's money under false pretenses."

Evan hung his head. I waited silently. Finally he said, "You're right. I've been struggling with that the last couple of days. I guess we have to tell that archaeologist where they really came from."

I rolled my eyes. "Whatever."

He looked up. "Listen to me. You have to understand I didn't see this coming. It never crossed my mind what it would mean if people thought the things were found here on Winter Haven. I mean, I had no idea what a big deal that would be, not until the other day when that archaeologist explained it. I just figured we'd put the stuff in glass cases and tell the world, 'Hey, look what we found,' and that would be true because we *did* find it. I never planned to make it seem like some big historic break-through or something, Vera. You've got to believe me."

I said nothing. I longed to know if he had truly failed to un-derstand where Siggy came from, if he had truly been ignorant of the efforts by the villagers to frighten me, if he had truly not considered the ethics of his choice to let people think the artifacts were from Winter Haven. I longed to know for sure that Evan Frost was not just playing a new role now that he had been found out. But I could not think of any question that would grant the certainty I wanted, because no matter what he said, I would not trust his answer.

I threw the blankets aside and struggled to get up.

He said, "What are you doing?"

"I'm going to the village."

"Now? It's pitch-black. You'll get lost!"

I considered what it had already cost to reach my brother's icy tomb. I stood, knowing for a fact that I would find my way.

Evan tried to stand as well, but I laid my palm upon his shoulder, feeling the warmth of him through the fabric of his shirt, knowing all sensation had returned to my extremities, if not to my heart. "Stay there. I'll be fine."

He looked up at me, both eyes struggling to hold mine. "You're going to leave the island, aren't you?"

"I wish I could trust you, Evan."

"When we had that picnic, it was the first time I'd been to the stone table on that day since my parents died. I wanted you to see it, to know about my family. I . . . I've answered everything. I've told you everything. Why won't you believe me?"

I looked toward the house. "Tell Evangeline I'm very grateful."

"Please don't go, Vera. *Please*."

He reached for me, but I had already started walking.

twenty-six

I LEANED HEAVILY AGAINST a piling at the village landing. It was nine o'clock in the morning, one week to the day since my arrival. The mail boat would arrive about noon. I waited, and in the packing shed across the way, Siggy waited, too.

The little harbor lay before me like a picture in a calendar, the peaceful water rippled only by a pair of loons at work among the lobster boats, the high-tide line along the far shore straight and true, black granite up above the line, dripping stone much blacker down below. One tiny cloud far to the west sailed alone beneath a dome of perfect blue. Between the standing rocks at each side of the harbor mouth I saw a slice of ocean. It lay flat and motionless, as if all storms everywhere had ceased and nothing else now dared provoke the depths. I almost believed a child on another continent could toss a pebble in that ocean and it would ripple clear across to Winter Haven.

Within me was a disturbing kind of peace. I took cold comfort from the fact that no Viking ghosts or Pilgrim witches ever walked the shores of Winter Haven. Maybe I would be allowed to resume my uneasy truce with madness, after all. Just last week—a lifetime ago—I had languished in my cubicle in Dallas, worrying at depreciation schedules and fantasies of Kenneth, humiliated by smeared mascara, longing for the dismal sanctuary of a dead-bolted apartment door and a pizza and a video I could watch alone. Now I stood in full view of beauty and tranquility beyond all imagination and I worried about nothing, longed for nothing, dreamed of nothing. I was stranded in my own kind of whiteness, the serenity of shock.

To avoid the Widow Abernathy I had spent the night at Steady Wallis's house, braving the possibility of contracting his wife's lingering flu. Morning came, and I had showered and accepted breakfast and a fresh change of clothes—more of Isaac's, I imagined, although I did not ask. I had explained everything to Steady—the glacier, the iceberg, the bodies, the polar bear—demanding that he let my brother go. Steady had agreed, promising the help I needed to get Siggy to the boat.

A strange thing happened when I left the Wallis home. I had passed two women on the way, and both of them spoke to me. The first had simply nodded and offered a "good morning," but the second stopped me on the path and asked about Siggy, offering condolences. Then, a little farther along, a man had touched his cap and mumbled, "Sorry 'bout your brother, miss." I stopped to stare at the man's departing back. It had been confusing.

On the landing now, I waited.

The loons were most amusing, diving so abruptly, popping up again a dozen yards away, cocking their heads to look around as if to say, "My, I did that well." I wished I could smile. I might again someday. But even if I didn't, at least I knew I would not cry again, not over men like Kenneth, not over lonely weekend nights in my apartment, not over remarks about my makeup . . . not even about Siggy. My freeze and thaw on Winter Haven had put everything into perspective, and if my soul could just regain sensation, I would soon be fine.

"Miss?"

I turned to find a small group of people walking toward me, mostly men, with Nathaniel in the lead. Immediately panic set in. They had trapped me on the landing with no place to go but over the side. I glanced down at the water. The tide was out. I wondered if I could survive the leap.

"Miss, ya think we might have a word?"

The little crowd closed in on the landing, spreading out enough to cut off my escape. Yet there was no hint of threat in anybody's face. In fact, Nathaniel and some of the others had removed their caps and held them awkwardly, as if standing in a hallowed place. Had they come to ask me to keep silent about what I knew and about what they'd done? Would they ask me not to lay claim to my brother's treasure? I raised my chin to stare at them defiantly. "What do you want?"

Nathaniel looked around at his companions. "Uh, the thing is . . ." He cleared his throat. "We come to apologize."

"I'll bet you have."

"Miss?"

"You want me to keep quiet about the iceberg, right?"

Several of them shook their heads. Nathaniel said, "No, miss. The boys, uh, they asked me to do the talkin' here, an' the thing is we just wanna say we's sorry for scarin' ya the way we done, with the tricks an' all."

I frowned, remembering my terror. The hisses and whispers I could overlook. Poor Evangeline was not responsible for her effect on people. But rocks from the sky? The bleeding limbs of trees? I said, "You call them *tricks*?"

"Well, I guess . . . prob'ly."

"You might as well call that thing out in the cove an ice cube."

"Was just some tiny pebbles and a bit of fish blood, miss. But I'll allow as how they was a little worse than tricks."

I crossed my arms. "It's too late to make me keep your secret. I already told Mr. Wallis everything."

"That's all right, then."

"So? What else do you want?"

Nathaniel turned to the man beside him. "Give it to her, Zeke."

I remembered the one he called Zeke, the one on the village green who had refused to tell me how to reach Bleak Beach. I had seen him with Nathaniel in the church, the two of them whispering together, both of them staring back at me. He was short and broad and walked toward me with the same strange rolling gait I had noticed before, as if even in that moment he was crossing the ship's deck where he worked with Evan Frost. Drawing near, he extended a small package to me. I remained motionless with my arms crossed, forcing the short man to stand before me with the object in his outstretched hand. "What's this?" I asked.

"We found that there thing in the ice this mornin', miss. Thought ya oughta have it."

The bald man's hand remained extended. He said, "Your brother. He was quite a fella." There was a general murmur of assent from the others.

I frowned. "How would y'all know that?"

Nathaniel said, "It's in that there thing, miss."

Relenting, I took the object. I unwrapped it to reveal a soggy copy of *The Mighty Thor* and some kind of notebook. Opening the notebook I saw pages filled with drawings and cryptic notes in a handwriting I did not recognize.

Nathaniel cleared his throat again. "Miss? I understand if ya don't feel much like forgivin' us. But ya shouldn't blame the cap'n."

I kept my eyes upon the notebook. "That's none of your business."

"No, miss. But ya still ought not ta do it. He's a good man. He don't mean no harm to anyone. He just tried to find a way to let us keep our homes and family ground."

I looked up from the remnants in my hands to search their faces. "I'm sorry about your troubles. But that doesn't mean y'all can lie to the whole world."

Nathaniel nodded. "That's what the cap'n said. Ain't nobody gonna lie no more—ya can be sure of that."

"Glad to hear it."

"But miss, ya need to know . . . Topsider, that is, the cap'n, he didn't know nothin' 'bout what we was doing, the tricks an' all."

"How am I supposed to believe that? Even his sister tried to scare me off."

"How's that, miss?"

"Don't pretend you don't know. Making those awful hissing sounds while y'all threw rocks at me."

"Oh no, ma'am. I believe she was tryin' to warn ya."

"*Warn* me?"

"Yes, miss. We couldn't get her to stop it, neither."

I sensed the truth of this and felt a sudden flood of shame for having so misjudged a mind confused by too little oxygen and too much guilt and grief, a voice damaged by the very hand that saved her. I had assumed the worst, when the woman's only crime was curiosity, her only goal to protect a stranger. Evangeline, alone on all of Winter Haven, had been my only steadfast ally all along.

I am not dangerous.

The man, Nathaniel, turned his hat in his hands. "Me and the fellas here, we just feel awful. We do, miss. We really do." He paused, looking at me expectantly. When I said nothing, he continued. "Miss, the thing is, the cap'n, he's awful broke up 'cause you're leavin', and we wanted to ask, just kinda make a suggestion, see, that ya stay a little longer. Try workin' things out with him."

I stared at my feet. "Did he send y'all here?"

"No, miss. He don't think it'll do no good. That is, he don't seem to think ya care much about him."

I nodded. "Okay, y'all had your say. Now let me wait for the mail boat in peace."

"You're still goin'? Without making things right?"

"I can't fix what's wrong here."

"Do ya think your brother would approve of ya runnin' off this way?"

I glared at them. "Leave my brother out of this! You didn't know him!"

"No, miss. An' that's our loss, for sure."

Around Nathaniel, all the others nodded somberly.

I turned my back to them. I stared out toward the narrow gap at the harbor mouth, at the perfectly still sea. "Please," I said, begging now. "Please, just leave me be."

"Ain't there some way we can make this up to ya? Somethin' we can do?"

Staring at the ocean, I saw Siggy setting out at four-fifteen exactly by the tolling of the steeple bell, searching for his dream, an autistic child alone but somehow, miraculously really, making it across half a continent to stow away on a seaplane, actually arriving on Greenland to be among his precious Vikings, and then sailing like a warrior back across the wide Atlantic in the leavings of a glacier. I saw the comic book cover behind the ice, bright colors in the whiteness, and the little Viking ship they found in Siggy's pocket, and suddenly I knew I could not simply take my brother back to Texas. I turned to face the repentant villagers of Winter Haven. "There is one thing . . ."

"Anythin', miss," said Nathaniel. "Just name it."

So I told them what I wanted, and as they left me on the landing to go about their work, I settled down onto a cardboard case marked *Engine Oil* to read the notebook they had found that morning in the ice.

A little later, just as I finished reading Aden McAllister's last words, Dr. Edward Thorndike arrived. The archaeologist was also going home now that he knew the real source of the artifacts. Below the landing where the doctor and I waited for the mail boat, the Winter Haven villagers made preparations at the water's edge, bringing a small rowboat around to the floating dock, securing a rope to its bow, and lining it with verdant branches taken from the ancient evergreens of Winter Haven.

When the mail boat arrived, I watched from the landing above as Nathaniel spoke to the woman at the helm. I assumed he was explaining the plan. She did not seem surprised, probably because of long experience with their peculiar ways.

Then at last the time had come. Steady Wallis and three others entered the old packing shed and emerged with Siggy's body. He lay on a piece of dark brown canvas, which the men gripped at all four corners. They bore him to the landing with as much dignity as possible. They tried to walk in step between the two short rows of villagers who stood in solemn silence with hats in hand to watch the body pass. A woman came to me with a small bouquet of wild flowers. I took them with a nod and followed the four men and Siggy down the ramp onto the floating dock. There, I stood by as they laid him in the rowboat. On his back my brother faced the sky, his hands together at his chest, that strange smile still upon his face. Other women came to lay more flowers on the boughs of evergreens that lined the boat, his little resting place. I knelt upon the dock and slipped a parting gift beneath his hands, *The Mighty Thor*.

With Siggy thus prepared, I boarded the mail boat, along with Dr. Thorndike. Many others rowed out to the harbor's lobster boats. The woman at the mail boat helm brought the engine rumbling to life, a villager cast off the lines, and we began our slow departure. Riding in his little rowboat at the end of the long rope, connected to our vessel by that slender line, Siggy followed.

Near the harbor mouth, I spied the Widow Abernathy standing alone above the cliff, the old woman's black dress luffing like a ghost ship's sail in the offshore breeze. She stared down on Siggy. A camera with a long telephoto lens hung by a strap around her skinny neck. She saw me looking up, raised the camera to her eye, and turned to aim it inward at the island.

I never left the stern deck of the mail boat. I stood watching my brother's final journey as he followed me out between the granite sentinels at each side of the harbor mouth. The signal bell on the rusting buoy chimed high and clear in the sunshine as our sparkling bow wave passed beneath it, and again when the buoy rode up and over our wake behind. The woman pushed the throttle forward. The mail boat picked up speed, heading toward the unseen mainland. Following one after another, all seven boats in Winter Haven's small fishing fleet emerged from the harbor. They fanned out to trail the mail boat, each of them riding differently across the water, one with its bow pointed up and its stern digging deep, another sitting almost level, a red hull, a blue one, others white and black, all of them with many passengers who, like me, stood on the stern decks, watching Siggy glide across the ocean like a Viking warrior, proud and undefeated.

"Vera? I don't mean any disrespect, but why are they doing this?"

Thinking about Siggy's final battle, I glanced at the archaeologist. "It's for my brother."

"Sure, but they didn't know him, right? So . . . why all this?"

I turned back toward the little fleet behind. I felt something rising up, an old sensation I had felt before, but not for a long time, something I could not quite identify. "Did you know Aden McAllister?"

"Not really. He disappeared while I was an undergraduate, but I did have one class with him. He was a great teacher."

"Would you say he was a man of faith?"

"Dr. McAllister? Faith?" The archaeologist's eyes, already magnified, went even wider behind his thick lenses. "Faith in science, I guess. But you mean faith in God, right?" He shook his head. " I doubt it."

I thought of what I'd read in Dr. McAllister's notebook, after all the other pages crisply filled with professional notations about a long-dead people, those last few scribbled observations of a life much more mysterious. I thought of how his handwriting had changed as the end drew near. Remembering my swim out to the iceberg, I understood the uncooperative extremities, his fingers stiff and useless. I marveled that he had managed to write anything at all. But he had been a scientist until the very end, determined to record the facts as he observed them. And thinking of what he had observed, I suddenly identified the sensation rising up within me.

I was so very proud of Siggy.

I recalled the facts I too had observed, for now I knew that I had also somehow been there in those final moments, when all was white except for Siggy with his colors, his rosy cheeks, his emerald eyes with flecks of red. I heard Siggy shouting, " 'The mighty are afraid! The arrow cannot make him flee! He laugheth at the shaking of a spear!' " and the awful sound, a monster's howl of rage, and the presence of an awful thing, invisible as white inside a world of white.

After reading Aden McAllister's notebook, I knew my visions were not madness, after all.

Somehow I had truly watched my brother flee, his slender form becoming smaller in the field of snow below him and above him and all around, Siggy getting smaller until that dreadful moment when he simply vanished. Now I knew the awful thing for Siggy had been a polar bear, chasing him and Aden McAllister through the blizzard, the two of them stumbling in the whiteout, desperate to escape the raging bear, struggling against the shrieking wind, the rising snow, the utter blindness of a colorless world. Pursued by the largest carnivore on land, they had strayed onto the glacier. Blinded by the driving snow, they had fallen into the crevasse. Sitting on the front pew at my father's church, the little girl I used to be had truly seen my brother step into the air and fly, arms wide like a dove. I had seen him dip and roll and soar through perfect white, and stop, all of a sudden, when the pure white ice of that glacial crevasse stopped his fall. I had known somehow an awful thing was coming, and being there in spirit I had called out, "Siggy! Siggy, please get up! We have to run away!"

Thinking of what I had seen, both in the visions of my youth and in Aden McAllister's notebook, remembering the human bites along the legs and belly of the polar bear, I knew the creature had also tumbled blindly down into the crevasse, following its prey, and perished in the fall. I knew Aden McAllister had tried to gather nourishment from it, tearing at it with his teeth. I knew what that had cost the man, with both of his legs broken. I knew he had tried to make my brother climb out of the icy chasm, to leave him there to die. I knew Siggy would not have budged.

"*'I go to prepare a place.'*"

At last I thought I understood the reason why.

I heard my brother speak from memory to the man who had no faith. I heard him say the only things worth saying in those final hours—*for God so loved the world*—and I knew I had been wrong to think it meant my brother doubted my salvation. It was Aden McAllister whom my Siggy had left home to save, Aden's soul he feared was damned, and never mine at all.

Suddenly I realized this might mean my Siggy never knew that I was watching. What if, when he shared his emerald eyes with me that one and only time, he had not really seen me? What if, when he showed me flecks of red like drops of holy blood, he himself had only seen the empty ice, instead of me? What if my lonely Siggy never really shared his eyes?

Filled with loneliness, I lifted my own ordinary eyes from Siggy's Viking funeral to watch the isle of Winter Haven slowly shrink behind the little convoy, the impregnable granite and majestic forest merely distant streaks of black and green on the horizon. Someone's voice crackled on the radio behind me. The mail boat began to slow. The other boats came to a stop together, all of us around the little craft that held the valiant warrior. Then the woman at the helm came back and untied the rope.

Siggy was adrift.

"I didn't realize your brother meant so much to all these people," said the archaeologist.

I looked around at all the hardened seamen and their women in the boats. They watched my brother with attitudes of deep respect. It confused me for a moment. Then I remembered they too had read the notebook's final pages, the clinical analysis of Aden McAllister's situation, his broken legs, the steep ice walls, the nonstop blizzard raging up above, and the strange boy raving on and on in King James English. Like me, these Winter Haven men and women had seen the man's words slowly changing to wonder at the boy's unfailing cheerfulness, and amazement as belief that Siggy did not understand their situation gave way to certainty the boy did understand, and yet was unafraid. Like me, the Winter Haven people had read the notebook's final entry, written at the bottom of an icy crevasse, and barely legible in a shaky hand:

> These words he says are true. I don't know how I know, but they are clearly true. For the first time in my life, I believe in something I can't see or hear or understand. God, forgive me for ignoring you all these years, and thank you for this boy—this angel that you sent from out of nowhere.

I saw Steady Wallis bring his vessel alongside Siggy's. He turned to look toward me. I saw his liquid eyes and knew his mind was filled with memories of another boy in another boat at another time. I nodded to him. He leaned across the water toward the little rowboat and reached into it, doing what he must. Then he pushed Siggy's boat away.

A wisp of smoke rose as my brother slowly spun across the glassy water. Flames caught in the boughs of ancient evergreens. Siggy was engulfed in the inferno, hot as heaven.

From one of the lobster boats, a deep voice sang out. I looked, and saw Nathaniel staring at the flames. As he sang, I stared into the flames as well, seeing Siggy Gamble and Aden McAllister, brothers at the end, entombed inside the glacier as the blizzard sealed their resting place deep within the ice, riding slowly toward the sea for more than a decade after that, a decade's journey of a mile or two, then sailing off together as the glacier broke away to become an iceberg, only to be found by Evan Frost and these men here, who had gathered now to send my brother on yet another ocean journey. I pondered the improbability of it, the miracle of it, really, as the others joined in singing Nathaniel's hymn, and their holy words rose with the smoke, lifting up my brother, prophet, friend and angel, The Mighty Siggy, going home.

twenty-seven

I T WAS NOT ENOUGH.

I longed to accept what had been shown to me, the secret in the whiteness, but the awful thing remained. My mother's death and my brother's disappearance still left me with one unanswered question that would not let my spirit pass, which thirteen years ago had frozen my heart just like Siggy's undeveloped body in the ice, the question I had shunned in a burning attic paradise, which bound my spirit even now. In spite of all that I had seen on Winter Haven, I still wanted God to tell me what could justify such suffering and sorrow.

My father's condemnation of my visions still rang true: *"You must be punished. Your sanity depends on it."* Yet in frozen agony at Gin Gap Cove I had overcome my fear and boldly risked my life to ask, only to receive an answer that still left me numb. Through visions fulfilled and a few lines in a notebook, I understood the hapless miracle of an autistic boy preaching Jesus at the bottom of a glacial crevasse, and now I was supposed to accept the salvation of Aden McAllister, as if one immortal soul was worth the cost.

No, it would not do.

It was not enough.

I wished to be a good Christian. I wished to accept the infinite value of a single soul. But what of Siggy's loss, and mine? What good had Aden McAllister done with the gospel for anyone besides himself in the final hours of his life? Maybe he was up in heaven now because of Siggy's courage, one lost lamb recovered, God and all his angels happy like the Bible said, but where was the justice in it? There should be something greater, some kind of benefit more universal, something much more cosmic to the balance.

I watched my brother's boat burn to the waterline, until only a few planks remained floating in the Gulf of Maine. The people of Winter Haven set out for the island they would surely lose, and the mail boat turned to take me to the mainland and a rental car and a flight to Dallas, where my cubicle and dead-bolted apartment awaited.

On the bench inside the vessel's cabin I pondered the alleged answer. There was no hint of seasickness this time, just a different kind of ache that would not pass. The woman at the helm and the archaeologist said nothing, no doubt in respect for my loss. I could not stand their heavy silence. I moved back to the stern and sat beside the bulwark, seeking solitude in my misery, continuing my attempt to understand. But no matter how I turned it in my mind, it was not enough.

The mail boat moved much faster on the trip back to the mainland since the sea was calm this time and there was no fog. I was surprised how soon the engine slowed. Sitting up straight, I could see the Pemaquid harbor over the top of the bulwark. In twenty-four hours I would be back at my so-called home. It would be as if nothing much had happened. I had returned to the real world, and it was still not enough.

How was I supposed to live with that?

I replayed the visions in my mind—all of them—from the first encounter with Siggy in the whiteness, to his last words as my visions faded, the words that robbed me of all hope that I would ever understand, for they had been spoken in a foreign language. Then the final words of all, not Siggy's but the deeper voice of someone else:

"THIS IS WRONG."

I had always assumed it was the voice of God I heard, or perhaps an angel, because I had always assumed Siggy was alone inside the whiteness. But now that I knew he had a companion, suddenly I wondered if that booming voice had belonged to Aden McAllister.

I roused myself. "Hey, Eddy."

The archaeologist seemed surprised to hear me speak his name. "Yes?"

"Do you know Latin?"

"Of course."

"What does *liberabit vos* mean?"

"Uh, 'to make you free,' or even better, '*will* make you free.' Why?"

It made no sense. I heard Siggy's final words as if he had just spoken them to me: "Vera, *liberabit vos.*"

"Why would someone say something like, 'Eddy, liberabit vos'?"

The archaeologist shook his head. "They wouldn't."

"But somebody said that to me once. He said, 'Vera, liberabit vos.' "

"Oh, you probably mean *veritas liberabit vos.* That's 'The truth will make you free.' It's pretty famous. From the Bible I think, or maybe Shakespeare. But the word *vera*, that means 'in truth,' not 'the truth.' "

"So it's wrong? *Vera liberabit vos?*"

"Yeah, definitely. It's bad grammar, like saying, 'In truth will make you free.' "

I heard those final words, booming like the voice of God. "*This is wrong.*" If I had been mistaken about who the voice belonged to, might I also have mistaken what it meant? Always I believed the "wrong" thing was me—my failure to stop Siggy when he walked away, my deluded visions, my blasphemous questions. But what if it had been much simpler than that all along? What if it was only Aden McAllister, archaeologist, well-educated man, saying Siggy botched the Latin?

But Siggy never botched the Latin, or the Spanish, or any of the other seven languages he could use to quote the Bible. He might get the pronunciation wrong, but he never got the words themselves wrong. Never. Not one single time. Which could only mean one thing.

Siggy used my name on purpose.

The one and only time my brother spoke in his own words, he somehow reached into his mind and substituted "Vera" for *veritas*. He was thinking of me. He made a little joke for me, and that could only mean he knew I would be watching. It meant my brother had looked into my eyes on purpose. It meant the prophet in the whiteness and the brother whom I loved were the same boy, after all.

Yet of course he was still gone, so even this was not enough.

The woman steered directly for the town landing, where she made short work of tying off the boat. She helped me and the archaeologist step ashore. No one waited there for me, but a man with thick gray hair called Dr. Thorndike's name. On the small dock I could not help overhearing them. It seemed the gray man was a reporter for the *New York Times*. His editors had dispatched him to meet the archaeologist in hopes of learning more about the amazing discovery of a Viking colony in Maine.

After the archaeologist explained the facts, the reporter said, "You mean it isn't true?"

"I'm afraid not," said Eddy Thorndike.

The older man sighed. "You're absolutely sure it turned out to be nothing?"

"Well, not nothing, exactly. They do have quite a few artifacts."

"Yeah, but they all came from Greenland, right?"

"It looks that way."

"Viking artifacts from Greenland, that's material for the *Smithsonian* or *National Geographic*, maybe, but it's not the front page news I was hoping for."

I said, "Excuse me. I couldn't help overhearing. Are you saying it would have been on the front page of the *New York Times*?"

The reporter glanced at the archaeologist, who explained, "This is Vera Gamble. She just spent a week on the island. Her brother was involved in finding the artifacts."

"Oh, okay. Well, no, I was exaggerating a little bit. Not the front page. But they probably would have led with it in the science section. I mean, Viking artifacts in Greenland isn't exactly a scoop, but a settlement in Maine? Yeah, that's quite a story."

"You think it would have made a lot of people interested in Winter Haven?"

Both men chuckled. Eddy said, "Vera, it would have been the archaeological discovery of the year, like I told you before.

Maybe even the decade. Yes, a lot of people would have been very interested in Winter Haven."

The two men continued talking as I followed them off the landing and across the parking lot. Passing by a pickup truck, I saw a raven light upon the cab. It cocked its head and watched as I drew closer. I wondered if it was related to the birds I had seen on Winter Haven. Perhaps it had followed me from there. Suddenly angry, I raised my arms and ran at it, shouting, "Shoo!" It rose into the air but only flew a little ways before landing again upon the harbormaster's office, a small shack covered with shingles and multicolored lobster floats. There it resumed its cold inspection of me. I glared at the bird. Dismissive, it shifted its attention to a strange clock just beneath it on the wall. In addition to the usual circle of numbers, around the clock's perimeter was a second, outer circle with the numbers thirteen and then fourteen and so on up to twenty-four. I had heard it was the way mariners kept track of time. One in the afternoon was thirteen hundred, two was fourteen hundred, and so forth. The logical system appealed to my love of numbers. Deliberately ignoring the raven, I paused to examine the clock. Beside the five I saw the number seventeen.

"... it was seventeen-fifteen on the dot, and I was sitting on the vee-berth—and the next second I was slammed against the overhead, looking at a granite boulder sticking through the hull."

Seventeen-fifteen was five-fifteen in the evening. It was right there on the clock. But something else was there, something important. If I could only see . . .

Time zones.

Seventeen-fifteen was five-fifteen.

Five-fifteen in Maine was four-fifteen in Texas.

"She has spent thirteen years standing on the shore and staring at those rocks."

In a flash I understood the rest of what had happened on the day Evan and his family gathered at the stone table to remember his grandmother's birthday, the one day each year when a momentary heart-shaped light bathed a little part of Winter Haven, the one day that was also my birthday. On that one day, at precisely the same instant thirteen years ago, Isaac crashed into the rocks, the widow lost her husband and her art, Steady lost his son, Evan and Evangeline lost their parents, and in a small East Texas town two thousand miles away, may God forgive me, I let Siggy walk away. All of that had happened at four-fifteen exactly by the tolling of the bell of my father's church.

I thought of Siggy's parting words.

" 'I go to prepare a place for you. And if I go and prepare a place for you, I will come back and take you to be with me that you also may be where I am.' "

I turned to stare back toward the mail boat at the Pemaquid town landing, my last connection with the island of Winter Haven. I thought of Siggy's parting words, and Evan's hopes for Evangeline, to rebuild Weatherly as a hotel, to serve a few tourists and maybe earn enough to heal his poor sister's afflictions.

Would that be enough?

I thought of Siggy's parting words and all those men and women who had humbly come to me, hats literally in hand, begging forgiveness not only for themselves but for their captain, whom they clearly loved.

Had that been enough?

I thought of Siggy's eyes on mine, definitely on *mine* in the moment that he broke from his quotations just one time, just to speak my name. I thought of Siggy and his empty whiteness forced upon me as my father said, but not exactly as my father said, for I had received one vision after another, not hallucinations, not delusions, but *visions*. In spite of my unwise repentance in the burning heaven of dear Siggy's attic, in spite of my bitterness at God's apparent silence, in spite of my long refusal to have eyes to see, I thought of my Creator waiting for me as I grew from girl to woman, my Creator waiting to send memories of visions, even though I called them mad, patient with me anyway, sending revelation to me in the freezing hell of Gin Gap Cove, deigning to persuade me of my sanity with the comic book colors of a lesser god, *The Mighty Thor* in a wall of whiteness I could never climb alone.

What if I could not have stopped my dear Siggy's leaving even if I had tried? What if everything had happened just as planned? Would that be enough?

I thought of Evan's final plea. *"I answered everything. I've told you everything. Why won't you believe me?"* I remembered why I left him. No matter what he said, I would not trust his answer.

For thirteen years I had kept my distance from a wrathful god who would not abide a question, much less an honest doubt. I had feared to lift my questions to him, thinking I must take it all on faith. But what if my poor father had been wrong? What if real faith lay in asking, in being honest about doubts, in trusting for an answer?

If I could just believe God had stooped to set an answer into motion at four-fifteen exactly thirteen years ago, if I could just believe he sealed his answer in a place he had prepared, not only for me, but for all the brokenhearted people out on Winter Haven, how much good might come from such a faith as that? Might it spread out forever, wider and wider, touching countless people in generations still to come?

I had wanted cosmic justice, but this answer was not that. The questions I had asked in Siggy's burning attic paradise remained in spite of everything. I might never know for sure if any of the outward flowing goodness I imagined was intentional, or if it was indeed just something I imagined. But Winter Haven had taught me there was more beneath the surface of this world than ever I imagined. I thought of everything I had seen and learned, and knew mere coincidence could never weave through so much time to bind so many strangers' lives together. So maybe if I simply chose to trust there was some kind of balance coming, some kind of common goodness planned in the beginning that made all suffering worthwhile; maybe then I could spread that goodness just a little wider, here and now, and maybe then this numbness I had felt for thirteen years would disappear.

Surely that would be enough.

I knew exactly how to start. I called, "Hey, mister! Mister *New York Times* guy!" The reporter, who was entering his car, paused to turn my way. As I strode across the parking lot, the raven on the harbormaster's shack cawed with outrage, for at last the awful thing was dead. "Hold on a minute!" I shouted. "Hold on! I have another story for you."

I told him of a call I got at work, of a miserable ocean crossing, and the way an island first appeared beyond an eerie whiteness. As I spoke, the skepticism in his eyes began to change. I saw interest rising there, not interest in Viking artifacts, or in Puritans, or witches, but in the story of a little boy who had no fear of anything, a prophet who had cast a pebble on the far side of an ocean full of faith, sending ripples across time to caress his sister's thawing heart.

twenty-eight

I SAT ALONE, STARING at the general ledger on my computer screen. There was an error somewhere, but the flaw eluded me. Lately it had been so hard to concentrate. The mathematics of my chosen profession no longer offered comfort because I could not seem to lose myself in numbers anymore. But this thing on the computer must be correct by Tuesday or the quarterly filing would be late and penalties would accrue, so I sighed and redoubled my efforts, watching the little blinking cursor as it obeyed my taps upon the keyboard, running up and down the columns, seeking the anomaly. Soon the cursor blurred and faded as my mind drifted off again to other things. I gave up. I had done my best to remain focused— I really had—but it was just impossible, especially with all the noise.

Looking up, I saw the source of the commotion, the little boy who ran across the lawn with a toy airplane in his hand, growling out engine sounds and the *rat-a-tat-tat* of machine guns as the plane rolled and banked in his imaginary dogfight.

"Young man, do *not* get so close to that cliff!" I called.

A slender woman in a bright orange and yellow sundress dashed over to the boy and swooped him up into her arms. Tickling his stomach, she carried him straight to me, where she set him down giggling on his feet. I shielded my eyes from the sun with one hand like a salute, looking up at the woman. She stood awkwardly before me. Her hands shook just a little. She clasped them together. I said, "Thanks, sugar."

Evangeline's sudden shy smile was every bit a match for her bright sundress. "You're welcome." Her voice was low and husky, as if she'd smoked too many cigarettes, but at least she had a voice, thanks to the surgeries. She cast a glance at her nephew and then ran across the lawn to the Adirondack chair where she liked to sit alone, both feet carefully planted side by side on the grass, each hand identically placed on the wide arms of the chair, her head the only thing moving as she watched the world around her, not completely well but mostly free of Isaac now, and getting better.

I bent in my seat, putting my elbows on my knees, dropping down to my son's level. He ignored me, spinning round in circles with his airplane. "Hey, you," I said. "Look here." The boy kept his eyes on the plane but inched a little closer. I said, "What did we talk about this morning?"

"I don't know."

"Look at me." My son's eyes stayed on his toy, on the ground, the sky . . . anything and everything but me. How I wished my parents could have lived to see this child. My parents, and my Siggy. Ah, well. No matter. We would all be together in due time, even Father, for I knew the God I loved would never hold that old man's needless fear against him.

Again I said, "Come on, look here." But my son would not put his eyes on me. I reached out to touch him. "You do too know what we talked about. Come on now. What did I say?"

Round and round the boy went, eyes on his toy plane. "Nothing . . ."

"You want to go inside?"

"No!"

"Then tell me what you promised."

"I mustn't play close to the edge."

"That's right. And do you remember why?"

"'Cause I can't really fly."

"And do you remember why?"

"'Cause God didn't give me feathers."

"Or wings," I said, smiling now.

"Yeah! Or wings!"

I sat back. "Okay, so please be good, and don't be bad, and no whining"—the boy finally looked fully into my eyes as he joined in with our funny little saying—"and no complaining and don't ask for any money!"

He laughed, and I laughed, and I said, "Okay, you. Go play."

As my boy ran off, I tried to dig into our tax return again, but somehow the pursuit of perfect reconciliation did not matter anymore. It was just too beautiful outside on the patio. I decided to make an adjustment, accept the flaw, and move on to more important things.

I loved the way the new dining patio extension curved toward the cove, and the white cast-iron tables and chairs, so elegant below the dark blue canvas umbrellas. I loved the fact that almost every seat was taken by guests from all around the world. I loved hearing them speak French and Spanish and German. I loved the English accents. I loved the fresh façade of Weatherly, Maine's newest resort, and the sight of the reddish cedar shingles, the crispness of the white painted trim, the taut canvas awnings, the sturdy columns, all of it so absolutely perfect—just what you'd hope to find on an island off the coast of Maine on a beautiful summer afternoon, kites flying above the field beyond the lively fountain on the hotel's far side, yachts moored inside the jetty down below, and this gorgeous man now weaving his way toward me through the tables, greeting guests.

It had been almost five years since the *New York Times* article about Siggy became one of those little human-interest stories that somehow grow and grow and reach a tipping point to capture the whole world's imagination. A famous author up in Bangor wrote a novel based on it, and then there was the motion picture *Winter Haven*, which was filmed mostly on the island. It was not the first time a novel and a movie had made an island famous. Comparisons were sometimes made to Hemingway and Key West, Bogart and Key Largo. It was Steady Wallis's worst nightmare come true. Ex-lobstermen now ran restaurants and rented out bicycles, and the main problem on Winter Haven was how to keep up with the electricity demand. But the people of the village had a plan for controlled growth. The forest, for example, would always be off-limits for development.

Across the dining patio, a guest stopped Evan with a question. My husband flashed his amazing smile, and I heard him say something about Vikings, and I heard the word "iceberg," and I knew he was telling the whole story once again, the one they always wished to hear, the one that had put Winter Haven on the map. He never seemed to tire of it, yet still he glanced my way as if both his good eye and the one that sometimes wandered could not get enough of me. For five years now, this handsome man had called me beautiful. Lately I had begun to think perhaps I really was.

Finally, Evan made it to my table. "Hey, honey," he said, bending down to give a kiss. I turned my face up to him and reached to cup his cheek, inviting him to linger just a moment. He did, and then he sat and touched the paperwork beside my computer. "Working on the books?"

"Ayuh."

Smiling at my affectation of the proper Maine affirmative, he replied, "When do *y'all* think *y'all* is going to be finished?"

I laughed. "Maybe tomorrow. I'm having a little problem with my concentration."

"Is she kicking again?"

I touched my stomach. "Just a little."

"Gonna be a lot of trouble," said Evan. "Like her aunt." I followed his gaze across the patio, to see Evangeline had risen from her seat to make dramatic gestures toward a waiter we had hired on for the summer.

I turned toward Evan. "Have you told her about the name we picked?"

"Naw. I think we oughta spring it on her at the hospital."

"Two Evangeline Frosts on one little island. Might be confusing."

"Confusing? Winter Haven? Never."

I laughed again as the new waiter brought our food. We began to eat our lunch together as we always tried to do, although it was not often possible with so many details to attend to during the busy season. I saw Nathaniel approaching our table from behind Evan. The big man's jeans and shirt were smeared with mud.

He said, "Cap'n, will ya look at this?"

Evan turned. "What's up?"

"Ain't sure, exactly. Me and Zeke, we found this in the trench."

"What trench?" I asked.

Evan said, "They're digging that new east wing septic system."

Nathaniel handed the object to Evan, saying, "Think this mighta been a shoe?"

Evan turned it in his hands. It was clearly leather, bunched and filthy, with stitching visible in places. "What do you think?" he asked, looking at me.

I reached for it, and as he passed it over, something fell onto the table between our plates. It was a rectangular piece of metal. I picked it up and wiped it clean as best I could. As the soil fell from it, Nathaniel said, "That there thing's a shoe buckle."

He was right.

I looked up at Evan. Our eyes met. He said, "No way."

"There's more stuff like this down there," said Nathaniel. "If ya wanna see."

Evan and I both leapt to our feet, and the three of us set out for Weatherly's east wing. But before we reached the door, my son ran up with his toy airplane.

"Momma," said the boy, trying to keep pace with me, "how *come* God didn't give me wings or feathers?"

I slowed for him, but only just a little. "Well, I don't know exactly, sugar. What do you think?"

"You don't know? Really?"

"Nope. Got no idea."

"Who *does* know?"

"Well, God does, I guess. Maybe you should ask him."

"Can I ask him things like that? Really? Will he answer me?"

I stopped walking.

"Hurry up," said Evan.

"Go ahead," I said. "I'll be there in a minute."

I knelt down very close to look full into my little Siggy's remarkable emerald eyes, flecked as they were with tiny bits of red. I looked deep into those lovely eyes of his, gaining his attention, and I took time to gather up my thoughts. Proof of Pilgrim colonies could wait. It was so much more important that I got this next part right.

about the author

ATHOL DICKSON studied architecture, painting, and sculpture at university, followed by a long career as an architect and then the decision to devote himself to writing full time. He is the author of six novels, including *The Cure* and *River Rising*, winner of the 2006 Christy Award for suspense. He has also written the bestselling memoir *The Gospel According to Moses*. Athol and his wife, Sue, live in Southern California.

www.atholdickson.com

More Superb Storytelling From Athol Dickson

In 1927, Pilotville, Louisiana, was an isolated outpost on the Mississippi River, an island of brotherly love in sea of racism. But in the swamp beyond the cypress the tupelo, veiled by Spanish moss, lies a lingering ev and it will sleep no more. It will rain down on Pilotvil and nothing but a miracle can stop this awful flood.

River Rising by **Athol Dickson**

Riley Keep, former man of God, lost everything in a single act of wickedness. As a last bid for survival, Ril sets out for a small town in Maine where miracles are happening…but sometimes the disease is not nearly dangerous as *The Cure*.

The Cure by **Athol Dickson**